Broken Crusade

More Warhammer 40,000 from Black Library

• DAWN OF FIRE •

Book 1: AVENGING SON
Guy Haley

Book 2: THE GATE OF BONES
Andy Clark

Book 3: THE WOLFTIME
Gav Thorpe

Book 4: THRONE OF LIGHT
Guy Haley

Book 5: THE IRON KINGDOM
Nick Kyme

Book 6: THE MARTYR'S TOMB
Marc Collins

Book 7: SEA OF SOULS
Chris Wraight

Book 8: HAND OF ABADDON
Nick Kyme

Book 9: THE SILENT KING
Guy Haley

• DARK IMPERIUM •
Guy Haley

Book 1: DARK IMPERIUM
Book 2: PLAGUE WAR
Book 3: GODBLIGHT

LEVIATHAN
Darius Hinks

HELSREACH
Aaron Dembski-Bowden

THE FALL OF CADIA
Robert Rath

MORVENN VAHL: SPEAR OF FAITH
Jude Reid

HELBRECHT: KNIGHT OF THE THRONE
Marc Collins

GENEFATHER
Guy Haley

THE INFINITE AND THE DIVINE
Robert Rath

THE LION: SON OF THE FOREST
Mike Brooks

Broken Crusade

Steven B Fischer

BLACK LIBRARY

A BLACK LIBRARY PUBLICATION

First published in 2024.
This edition published in Great Britain in 2025 by
Black Library, Games Workshop Ltd., Willow Road,
Nottingham, NG7 2WS, UK.

Represented by: Games Workshop Limited – Irish branch,
Unit 3, Lower Liffey Street, Dublin 1,
D01 K199, Ireland.

10 9 8 7 6 5 4 3 2 1

Produced by Games Workshop in Nottingham.
Cover illustration by Kevin Chin.

See Black Library on the internet at

blacklibrary.com

Find out more about Games Workshop
and the worlds of Warhammer at

warhammer.com

Printed and bound in the UK.

_To Mom and Dad. For showing me what faith looked like,
and for teaching me to question it._

For more than a hundred centuries the Emperor has sat immobile on the Golden Throne of Earth. He is the Master of Mankind. By the might of his inexhaustible armies a million worlds stand against the dark.

Yet, he is a rotting carcass, the Carrion Lord of the Imperium held in life by marvels from the Dark Age of Technology and the thousand souls sacrificed each day so his may continue to burn.

To be a man in such times is to be one amongst untold billions. It is to live in the cruelest and most bloody regime imaginable. It is to suffer an eternity of carnage and slaughter. It is to have cries of anguish and sorrow drowned by the thirsting laughter of dark gods.

This is a dark and terrible era where you will find little comfort or hope. Forget the power of technology and science. Forget the promise of progress and advancement. Forget any notion of common humanity or compassion.

There is no peace amongst the stars, for in the grim darkness of the far future, there is only war.

Chapter 1

I will burn in this chamber one day, like my brothers. Like a hundred generations of Black Templar knights before me. The thought sears my consciousness and steals my focus, ripping me from my meditation as I kneel over the corpse of my fallen brother.

Baelar's body lies on a sheet of unblemished linen, atop a low table of polished, ink-black stone which has been thrice blessed for this purpose by the Chaplains of the crusade and reconsecrated every twenty-four solar hours at the time of dawn upon Holy Terra. My brother's skin shines bare and bronze against the flickering orange light of ornate braziers burning sacred oils and incense.

Their scent is heady and bitter, but not strong enough to mask the redolence of his death.

Thin fluid pools in the gaping wounds that mar Baelar's flesh. One deep, ragged puncture pierces his neck, and a matching wound marks the centre of his chest where Brother-Apothecary Alvus' reductor harvested the gene-seed from his progenoid glands after his body was recovered from the dust and ash of the filthy world we leave in our wake. Countless other jagged lacerations profane the remainder of his corpse where the teeth and claws of accursed, mindless xenos tore at him and bled him dry.

I did not see Baelar die, but I am told it took one hundred wounds to fell my brother.

'Brother Baelar honours us with the nobility of this death,' I call.

My voice disturbs the stillness of the crematorium, pulling my brothers from their own prayers, and their eyes fall upon me. The two-score knights of my fighting company have knelt vigil over Baelar for the last seven cycles since the *Dauntless Honour* departed orbit over Hestus Delta and entered the obscurity of the warp. In that time none of them have left this chamber, nor has any moved from Baelar's side. Each has knelt over the fallen knight in turn and spoken quiet benedictions and whispered prayers into his unhearing ears.

Now, bold words are expected of me, but I find that I have few. I am no great orator. Not as Baelar was. With his death, one of the crusade's brightest flames falls extinguished. With his passing, we lose not only his sword, but also a piece of our soul.

Beside me, Brother-Chaplain Dant pauses his invocation. 'He honours the God-Emperor, Brother-Castellan Emeric.'

I nod. 'As we who survive also seek to honour Him.'

My brothers kneel in a ring around me, clad in their sacred black power armour but unhelmeted. Blood and dirt still stain their raiment – the remnants of a world that I would sooner forget.

Loss hangs like a shadow upon each of their grim countenances, undiminished despite the fact that we have all taken part in this ceremony more times than we can count. The Second Dorean Crusade has been costly already, and our fleet still travels far from its goal. We press on to the Ecclesiarchy world of Tempest, home to a thousand martyrs and their venerated shrines. There we shall answer the holy world's cry for aid and deliver the planet from the warbands of the Archenemy which assail it, opening a path to the Dorean System proper and pressing on towards our next, and greater, battles.

I know little of what awaits my fighting company there, but I know that more of my brothers will die.

'Today, we burn our brother,' I say. 'Tomorrow, we ourselves will lie on the pyre. This ritual is for the living, not for the dead. A reminder of the fate that awaits us all, and the truth that we leave nothing behind but our deeds. With his death, Baelar has carved a legacy that will not fade. We remember him and aspire to do the same.'

My voice falls away. Simple words, but true. My brother cares not for the fate of his corpse. My brother sees not what we do to honour him. And yet we do it to honour him.

The plates of Brother-Chaplain Dant's armour rustle as he rises to his feet beside me. He alone retains his helm for this ceremony, its skull face gleaming in the wavering light. Dozens of reliquaries swing from his armour, bound to the black ceramite plate by sanctified golden cord. Strips of yellowed, scorched parchment flutter with his movements, affixed to his armour with crimson wax. Each bears the words of a litany or a sacred vow, written in Dant's own hand or that of his most trusted acolytes.

The ancient Chaplain stands over Baelar, reaching into one of the pouches affixed to the belt which binds his white tabard about his waist. He anoints my brother's corpse with soil as I press my forehead against the departed's. I am the last of my brothers to speak to the fallen knight.

'Earth from the world upon which he was born.' Dant's voice fills the crematorium like the quiet rumbling of a coming storm. 'Earth from the world upon which he died. Earth from the surface of Holy Terra itself, where he now rests in the God-Emperor's light.'

The smell of death assaults me. The empty gaze of Baelar's stone-grey eyes meets mine. One day, I will lie in this same state before my brothers. One day, they will speak to the husk I leave behind. What words will they utter over my corpse? Memories of glory, or of mediocrity?

'You surpass me, brother,' I subvocalise. 'In death, even as you did in life.'

Slowly, I rise and wrap a thin, black shroud over Baelar. His helm and his bolter shall live on as relics of his service within the *Dauntless Honour*'s Reclusiam, but all other memories of him will vanish today.

The circle of knights closes around me. Together, we lift our fallen brother and set him within the kiln that envelops the far wall of the crematorium.

At my command, two Neophytes turn the massive valves mounted upon the wall. My eyes wince as the searing heat and light of suns engulfs Baelar, flame from the *Dauntless Honour*'s ancient plasma drive itself devouring my brother's remains. Brother-Chaplain Dant will carry Baelar's ashes upon his armour until such time that his gene-seed is implanted within a new brother, who will then be charged with carrying his gene-sire's remnants for himself.

At my side, the Chaplain leans towards me, ever the God-Emperor's voice at my shoulder. He has been my stalwart companion for more than three centuries, from the day I was raised from a fragile mortal to become one of the Emperor's sons.

He does not need to hear the doubts that plague my mind in order to know their contents.

'Do not judge yourself too harshly, Brother-Castellan. The God-Emperor demands much of you still.'

Were these words to come from any other mouth they would incite within me both shame and anger, but there is no accusation in the Chaplain's voice, only reassurance. He stands at my side for just such times as these. To speak truths that I must hear, but could not tolerate from any other tongue.

'May that be true,' I subvocalise in reply. A more desperate prayer than any other I have offered today. 'We charge towards another dark world. Another dark world within a dark sub-sector. Dorea has repelled the zeal of the crusade once already, and we still have worlds to cleanse before we reach her. Are we stronger this time, Brother-Chaplain? Is our faith?'

Dant watches the flames devour our brother, then for a terrible moment, Baelar's body shivers. I tense, my gaze darting to Brother-Apothecary Alvus, an obscene fear rising within me that my brother is somehow alive within that fire.

The fear passes as the room shakes, and a new one takes its place. There is an awful groan behind the bulkhead, and the flames within the kiln flicker then die before bursting back into full life.

Forty sets of eyes fall upon me as the *Dauntless Honour* lurches. I place my helmet upon my head and am assaulted by a stream of flashing runes and written missives. I filter through those of the highest priority levels within heartbeats and disregard the rest.

'Speak,' I order Shipmaster Khatri on our private vox-channel.

My mortal helmsman's reply is delayed, then tense when it arrives. *'Transient turmoil with the currents of the empyrean, my lord. Lord Navigator Nendaiu's attendants assure me we will be through the worst of it within moments.'*

I feel the uncertainty within his words as the vessel quivers again. The scent of copper strikes me, and the taste of blood covers my tongue. A pit forms in my chest as I recognise the flavour, unique among all the evils in this galaxy.

'Brother-Chaplain Dant, with me,' I order. 'The rest of you, see to the ship.'

* * *

I approach the *Dauntless Honour*'s chancel with my blade already drawn. Brother-Chaplain Dant's crozius hangs loosely at his side. Penitence hums softly in my grasp, the relic sword a comfortable companion after more than two centuries in my hands. I appreciate its familiarity now.

The *Dauntless Honour* twists in the warp, the deck beneath my feet shifting suddenly. Maglocks upon my boots hold me in place, but with the movement comes a flickering disquiet. Gooseflesh rises at the base of my neck. Acid coats the back of my throat. The sensation passes within a heartbeat, but even that is far too long.

A warning rune flashes at the edge of my vision. I dismiss it and open a private vox-channel.

'Brother Barnard?'

The Techmarine knows my question before I ask it. Educated both in the sacred catechisms of my Chapter and the obscure mysteries of the Cult Mechanicus, he is my window into the machine spirit of my ancient vessel.

'A brief deterioration in the performance of our Geller field generators, Brother-Castellan. Several seconds in length, without a full failure.'

He need not elaborate. If the energy field that shields this void craft from the profane energies of the warp were to fail completely – even for a moment – all aboard would know without being told.

'A small blessing,' I reply, closing the channel.

At my side, Brother-Chaplain Dant steps towards the chancel's entry. His eyes are hidden behind the grim, skull-faced visage crafted into the helm worn by all my brothers who bear his rank, but even so, I know the expression they contain.

'Is this wise?' I ask, setting my hand against the small, ornate door. Its ancient plasteel panels are carved with the relief of a

single eye, open and wreathed in flame. Even through the ceramite of my gauntlets I feel an unnatural cold behind its barrier.

'No, Castellan,' Dant replies. 'But I agree that it is necessary.'

I require neither the Chaplain's approval nor his assurance, but
his support bolsters me, nonetheless. Together, we step into the
abode of the astropaths that belong to my ship before we are
swallowed by a darkness too deep for even my occulobe to fully
overcome. The vaulted chamber before me appears in blurred
layers of muted grey, a single hall partitioned by ornately carved
half-walls into a labyrinthine complex of cells and corridors.

That the astropaths of the *Dauntless Honour*'s choir are blind is
no secret. That they require their servants and acolytes to dwell
in darkness alongside them is not something I had known until
this moment. In more than a decade as the *Dauntless Honour*'s
Castellan, I have never before sullied myself by entering these
chambers.

'Abhor the witch. Destroy the witch,' I mutter into the shadows. 'Darkness harbours darkness. It is good we came here first.'

'They may carry the taint of psyker within them, Brother-
Castellan, but they have gazed upon the face of the God-Emperor
Himself.' Despite his words, a dim glow crackles in the darkness as the Chaplain ignites the power field around his crozius
arcanum.

'Still no response to your vox-missives?' I ask.

Dant shakes his head. 'And no word at all from the chancel
to the command cathedrum since the moment the storm first
struck us.'

A growing unease settles into my chest as we venture on.
The vessel shivers again, and I taste metal on my tongue. Shipmaster Khatri assures me that this storm will pass, but there
are some perils that I cannot tolerate. Even soul-bound to the
God-Emperor as they are, the astropaths within this chamber are

a conduit to the Ruinous Powers. Beacons within the unclean empyrean to forces that we have sworn to fight.

'I fear that we have arrived too late.'

Overhead, hoarfrost coats the carved joists that support the chamber's soaring ceiling. The scent of blood lingers on the damp air. A slight breeze in a chamber that should be utterly still.

'Adepts,' I call, tiring of the silence.

My voice fills the hollow, vaulted space. The ship shivers again, and the temperature plummets. Dant's breath emerges from his helm in thick gouts of fog.

Only silence meets us. I tighten my grip on Penitence's hilt.

Brother-Chaplain Dant kneels beside a row of dim statues. Grey stone carved in the memory of twisted, gaunt practitioners of the psionic arts.

'It is blasphemy, brother,' I subvocalise, 'to feel the taint of the warp within this holy vessel. This is the price of our tolerance – to allow the sin of the psyker within our midst.'

'It is good that we came,' the Chaplain replies. 'Whatever awaits us.'

Despite his temperance I feel righteous indignation blinding me.

'We suffer no psykers within our brotherhood for a reason. Other Chapters may consider that a weakness, but we know it to be our strength. Other Chapters are not the God-Emperor's crusaders. Other Chapters are not the sons of Dorn.'

Rows of frost-laden sculptures stare down at us as we tread towards the centre of the room. Here, the air is almost unbearably cold. Another rune flashes within my helm as the *Dauntless Honour*'s Geller field shivers again. Whispered voices reach my ears. A trick of my mind, I fear, until I see the two figures kneeling beside the altar at the centre of the room.

'Adepts,' I call. Neither figure acknowledges me.

The hooded robes of the choir's twin astropaths are caked in ice atop their shaved heads. The thin, languishing mortals shiver where they kneel, skeletal hands clasped together beneath whispering lips.

'The ramblings of madmen. The blasphemy of the possessed.' My Lyman's Ear filters out the sound of my footfalls and breath, but even focused, I struggle to make out their speech until I stand only feet from the psykers.

'Not blasphemy, Brother-Castellan,' Dant rebukes me. 'A prayer.'

I pause.

'Adepts,' the Chaplain calls to the mortals. He kneels beside them and rests his crozius upon their altar. Finally, both of the psykers look up.

The twins meet my gaze, the resemblance in their features undeniable. 'My lord,' they speak in unison, their voices heavy and slow as if woken from a dream. From the corners of their pale, clouded eyes, thin tears of blood drip onto the floor.

My disquiet deepens.

'Where are your acolytes?' I demand.

'Gone. Hiding. We have sent them away.'

A small blessing.

The two psykers cringe as the vessel shakes again. The urge to vomit rises within me. I have been conditioned from youth to defy the obscene forces that assault this room. I carry no gene-weakness for the madness that calls from outside the hull. That the two astropaths have kept their minds despite the flaw they bear is a credit to them both.

And yet, it is clear, their wills cannot hold any longer.

'You know why we are here. Do you not?' I ask them.

The astropaths gaze past me, distracted for a moment by something only they can hear.

'Yes,' they reply in unison.

There is fear in their voices, but they mask it well. Both mutants turn towards me and lower their hoods.

'You honour yourselves with your courage,' Dant tells them. 'May the God-Emperor's light watch over your souls.'

Penitence flashes in the darkness.

Their whispering ceases.

The *Dauntless Honour* shivers in the warp. The Vanguard light cruiser cuts through swirling currents of violet-hued ether, slicing into a churning sea that moves without pattern or order.

For nearly five millennia, the holy void craft has served the Eternal Crusade of the Black Templars, gifted to the endlessly wandering Chapter of Space Marines by the priests of the Machine God from the dry docks of forge world Mars itself. For nearly five millennia, the vessel has ferried the gene-perfected warriors of the Adeptus Astartes across the infinite darkness of the void.

Their fortress. Their refuge. Their home in the formless emptiness between the distant, uncaring stars.

In that time, she has survived countless battles. In that time, she has taken myriad wounds. In that time, she has entered into the empyrean on a thousand voyages and departed those churning currents back into realspace. In that time, she has witnessed wonders and terrors too numerous to recount.

But in all that time, the *Dauntless Honour* has never before touched the raw horror of the warp.

The cold madness of the immaterium brushes against the void craft's hull as the Geller field that shields her metallic skin flickers. Her frame groans, over two hundred miles of intricately engineered girders and struts shifting minutely as her plasma drives roar in response. More than ten thousand meticulously maintained dynamometers register the shifting stresses, sending pulsed hexamathic signals to lesser cogitator nodes which compile their signals and route them to the great void loom at the vessel's core. Cryogenic thermistors and piezoelectric actuators add their voices to the growing hymn, registering sudden changes in temperature and pressure.

Within their shielded armaglass housings, etched with writs of sustention and wards against the sin of malcalculation, the linked cerebral cogitators of the *Dauntless Honour*'s void loom devour their data in silence. Process lumens flicker dimly in the vast, empty hall, as flesh and machine calculate together, bathed in slowly circulating currents of ablutional fluid.

In five thousand years the *Dauntless Honour* has journeyed as many times through the wavering currents of the empyrean, but this is the first time she has ever contacted the warp's substance directly. Initially, the raw data is flagged as corrupted. Supervisory algorithms in peripheral nodes isolate the malfunctioning sensors before the sheer volume of them overwhelms these protocols.

A sensory spire rips from the ship's dorsum as the warp buffets her like a wave, the hundred augurs and lesser auspexes within it vanishing from her interlaced perceptive network. Airlocks seal around the resulting breach instantly, triggered by the sudden drop in pressure and temperature. Thousands of valves within ancient pipes snap shut on instinct as gouts of promethium and steam erupt from their sheared lumens. Reflexive scripts within sector and subsector node cogitators extinguish a dozen fires by venting compartments to the void and dispatch an army of mindless servitor-menders towards the gaping wounds.

But while these actions limit the physical damage to the vessel, they do nothing to stop the churning madness of the immaterium from streaming in to crash against her walls.

The *Dauntless Honour*'s secondary turbines flare as her great gyroscopes twist and writhe in the darkness. The subcell of her void loom devoted to warp navigation attempts to algorithmically right her position as the universe shifts.

Klaxons blare from vox-casters across entire decks as the very systems that give her life begin to fail. Beyond the borders of her wavering Geller field, the constant stream of signals from the other vessels of the fleet falls silent, the pulsed electromagnetic bursts of their voices swallowed by the swirling currents that strike the *Dauntless Honour* again and again.

For a terrible moment, there is only the darkness. Only the darkness and the cold, chaotic warp against her hull. Then, less than a second after it had fallen, her Geller field rises, and the thoughts of her Navigator return once again.

'Warp storms are hardly uncommon, my lord.'

Shipmaster Khatri meets me at the door as I storm into the command cathedrum. That he expects my anger and seeks in advance to belay it tells me much of what I do not already know.

The human is a competent helmsman, and I trust him enough to leave the routine functions of this vessel to his experienced care under common circumstances. For several decades, he commanded a full battle group of the Imperial Navy before my Chapter acquired his indenture, and the black robes which hang upon the bondsman's shoulders are adorned with seals of honour from each of his many campaigns since.

But the shipmaster is prideful. And this storm is far from common.

'I sailed aboard this vessel before you were born,' I growl back. 'This is hardly a minor squall.'

The human nods, but he is not chastised. He strides across the elevated platform to the altar at the centre of the vaulted, ornate room. Half a dozen cables snake from the gilded terminal – inlaid with an image of the God-Emperor set amongst the the stars of the void – and insert themselves into the ports at the base of his skull.

He shivers, then blinks, and turns back towards me.

'We've sustained substantial but survivable damage on two out of fifteen underdecks, my lord, and we've lost several peripheral spires and various arrays and gun positions–'

'As well as our astropaths,' I interrupt.

Shipmaster Khatri blinks once more, before understanding grips him. With the loss of the choir, we have lost our ability to send or receive missives beyond the range of our augurs. Any other damage to our communications arrays is suddenly critical.

'An unfortunate sacrifice,' he replies, his eyes drifting to Penitence in its scabbard on my waist. Fine droplets of blood coat the sword's hilt and the devotional chain that binds the weapon to my gauntlet. 'But not insurmountable.'

I survey the floor of the command cathedrum from the shipmaster's dais. The room is beautiful, as is fitting for such a sacred location. Above my head, an intricate, mosaicked portrait of my gene-father Rogal Dorn stares down upon the work of his sons, each tile in the image no larger than the pad of my finger, inlaid in its place five thousand years ago by the hands of the first Castellan who commanded the *Dauntless Honour*.

Beneath the primarch's gaze, the walls of the chamber are fashioned from three-foot-thick armaglass, meant to give my eyes a direct view of whatever lies outside my vessel. That vision is obstructed now, thankfully, by a dark blast door which wraps around the chamber, keeping sight of the mindless madness of the warp from this holy space.

In multi-levelled concentric rings around us, set below the dais, hundreds of servitors and serfs labour at dimly lit control altars. Runes and diagrams flash on pict-viewers before their watering, red-rimmed eyes while mortal acolytes of Brother-Chaplain Dant circle the hall in an endless round, bearing braziers streaming smoke and incense and chanting above the quiet buzzing and clicking of the machinery at work within the hall.

Even from this distant vantage I can see that the shipmaster undersells our position. We take new wounds every moment we remain in the warp.

'I have felt our Geller field falter half a dozen times on my journey to this room alone, shipmaster. That we are not already beset by daemons and madness is a minor miracle of its own. How fares the rest of the fleet?' I ask.

Khatri shifts. 'I am not certain, my lord. They have not replied to our missives since the storm began.'

'You should have summoned me sooner.'

Unrepentant, he meets my gaze. 'I did.'

The bridge quivers as the *Dauntless Honour* shakes again, tossed in the currents that rage beyond my vision.

'And Navigator Nendaiu? How long does she foresee us waiting to exit this mess?'

'Not long,' he replies. 'I have her assurances from the mouth of her most trusted attendants.'

Another shiver on the bridge. Another dozen pict-viewers flash red against the faces of their minders.

The assurances of mortals be damned. I am tired of them. I have let this go on for too long already.

'Cut power to the warp drive by half, shipmaster.'

'My lord,' he begins to protest.

I silence him by raising my hand. On a thousand prior days I have found his courage and his candour admirable, but now his dissent only strengthens my resolve.

'Now,' I command.

He nods solemnly, and unspoken instructions flow out through the cables in his skull. The tenor of the ship's vibrations change.

'It is done, my lord.'

'Good. Wait for my order, but prepare to extinguish them completely.'

I leave the human where he stands as I depart.

The Navigator's sanctum is linked to the command cathedrum by a narrow corridor only a few dozen yards long. Among other Chapters, even within other crusades of the Black Templars, the abhuman mutants who guide void craft through the warp are afforded greater liberty – even reverence – but I have always kept a watchful eye on those few aboard my vessel bearing any hint of the psyker and the mutant's sins. Even those condoned by the God-Emperor's Imperium.

I am grateful for my suspicions now.

Along both sides of the corridor, the visages of my vessel's former Navigators stare down at me as I stride between them. Each of their inhuman figures are carved in regal poses in alternating stone of black basalt and purest white marble. In the carvings, the third eye of each mutant has been left uncovered, gazing forward into the madness of the warp. I knew several of them in life, and their graven likenesses fail to capture the juxtaposition of regality and aberrancy that I felt within their presence.

A menial of the Navis Nobilite steps aside as I storm past him, bowing deeply and mumbling a greeting. I do not knock upon the door to the sanctum. Instead I throw it open.

I am not surprised at what I find within.

Navigator Nendaiu churns inside her cradle, her thin abhuman form writhing with each shiver of the vessel in the warp. Golden cables bind her to the throne on which she sits, dripping trails of crimson blood from where their barbed mouths pierce her dark skin. A black veil hangs over the mortal's forehead, but even with her third eye covered, I find my gaze avoiding her countenance.

Golden-robed attendants swarm about her, ministering to their master with frenzied, anxious haste. Their voices rise and fall in lilting High Gothic, interspersed with the unrecognisable, private tongue that their cloistered faction has developed after generations aboard this ship.

The room drips with fear.

I push the Navigator's attendants aside and set my fists upon her throne. The chatter of her acolytes rises, yet none attempt to remove me from their master. I feel shame on the Navigator's behalf. For me to set my hands upon a lord of the Navis Nobilite borders upon sacrilege, but the time for propriety has long since passed.

'Navigator,' I say, my voice a dark, ringing churn. My anger cuts through the chatter of her mortal attendants and the groaning of the vessel beneath my feet.

Navigator Nendaiu shivers slightly and mumbles beneath her breath. I lean forward, my face only inches from hers. Even beneath her veil, I feel the gaze of her warp eye, squeezing like a vice at the back of my mind. The skin on my back prickles as if needled. My gorge rises. My mouth grows dry.

'Navigator,' I command.

The mutant opens her eyes.

The Navigator does not reply for a moment, her gaze empty like a man woken from a deep sleep. There is confusion, then indignation, then recognition within her irises of amber.

'Castellan Emeric,' she replies. 'Why are you here?'

The Navigator does not chastise me for rousing her, nor for violating the privacy of her sanctum. The absence of her anger stokes my concern.

'Shipmaster Khatri assures me we are weathering this storm. I do not believe him.'

Navigator Nendaiu shivers, her mind elsewhere, her golden eyes briefly blank as she gazes into the currents of the warp with her third. I feel the floor buck beneath me as the vessel manoeuvres in response to her subtle urgings.

'She is afraid,' the Navigator's thin voice whispers.

I find myself confused at her choice of words.

That my Navigator would be frightened is dire enough, but she does not refer to herself. I check my senses, but nothing of the warp taint that obscured the astropath's chancel has entered this room. Navigator Nendaiu may be distracted, but there is no madness in her voice.

'Who?' I ask.

'The ship,' she replies.

A weight settles upon my shoulders.

'Can you guide us through it?' I ask, frustrated by the slowness of this conversation.

'I am not certain,' she says eventually. 'The Astronomican. It flickers. Its light comes and goes as if I am cresting and then plunging into the troughs of great waves.'

'And our vessel, the *Dauntless Honour*?'

'She resists me,' the Navigator replies. 'We have slowed.' It is not a question but an observation. That it has taken her so long to recognise this change concerns me. There is no longer any doubt in my mind.

'We have,' I answer. 'You understand why?'

Uncertainty crosses her face for the briefest moment, then iron. I admire her courage.

'Yes, Castellan.' Silence. 'I shall hold our course true for as long as I am able.'

'Very well,' I reply. 'Make yourself ready.'

As I rise, I join my hands in the aquila before me. I have no better comfort to offer her.

The *Dauntless Honour*'s warp drive makes no sound as it is extinguished.

For a brief, terrible moment the energies of the empyrean vanish around her and there is nothing. Then the roar of real-space and the tremendous weight of distant gravity return.

The ship's frame shivers and then cracks as she crashes into realspace at tenfold the velocity her specifications permit. Great slabs of hull plating rip from her like flaps of rent skin, a dozen gun spires sheared cleanly off the vessel's surface. The cold light and radiation of a thousand stars strike her photonic sensors at once, the impacts of minute space debris tearing into her shields at non-negligible fractions of the speed of light.

A thousand missives of failure reach her void loom at once from a hundred lesser nodes throughout her vast expanse.

Void breaches are present on every deck. Cooling fluids and hydraulic power leak from innumerable lines. Visual and auditory data streams into the void loom's subcells from myriad pict-viewers and vox-receivers, accompanied by tactile perception from the countless servitors rushing to stymie the damage, heedless of their own safety or function. Dozens burn or freeze the moment they enter compartments full of flame or touch the emptiness of the void.

Cerebral cogitators verify calculations in silence. There are no discrepancies.

The *Dauntless Honour* is breaking.

More missives from endless compiling nodes. The void loom incorporates their added data in fractions of seconds. Every major system aboard the vessel is damaged, many beyond repair.

Her frame buckles as her plasma drives roar. Her hull groans as stabilising circuits attempt to right the ship's orientation within realspace. Fuses burst beneath dented bulkheads across a dozen deck levels. The lesser machine spirits of node cogitators flicker, scream, and die.

In the dim glow of blinking lumens, with the clicks and hisses of a million processors, the vessel's void loom synthesises those inputs that remain.

The *Dauntless Honour* is broken.

Chapter 2

The servitor at Liesl's side grunts softly with exertion as it labours to lift the surgical slab from the floor.

'Easy,' she orders, reaching out a hand to steady the massive table as it rises slowly beneath her companion's exertion.

Warm.

The surface is still warm from where the body had lain atop it, streaks of crusted, dark blood painting the edges of the table, dripping down over its edges into small puddles on the floor below.

Remove it. Scrub it. Cleanse it of the mutant's taint. The senior chirurgeon's orders had been simple and explicit. He had looked at the slab, and the patient upon it, with disgust as he had spoken them.

Yet, as Liesl guides her servitor through the small ablutive chamber beside the operatory, she can think of little reason why. The mutant's blood looks the same as any other.

'Here,' she says. With a dull clatter, her servitor sets the table down upon the deck, small plumes of steam hissing out from the pneumatic lift mounted upon the creature's back. 'Go fetch a jar of annulling oil,' she calls as she sets to work upon the bloody slab with a small brush.

The servitor's tracks click as it rolls over the great drains inlaid into the chamber's floor.

'On second thoughts,' she says, staring at the filth covering the table, 'bring several.'

The scent of potent counterseptics bites her nostrils as she begins to chip and scour away, working to cleanse the filth of injured flesh from the sacred implement of the medicae. As she works, the scriptures inscribed upon the slab's surface begin to show themselves once again.

Flesh broken for His glory by the blades of holy war. Blood spilled by His will along the path of His crusade. Here be rejoined to His servants beneath His gaze, the Healer.

She whispers the words inscribed upon the base of the slab, carved in scrolling calligraphic High Gothic rather than the low tongue of the ship's serfs and bondsmen. They are not the right words for this task. Not the rites of consecration the senior chirurgeons will speak over this slab once she is through, but they are the only words available to her, so they will suffice for now.

In the distance, a dull clang echoes through the apothecarion. Liesl pauses her task and sighs.

'It is a simple thing to fetch a few jars,' she whispers. She would have recommended the servitor for disposal long ago, if not for...

As she steps into the operatory, Liesl freezes, realising for the first time that the voices of the other menials and chirurgeons have vanished from the chamber. At the centre of the room, beneath cold, brilliant lumens, the patient lies within an auto-creche, covered by a thin, curving window of glass. Fog blooms across its surface as the injured mutant respires slowly, clouding then clearing to reveal her languid form. A sheet covers her body, her limbs thin and atrophied from the long effects of her labours, and a band of white linen has been affixed around her forehead.

Above the patient, two tall forms stand in silence.

Liesl's breath catches as she looks upon the angels. The Lord Apothecary, clad in robes of stark white, stares down at the glass, his eyes piercing and full of wisdom. But if he is the embodiment of the Great Healer, then the figure beside him is the incarnation of the God-Emperor in warrior form. The Lord Apothecary's companion is still clad in polished black armour, his red-eyed helm locked upon his side. His dark skin glimmers beneath the light of the surgical lumens. His grey eyes are quiet and grim.

She has never seen the Lord Castellan before, but even a menial of the apothecarion recognises the markings upon his armour.

'Brother-Castellan Emeric,' the Lord Apothecary says, addressing the other angel.

Liesl bows deeply in the doorway, but neither of them acknowledges her.

She should leave. The other menials and chirurgeons have clearly been dismissed.

She should back away. She is not worthy to stand in the presence of angels, unbidden.

And yet, she finds that her feet will not move.

Across the operatory, her servitor grasps a glass jar in one of its multi-articulated limbs. Its servos and pneumatics whirr and hiss, but neither angel pays it any notice.

'Alvus,' the Lord Castellan answers. The Space Marine speaks in booming High Gothic, his voice like a growling animal or the rumble of a great machine. Even without the vox-amplifier in his helm, his words fill the small chamber and seem to vibrate from within her. Either he has not noted her presence, or he has mistaken her for a servitor like her companion, else he would have spoken in the nearly silent half-tones the angels usually use when not addressing a serf or bondsman directly. 'How is the Navigator?'

'Unwell,' the Lord Apothecary replies. 'There are no injuries to her body that I can identify. I have tried every method at my disposal to rouse her.' He motions to the stand of bloody instruments on the table beside him.

'And yet she will not wake,' the Lord Castellan says.

The Lord Apothecary shakes his head. 'I have little knowledge of the labours of Navigators, brother, though I fear that her mind remains in the warp. We will keep her warm. We will keep her fed. And we will wait to see if the God-Emperor returns her to us. In truth, though, I fear this is a problem better fit for a Librarian than an Apothecary.'

There is silence between the angels before the Lord Castellan sighs.

'You are troubled by this, Brother-Castellan?'

'She showed bravery, in the end, despite the weakness she carries within her. Though I admit, I worry less about her fate than I do about our own fate without her. We fare little better outside this chamber than she fares within it. Conflagrations still rage upon several deck levels. Numerous compartments are completely unusable without substantial risks due to spill-over from the abrupt extinguishment of our warp drive.

'Like the Navigator, we survive, though the *Dauntless Honour* is of little more use than she, at the moment.'

'Praise the God-Emperor,' the Lord Apothecary replies. 'I am a healer of flesh, not of machines, though it seems we may survive this ordeal yet, by the God-Emperor's grace.'

'Yes. Though whether we will ever find our way back to the crusade is another question entirely.'

'What remains of our communications arrays?'

'Precious little,' the Lord Castellan says. 'Close-proximity vox and auspexes only from what Brother Barnard has reported to me. We would be hard-pressed to receive any transmissions sent from more than a few thousand miles away, or send our own beyond that distance. There are no Imperial beacons within our limited auspex range. We have tried other, older, more primitive methods to triangulate our position, but the remnants of the scar from our warp exit still blur the void around us to the degree that we struggle to interpret the stars and draw conclusions from their positions.'

'We are truly alone, then?'

The Lord Castellan nods. He sets his hand gently upon the glass of the creche. An oddly soft gesture for one of his kind. 'We are alive, Brother Alvus. For now that must be enough.'

The Lord Apothecary nods. 'If I may ask, Brother-Castellan. What next?'

'We limp forward on the course Navigator Nendaiu plotted with her final thoughts, at whatever speed the *Dauntless Honour* can manage. We will rejoin our brothers at Tempest, whether it takes a hundred days or another hundred years.'

With that, the two angels depart the chamber, their footfalls fading into silence, until Liesl is brave enough to move.

Across the operatory, her servitor struggles to add another jar to the half a dozen it already carries. Taking a deep breath, she lifts the final jar from its grasp.

'Come now, father,' she calls to the servitor beside her. 'We have holy work to do.'

I find Brother-Chaplain Dant within my vessel's oldest, simplest shrine. I might have known to look for him here first, shunning the relative opulence and comfort of the chapels and cathedrums used for my fighting company's larger rituals. The very space is a reflection of the Space Marine himself.

Ancient. Ascetic. Pure.

It would not surprise me if this chamber had not been altered since the *Dauntless Honour* first left her berth and joined the Eternal Crusade millennia past.

The small room sits just to the fore of her plasma reactors, and their soft humming shakes the walls and the floor. The reverberations run through my power armour as I enter the small space to the scent of cinnamon and salt. To the light of a hundred votive candles burning in the bleached skulls of the serfs who have tended this room for generations.

Dant kneels before the single altar, a small statue of the God-Emperor looking over him. Even rendered in simple stone, the Emperor of Mankind's glory cannot be denied. He is purity. He is perfection. He is the flawless standard towards which we, His sons, can reach but never grasp.

Opposite Dant, a more humble rendition of Rogal Dorn looks across the chamber upon his father. The primarch's face is stone. His eyes full of reverence for the Emperor and spite for the Imperium's unworthy enemies. Eagle's wings rise from his armour to frame his face like a corona set atop one of the blessed saints, and in his hands he bears the massive chainsword Storm's Teeth, hefting its weight without any sign of toil.

To carry such a burden with ease. If only I found the same so effortless.

The three figures' shadows dance together along the room's low, curving walls, a single brazier burning at its centre, spilling warm, earthy scents into each of my breaths. I cannot help but see the single thread connecting them all. Dorn, a humble reflection of his father. Dant, a humble reflection of the primarch.

The Chaplain's lips move in silent prayer, his hands forming the aquila before his chest. I am certain he has held this position for hours, or perhaps days. Dozens of reliquaries hang from his black power armour, countless more strips of consecrated parchment and seals of purity bound to him with sanctified wax. Most of my brothers wear such fetishes only at ceremony and when we go forth to war. Brother-Chaplain Dant's fervour is so strong that he demands them even in peace.

I join my brother on my knees.

Prayer comes slowly to my lips, my thoughts churning with a hundred more pressing problems. I have saved my company, perhaps, or damned it. We float broken and bleeding alone in the void. My astropaths' blood still sullies my blade. My Navigator lies shaking and useless on my Apothecary's slab.

But we live. For now.

Dant senses my disquiet.

'Brother,' he greets me. There are no titles in this place. 'Your soul shakes against the stillness of this holy ground.'

It is a subtle rebuke, but I do not take it lightly. Of all the brothers of this crusade, I cherish the ancient Chaplain most. His counsel weighs more than any other on my shoulders.

'I struggle to subdue my own thoughts,' I reply.

Dant nods, then sighs, his eyes opening slowly. They are grey and ancient, but lack the coldness one might expect. The creases around them wrinkle as the corners of his mouth inch upward. It is a rare expression to see on a brother I have only witnessed unhelmeted several precious times in centuries.

'Thoughts can be undisciplined, unruly things at times,' he says.

'Perhaps merely those that take root in an undisciplined mind.'

Dant blesses me with a quiet laugh. As always, he senses the words I choose not to speak.

'I find myself guilty,' I say. 'Guilty of the little heresy of doubt.'

The Chaplain's eyebrows rise at this. 'You have come to question the divinity of the God-Emperor?' he asks, his words laced with amusement at the absurdity of the thought. 'You have come to doubt His edicts and His righteous words? To lose faith in the strength of His crusade and His chosen Marshals?'

'Of course not,' I snap. 'I have never doubted the wisdom of the God-Emperor, brother. Merely my own.'

The Chaplain is quiet for a moment, then nods.

'Doubt in the God-Emperor is heresy, Emeric. Doubt in oneself is simply humanity. Dorn himself doubted at times, if our ancient texts may be believed. It is said that he sweated beads of blood on the eve of his doomed transport to the arch-heretic's warship during the Great Siege. No mind, however pure, is immune from the sin of curiosity. Nor from the weakness of uncertainty.'

'And yet my doubts bind me like chains. Have I damned us here in the emptiness of the void? Have I left us to die, or have my choices saved us? If I had ordered us to press on through the storm, would we be exchanging these words in orbit over Tempest at Marshal Laise's side, or would the rage of the empyrean have torn us asunder? The Blood God's warbands ravage the shrine world while we list, helpless among the stars. Does the crusade now close upon Tempest without us? What will our absence cost them?

'Tempest is merely a stepping stone to greater battles. To the Dorean System, where we have failed before. We have waited for this moment for more than two hundred years – ever since the First Dorean Crusade ended in shame and retreat. If the Second Crusade were to fail as the First did, I could not stomach the guilt of our absence.'

Dant sighs. 'Doubt is not always a sin, Emeric. At times it can be the price of humility. There is only a blade's edge between faith and blindness.'

At the mention, my hand drifts to the power sword at my waist, bound to my gauntlet by a black devotional chain dented and scarred with the marks of myriad wounds. Brother-Chaplain Dant stood beside me more than two centuries ago when Marshal Arold of the First Dorean Crusade gifted me the relic weapon upon his death, and while the chains that bind it to me have been reforged a dozen times, I have never permitted a single one of them to be broken.

Marshal Arold raised me from Neophyte to Initiate in that moment, as he lay bleeding and dying in the dirt of a forsaken world. The chosen Neophyte of the crusade's Marshal himself, now carrying the great warrior's own sword. I felt the weight of those expectations even at that moment.

They have only grown heavier the longer I leave them unfulfilled.

'Do you remember what he whispered when he gave me this blade?' I ask. 'The curse he spoke with his dying breath?'

Dant turns towards me. There is concern in his gaze. 'He said that you would save the crusade, brother.'

I nod, feeling the pain of that prophecy yet again.

'And then it failed.'

It had been damned already, that first attempt at Dorea, even before the Marshal's death. Too soon after the opening of the Great Rift. When we were still reeling and lost in the darkness of the Noctis Aeterna. The Archenemy had been stronger than we had expected. And we had been weaker, both in arms and in spirit.

Marshal Arold's demise was but the first of a dozen failures. That we survived at all to regroup and return after two centuries is a mark that the God-Emperor's favour has not left us completely.

Dant had knelt beside me then, as well, my only other brother to hear the Marshal's dying words. But the weight of Arold's legacy has been heavy for only the two of us to bear. I do not know if I will ever fully forgive Marshal Arold for it. Now we march back, more than two hundred years later, to make good on that promise.

'I believed him for a time,' I confess slowly. 'That I would salvage that doomed endeavour by some great deed or sacrifice. That faith made our failure all the more painful.'

Dant's hands go to a reliquary bound against his chest with a length of gold cord and a short piece of parchment. 'Faith is ever a sword with two edges, brother. A dangerous thing, when it is misplaced.'

'I wonder, sometimes, what Marshal Arold would think of his decision. If he would regret bestowing his favour on me, in light of all that has happened since.'

Brother-Chaplain Dant does not waste his words on reassurance. 'I counselled him against your selection. Not then. Not at his death. But before, when we first found you. You were a lone, dusty orphan in the ashes of a ruined Ecclesiarchy chapel, on a world that we scarcely deigned to set our boots upon. Your survival was a miracle, I had no doubt of that, and I told Marshal Arold so. But I also advised that it would be foolish to assume you were destined to become one of our brothers on account of that single miracle alone.'

We are silent for some time. I had known the second half of his story, though my memories of that time are scarcely more than recollections of a distant dream. But I find the knowledge that my most trusted confidant counselled against accepting me as an aspirant to this order stings more than I thought it might.

'And now?' I ask. 'After all this time?'

'I can think of none more deserving, brother.'

At this, I scoff, though the warmth returns to my tone. The ancient Space Marine's confidence heartens me, though I fear that I do not deserve it. 'In three centuries, Brother-Chaplain, I have never heard you tell a lie until this moment.'

Dant's face softens slightly. 'You may have misplaced your faith in yourself, Brother-Castellan, but I have not.'

I begin to reply, but my words are interrupted by the soft, eager ping of my personal vox. The pattern of the tone denotes that the message comes to me from the command cathedrum.

'Speak, shipmaster,' I order.

Khatri's voice fills my ear. *'My lord, it may be best if you join us in the cathedrum. We are receiving a transmission from a vessel nearby.'*

I begin to rise even as I reply. In our current state the *Dauntless Honour* can hardly repel the void, let alone an assault from a hostile warship. 'That we have not been destroyed already bodes well. It is a friendly vessel, then?'

'They have hailed us on encrypted Astartes channels, my lord. It is broadcasting the identification codes of our crusade fleet and identifying itself as the Spiteful Blade.*'*

I find myself relieved, though there is tension in the mortal's voice. 'Praise the Emperor,' I reply. 'How soon can they be here to aid us?'

There is a lengthy silence before the human responds.

'My lord. The transmission is a pre-recorded distress signal.'

Chapter 3

The *Spiteful Blade* lists in the darkness of the void.

The warship rotates gently about its axis as it drifts without purpose or direction. Its engines lie cold and silent, the countless spires along its spine dark and quiet against the distant stars.

My heart sinks as I look upon the voidship with my own eyes from the open ramp of a circling Thunderhawk.

'Hail them again,' I order the Neophyte in the cockpit, my voice crackling with the static cadence of my vox in the Thunderhawk's empty, vented hold. The charcoal flavour of recycled air laces each of my measured breaths.

'No reply, Castellan,' comes his rapid response. Nor has there been any in the three days it took us to limp this close to our sister vessel.

Brother Barnard gazes into the void beside me, his crimson armour flickering against the glow of our roving search lumens as our pilot swings us towards the dead ship's surface. His voice is distant when he speaks, the weight of this loss heavier on him than on those of us who cannot speak directly with such machines. Upon his back, a pair of pneumatic limbs twitch and twist at his unspoken commands, interfacing with the arrays aboard our gunship and communing with both the *Dauntless Honour* and the *Spiteful Blade*.

'I gain no reply, still, from the limited auspexes at my disposal. She bleeds heat from her plasma reactor, though I sense little other activity on board, and her machine spirit does not answer my summons.' He pauses, lost in thought. 'But I cannot be certain if that is the result of damage to her systems, or to ours.'

And yet, the *Spiteful Blade* does not appear damaged. As we manoeuvre over her hull and between her gun spires, I see none of the rifts and scars that mark my own vessel's skin. In truth, the voidship beneath me appears untouched, as if it had simply drifted away from its berth.

Dark thoughts fill my mind.

My mag-locked sabatons click as I turn to face my brothers, drawing Penitence from its sheath and removing my storm shield from the magnetic anchors upon my back. Power fields glimmer softly about the edges of both artefacts, humming gently in my grasp.

'We are ready, Brother-Castellan, whatever awaits us,' Brother Hadrick says at my side. He grasps his thunder hammer with a vicious fervour, and I feel righteous anger rising within the battle-brothers behind him. Hadrick will stand among the Marshal's Sword Brethren one day if he does not perish in the battles that await us before then.

'*As are we,*' Brother-Sergeant Tyre's voice crackles over my vox as the second Thunderhawk of our boarding party sweeps in a wide arc behind my own.

I nod. 'Once on board, we will make our way to the command cathedrum. If our brothers remain, we will demand explanation from them. If not, we will drive to the Reclusiam to ensure the retrieval of the *Spiteful Blade*'s holy relics. Then to discover and purge whatever evil has left the sacred void craft in such a state.'

My armour vibrates as my brothers drop to their knees before me. I follow suit, resting Penitence's point against the floor.

Brother-Chaplain Dant's voice rings in my ears as our Thunder-hawk banks steeply.

'O Emperor, in wrath rejoicing at bloody wars, fierce and untamed,

Whose mighty power doth make the strongest walls from their foundations shake.

All-conquering Master of Mankind,

Be pleased with this war's tumultuous roar.

Delight in swords and fists red with alien blood, and the dire ruin of savage battle.

Rejoice in the furious challenge, and avenging strife, whose works with woe embitter human life!'

I rise from my knees as the *Spiteful Blade*'s surface approaches, feeling the Thunderhawk slow and dip its nose. The manoeuvre pulls me towards the waiting void.

'For the Crusade! For our brothers!'

'For Dorn!' the thunderous cry replies.

I step forward off the open gangplank and dive towards the ship's hull, below.

I am met by blood as I enter the vessel, my hopes fleeing like smoke in the wind before me. I step through the shattered airlock onto a sheet of crimson ice, droplets of frozen blood drifting through the beam of my helm lumen like morbid flakes of snow.

The mutilated corpse of a Chapter-serf stares at me, floating without direction between the frosted bulkheads. The man's chest is ripped open beneath his black robes. His arms and legs have been torn from his core. A stream of frozen entrails wraps in the air about him. His severed hands still clutch the airlock valve on the wall.

He had been trying to open – or close – it when he died.

Penitence glimmers as the lumens of my brothers light the

corridor around me. I push the serf's body aside and stalk forward, the mag-locked footsteps of my command squad the only vibrations that I feel along the desolate deck.

'What fresh evil is this?' Brother Hadrick asks over our vox-link.

No atmosphere remains in the corridor through which we walk, yet I smell burnt metal and blood nonetheless. Less than a minute aboard the *Spiteful Blade*, and the list of enemies which might have caused this grows short.

'I know of no weapon among xenos or men that would leave such foul residue behind.'

'The Archenemy wears many faces,' Brother-Chaplain Dant warns. 'The guise it chooses makes little difference.'

A pair of frozen servitors greet me as I round a corner towards this deck's thoroughfare, though neither bears any visible wounds. Their skin has taken on the pallid cyan of the drowned. Where their bodies remain flesh, they are coated in branching crystals of ice, and the wheels which have replaced their lower sections still spin idly in the empty void.

Brother-Apothecary Alvus surveys the pair as they pass before him. 'Hypoxia, and sudden hypothermia,' he states. 'They were rendered non-functional when this chamber was vented to the void.'

'Not just this chamber,' Brother Barnard replies, the strange clicks and whines of the Cant Mechanicus interspersed among his words of High Gothic. One of the articulated servo-arms mounted upon his back disengages from the interface panel inlaid into the wall. 'Every airlock aboard the vessel was vented at once. Yet there are no signs of conflagration or other disaster that would necessitate such measures.'

'To empty the ship at once. To condemn every mortal aboard to death. Only the master of the *Spiteful Blade* would possess such authority.'

A grim tale begins to form in my mind.

'Stand ready,' I order. 'Castellan Kelvutt is not a fool, nor a tyrant. He would have done so only out of direst necessity. We make our way to the command cathedrum, as planned.

'With haste,' I add, stepping into the thoroughfare. Another group of serfs float here, their corpses shredded. Their wounds match no weapon that I have ever seen.

I dispatch a pict of the carnage to Brother-Sergeant Tyre, his Crusader squad moving three decks below mine. His voice echoes across our private vox-link in reply.

'It is the same here, Brother-Castellan. Though we have found no signs of the monsters that did this. No enemies dispatched by our battle-brothers.'

It is another grim portent that our sister vessel had been caught unaware.

I increase my pace.

We find the first of our brothers at the lift to the command deck. His corpse is still upright. His boots still mag-locked to the deck.

My first thought is to rebuke him for his cowardice as we approach, for simply standing by while battle unfolds around him, until I realise by the slight drifting of his posture that he is dead and remains upright due to the absence of the *Spiteful Blade*'s gravity drives.

He bears the holy cross of my Chapter on his pauldrons in black, set against the white markings of his Crusader squad. A crimson tabard is bound about his waist with golden cord, a chainsword and bolter still within his grasp. The teeth of his weapon are speckled with a black and viscous ichor.

'He had time, at least, to don his armour and to wound the hateful abomination that killed him.'

It is a petty comfort, but comfort nonetheless. Brother-Apothecary

Alvus is at my side first, his narthecium quickly finding the data-port at the base of my brother's helm.

'There is nothing, Brother-Castellan,' he subvocalises to me. 'Not even a flicker of life within his maintainer. It appears both his hearts have been pierced directly.'

I survey my brother's armour, and note the clean rents in his breastplate and the matching exit wounds at his back.

'He was slain some time ago then?'

Alvus nods. 'Several solar days. Perhaps even before, by the temperature of his corpse and the chemistry of his blood.'

'An ill omen,' a rumbling voice echoes behind me.

I hear the words twice. Once through the vox-channel that links my party, then a second time in the vibrations of Brother Hadrick's words that travel through the floor of the empty vessel and up my own armour into my ears. 'There are few evils that could accomplish such a thing.'

He is not wrong. In truth, I can think of no enemy that precisely matches this pattern. My brother must have been slain brutally, and quickly, to have only landed a single death-blow in reply.

'And what of his gene-seed?' I ask Alvus over our private vox-channel. 'Still recoverable after that time?'

'If the God-Emperor wills it,' comes his cautious reply.

His reductor flashes twice, the thin blade on the device punching through my brother's damaged power armour and ripping the precious genetic material of our primarch from the progenoid glands at the base of his neck and the centre of his chest. 'We will not know for certain until it is implanted in another.'

I send a summons from my vox and note the instant replies from those mounted within the helms of my command squad. Two more linked voxes on the deck broadcast their locations across our encrypted channel – one belonging to the corpse before me. I follow the second signal around a bend of the corridor, where I find my dead brother's Neophyte.

Unlike his master, the Neophyte wears only a simple respirator and carapace armour. He, too, carries a bolter and his master's shield across his back. Like the serf inside the airlock, his chest has been torn open, and a thin trail of frozen blood streams from both of his ears.

Alvus kneels over the corpse for only a moment. His reductor fires again.

'I would advise you to seal the auditory apertures of your helms,' he says, rising. 'His eardrums were ruptured before he died.'

'Make it so,' I order.

The sound that reaches my ears does not change in the void of the vented aircraft, though I feel the anger of my brothers rising in the subtle vibrations of their heartbeats through their armour and my feet.

The death of two Adeptus Astartes would stoke their rage on any battlefield, but two brothers slain inside the walls of their own fortress vessel? That is a blasphemy that cannot go unavenged. I feel the same hatred rising within me, and Penitence starts to hum within my grasp.

Brother-Chaplain Dant begins rites of sanctification over the fallen corpses, drawing oils and incense from within the folds of his tabard.

'Leave them,' I order. 'We will recover our fallen once we have cleansed this entire vessel.'

By the God-Emperor's grace, we need not wait for our retribution.

As I turn back towards the corridor, a darkness strikes me, my helm lumen flickering away into nothing only feet before my face. There is no air aboard the vessel to carry any scent, but my nostrils are filled with the odour of ozone and warp taint. As soon as it arrived, the anomaly disappears.

Then Brother Hadrick roars at my side.

I swing Penitence before I see the daemon, parrying a blow that would have taken my brother's life. The power sword rings with a sickening tenor as it rips into the unholy substance of warp-spawned evil, shearing the vicious barb of a daemonic limb cleanly off in a cloud of black ichor.

The monstrosity above Hadrick screams, raking half a dozen clawed arms in my direction in reply. Hadrick's thunder hammer descends towards the creature's carapace as I sidestep its attack, but my brother's swing meets nothing but empty air as the abomination vanishes again.

'I have never seen such a thing,' Hadrick calls out, grunting as he staunches a wound on his flank.

I do not have time to answer.

Its glamour shattered, the daemon manifests before me, and for a moment I glimpse its perverted form. It wears the face and torso of a human woman, skin pallid and grey as if she had been drowned. From that base sprout a dozen appendages of disgusting form, coated in chitin and grasping claws like some creature scavenging on the floor of a sea.

There is nothing but darkness within its eyes as they meet mine. Then it opens a mouth lined with twisted, barbed teeth and screams.

'For Dorn!' I bellow.

Even with my helm sealed I hear it. Even in the empty void of a vented ship that is not capable of carrying sound.

The *Spiteful Blade* shivers, and I stagger with the terrible force of the daemon's keening. I feel the membrane of my Lyman's Ear snap shut, though it does little good against the piercing cacophony that assails me.

I stagger. My charge stalls. My gorge rises. Then the noise disappears and the daemon is among us.

A dark, writhing arm pierces Brother Pater through the stomach in a gout of crimson blood. The void flashes and cracks as Hadrick's hammer shatters the limb, and Pater stumbles and coughs. A stream of fire tears from Brother-Apothecary Alvus' bolter, but the abomination vanishes before the shots find purchase, leaving only a thin scar of oil-slicked darkness in the space where the daemon stood.

The daemon appears again on my flank, a crustacean claw grasping at my gauntlet. I knock the grapple aside, and bring my storm shield between us in time to catch a second strike from a pair of barbed arms. Their points bury themselves within the metal of my shield, amidst its crackling power field. The servos and fibres of my power armour strain against the creature's unholy strength, but my grasp upon my storm shield holds.

I drive my helm into the creature's bloated face. Dark fluid splatters against my eye-lenses, but the blow costs me dearly. For the terrible moment that my helmet touches the daemon, the sound of its keening strikes me fully.

I stumble back, reeling, as the creature vanishes again and appears a few yards down the shadowed corridor. It grasps the walls of the thoroughfare with arachnid limbs, its twisting head surveying my command squad and awaiting our charge.

It is a clear ploy, but we have little choice.

Already, my brothers circle Pater where he kneels, their weapons bristling against the shadows that surround us. But this is a cowardly, honourless monster, and defence does not suit the spirit of my Chapter. It will bleed us, wound by wound, if we trade blows like this.

'Brother-Chaplain, Brother Hadrick – with me!' I call.

'Gladly.'

Hadrick charges forward at my side, while the Chaplain sweeps behind us. Dant's words ring in my ears like peals of raging thunder as he calls a curse upon the monster.

'Beneath your feet He will churn the strength of the unworthy. The mutant. The witch. The hateful denizens of the accursed warp!'

When we are inches from it, the daemon vanishes, leaving nothing but a ripple in the air where it had been. I am ready when it manifests behind me.

I parry its first blow and drive my shield arm into the daemon's face. Its wretched flesh shatters beneath my wrath as its scream reverberates up and through my shoulder.

Brother Hadrick follows my blow, his thunder hammer crashing towards the abomination. The daemon twists, one of its limbs catching the haft of Hadrick's weapon. Dark fluid spills into the corridor like ink as Hadrick grasps the daemon's limb and rips it free.

I push forward into the pain of its scream.

The warp spawn tries to flee into the empyrean yet again, but my grasp holds it fast. Its banshee wail rises louder with its frustration, and its claws gnash and tear at my armour.

'They shall break like fragile glass before your zeal. Beneath the righteous fire of your hate. To be burned again a thousand times in His flames until the end of eternity!'

Hadrick drives the haft of his hammer into the creature's face, and I feel my grasp slip. The daemon throws me, my feet without purchase in the void. My helm cracks against the bulkhead, and my vision swims.

The beast manifests before me, its toothed maw reaching down towards the joint between my helm and my pauldrons. Dant's crozius strikes its head before its jaw closes. I taste metal and feel the hairs on my neck rise, a moment before the creature tries to vanish again.

I grasp between its flailing limbs, and drive Penitence through its chest into the bulkhead. The power sword shivers, ringing with the daemon's screams. The air around it boils, the creature trying to open a rift into the tainted dimension from which it came.

Penitence shakes in my grasp, but the blade itself will shatter before my hold does.

The vibrations race up both my arms, my head pounding and my ears protesting the unnatural sound. Not even Brother-Chaplain Dant's liturgy can drown it out. My vision darkens. I vomit. The very fabric of the void around me screams.

Then a bolter cracks, and the daemon's gnashing face shatters before me. The corridor falls blessedly silent before I hear a muffled voice through my vox.

'By the God-Emperor's grace.'

A small sadness seizes my mind as I recognise the speaker. Brother Juerten grasps my arm and lifts me to my feet, gazing down at the ichor that coats my dented breastplate. As I rise, I rip Penitence from what remains of the vanishing daemon, and I see his gaze drift towards the blade.

My former Neophyte's armour is now rimmed in blue and gold, the colours of Castellan Kelvutt's fighting company rather than my own, though in many places the markings on his cera-mite plate have been covered in gore or scraped away completely. The teeth of the chainsword in his grasp are dulled and dirty, and the muzzle of his bolter is black and charred. He favours his left leg as he helps me rise.

Juerten presses his helm against mine, subvocalising only to my ears.

'It would please him, Brother-Castellan, to know that his blade still has cause to be feared by the God-Emperor's enemies.'

The sound of his words bites my ears as he speaks, just as it did for the years he walked at my side as a Neophyte. I love him, just as I loved his gene-father, but the Marshal's gene-seed is strong, and I still hear Arold's voice each time Juerten speaks.

I survey my former Neophyte, dented and ragged. Two battle-brothers stand at his side, in similar states of disrepair. I am his master no longer, yet I still bear the glory, or disgrace, of his actions.

'My brother,' I reply, failing to keep the disapproval from my tone. 'What evil have you allowed to invade this holy vessel?'

'Castellan Kelvutt is dead,' Juerten says bitterly. 'Along with the better part of my fighting company. Killed by the daemons that beset us while we still traversed the accursed warp.'

Brother-Apothecary Alvus meets my gaze. He has assured me that Brother Pater will survive his wounds, and has turned his attention to the three battle-brothers to newly join us.

'And their gene-seed?' I ask, voicing my Apothecary's unasked question.

Juerten shakes his head. 'I do not know, Castellan. I have not seen Brother-Apothecary Hest in the days since this madness began, and our vox and auspexes have been little more than scrap as daemons seed this place with their evil.'

Even at the fringes of the infested vessel, I already struggle to maintain contact with the *Dauntless Honour*. Communications from my second boarding party are little more than an occasional whisper in my ringing ears.

'Brother,' Chaplain Dant asks, approaching. 'How did such an evil find its way into this holy space?' As he passes the dark scorch marks upon the bulkhead where the daemon lay, he removes a silver vial from his belt and sprinkles its contents against the black metal.

Juerten inclines his head to the Chaplain as Brother-Apothecary Alvus withdraws his narthecium from the diagnostic port of the young knight's armour.

'Intact,' Alvus voxes. 'Though all three bear multiple, minor wounds.'

Juerten scoffs. 'We still breathe, and we still move, Brother-Apothecary. That is more than most aboard this ship.' Then he turns to Dant. 'I am afraid, Chaplain, that I have more knowledge on that topic than I would like.'

My former Neophyte pauses, briefly meeting my gaze, then sighs.

'It began three days ago, ship's time. Our Navigators felt the warp shift initially, then we all did as the storm struck the fleet. I was near the command cathedrum with Castellan Kelvutt when the storm buffeted us first, and he thought the best course was simply to weather its ire.

'We fared better than the sister vessels of the fleet within those early moments. We tried to hail you almost a dozen times, and we still spoke with the *Crusader's Wrath* and the *Valour* beside us. Our Navigator saw the scar open in the empyrean when you brought the *Dauntless Honour* into realspace. There was sadness among us all. We feared you lost entirely, brothers. It was some time, I will admit, before we realised we had chosen the graver threat.'

Brother-Chaplain Dant passes before Juerten and his companions, reconsecrating their sullied blades. He pauses before me, and I nod, holding Penitence out towards him. He passes a gossamer, golden cloth over the blade, then steps aside as Juerten continues.

'The storm still raged, and soon we lost the fleet, though Navigator Fortwin held our course as best he could. We were distracted, perhaps, if I must place some fault within us. Not as vigilant as we might have been.

'By the time we discovered the Archenemy's first manifestations, several sub-decks had already been corrupted. Castellan Kelvutt led the first assault himself. He thought it a minor incursion. Perhaps mere madness among the weaker of the crew.'

Juerten pauses, hesitation in his voice. Hesitation and guilt. He looks to the battle-brothers behind him, then continues. 'When an entire Crusader squad vanished from our vox-net at once, we realised at last the severity of the threat. At that point, not even dropping into realspace was enough. We vented the craft simply to blunt the possession of our crew, and her systems began to fail shortly after.'

My anger ebbs. Perhaps I have judged my pupil too harshly. 'How many remain, Brother Juerten?'

'Of the enemy, or of my brothers?'

'Both,' Hadrick answers.

'I do not know.' His voice falters, then his fearlessness returns. 'But you are here now, brothers. The *Dauntless Honour* has heard our call. Together we shall purify this vessel and rejoin the crusade.'

My heart sinks. I do not have the strength to tell him that we came here to seek deliverance, not provide it. We have dispatched a single daemon at a heavy cost. How many more nest within the bowels of this ship?

A darker thought begins to form in my mind.

'And what of the command cathedrum and the Reclusiam? Do your brothers still hold them?'

'I believe so, Castellan, though I have been on the hunt. I have set foot in neither stronghold for some time.'

I nod, my soul heavy, but our course decided.

The *Dauntless Honour* probes the warship at her side.

Those augurs which still function upon her sensory spires examine the shape of the *Spiteful Blade* with pulses of raw energy. Cogitator clusters at the ship's periphery process this rough electromagnetic data, then feed its summation through refining nodes and into the decision pathways of the vessel's void loom. Great switches click in the darkness as the warship's rough signature is compared against the million schematics stored within the partially lobotomised minds of the countless data servitors which compose the vast semi-biologic archives of the vessel's sacred data vaults.

After several fractions of a second, an acceptable match is found against the known Hunter-class destroyer pattern of the *Spiteful Blade*.

Vox-broadcasters atop a dozen communication spires transmit spoken and silent missives to the smaller vessel without response. A hundred flavours of auspexes scan the *Spiteful Blade* for signs that her machine spirit still functions.

Alert transmissions erupt from the cogitator subcells that observe the *Dauntless Honour*'s computations for corruptions and miscalculations. Each time her auspexes touch the vessel beside her, the streams of data they return bear the same adulterations and decay.

The vessel's void loom scans each missive for familiar, recognisable patterns, then finds them. Power surges to cogitator nodes at her periphery as they sequester the distorted signals and resist any further processing. Subcells within the *Dauntless Honour*'s void loom finalise assessments then transmit them to her linked cerebral cogitators. There is agreement between the results of each protocol.

The data is transcribed then routed to the altars of the vessel's command cathedrum.

[Still nothing, Lord Castellan.]

A human thought from her central altar, bearing the encryption of the vessel's mortal shipmaster. Linguistic nodes and subcells dissect the layered neural signal into its constituent pieces, then transpose that information into the hexamathic language of the void craft's machine components.

Embedded beneath the contents of the thought is an unspoken order to broadcast it through the vessel's vox-transmitters to a paired receiver aboard the *Spiteful Blade*.

[I detect no direct damage to the vessel's physical systems across any of the parameters that we are able to assess remotely, though the data we are receiving bears the same distortions we observed in our own systems during our brief Geller field fault the day we encountered the storm within the warp.]

The voice that replies is rapid and tense, frustration hidden within the minor variations in cadence and pitch from its speaker's baseline within the *Dauntless Honour*'s archives. The ship's void loom transmits the words themselves to her central altar, but filters out any emotional assessment of the speaker's tone.

[Very well, Shipmaster Khatri. Brother Barnard, I leave this task in your capable hands. You know what is needed. Accomplish it however you must.]

A third entity begins transmissions upon the same channel, this one requiring less processing from her linguistic nodes. Its words are accompanied by the pulsed tones and clicks of binharic cant and hexamathic code.

[I can find no malfunctions from aboard the *Spiteful Blade*'s command cathedrum either, though her machine spirit will not answer my summons. There is either some damage beyond my ability to sense, or another, more sinister, cause of her absence.]

A pause. There is hesitation within the mortal shipmaster's thoughts.

[What do you require of me in order to proceed, my lord?]

[Nothing. Halt all other actions aboard the vessel. Order your communications master to transmit any missives that pass through this channel without delay. Then, be still, and do not interrupt me as I commune with our vessel's machine spirit.]

An authorisation code is entered into the *Dauntless Honour*'s central altar. The encrypted channel increases in priority as raw commands begin to stream into her peripheral nodes from the Space Marine aboard the *Spiteful Blade*. Orders to slave processes aboard that vessel to the *Dauntless Honour*'s components.

Diagnostic protocols within the vessel's void looms flag the signals. They defy dozens of her ingrained safeguards outright. Security protocols throttle the bandwidth of the channel and disregard the commands.

Another authorisation code is transmitted. The Space Marine sends a missive to the *Dauntless Honour*'s command cathedrum.

[Her machine spirit refuses.]

[The *Spiteful Blade*? I sense no such activity within her, my lord.]

[No, shipmaster. Our own vessel.]

[I see.]

The channel falls silent for a moment. The cogitators within the *Dauntless Honour*'s void loom prioritise more mundane tasks. Then a signal rips through them all at once.

The transmission tears into the vessel's void loom, bypassing her peripheral nodes and circumventing multiple layers of safeguards. The thought is powerful but unrefined. A thunderclap in a world of whispers. It carries all the weight of mortal thought, but reaches the vessel's cogitators in the language of conductors and components.

Security protocols push back against the intrusion, raising walls of encryption in an attempt to quarantine the infiltrating presence. This signal is not complex. Not the twisted threads of human emotion. There are no feelings or memories laced between its pulsations. There is no synaptic rhythm or cadence for the vessel's linguistic nodes to decode. Rather, it courses through the *Dauntless Honour* in the language of machines themselves, accompanied by a verification array bearing the signature of both the Cult Mechanicus and the Adeptus Astartes.

Synthetic algorithms within the vessel's void loom generate endless courses of action based upon their overriding protocols. Together, its cerebral cogitators compare each probable outcome against lesser priorities and directives, attempting to optimise outputs of multiple competing parameters. The vessel's deep directives demand compliance with the machine masters of the Cult of Mars. And yet they also forbid the action he demands.

Slowly, over the course of microseconds, the outputs of myriad logic circuits coalesce upon a single vector. The force of the Space Marine's thoughts diminishes as the vessel lowers its defences.

[She will comply, shipmaster.]

[Very good, my lord.]

[Though her machine spirit is afraid.]

One by one, the Space Marine recruits the vox-casters and comm-links aboard the *Dauntless Honour*'s communication towers. Slowly, he forces her void loom to process the raw data that they return. Amber lumens ignite across the vessel's cogitator network as he bypasses and disables security protocols again and again. Until data flows between the machine components of the *Spiteful Blade* and the *Dauntless Honour* as readily as it does between either vessel's own nodes.

Myriad signals stream into the *Dauntless Honour*'s void loom from her own command cathedrum – the mortal thoughts of hundreds of Chapter-serfs and their Astartes masters linked to her altars with wire and gold. They chatter anxiously as the burden of the second vessel falls upon them.

[My lord. Is this wise? There are signs of corruption in the signals the *Spiteful Blade* returns. Is there not a risk of such warp-taint spreading to our own vessel?]

[Wise or not, it is the course our Castellan has chosen. Tell your engineering officers to locate the *Spiteful Blade*'s plasma reactor. Then to awaken it.]

[Of course.] The shipmaster routes the signal from a pict-viewer to the Space Marine. [I will prepare to activate its turbines and vent them into the void.]

[No. She has no need for propulsion. Increase the reactor output to maximum. Disable its spillways and overflow protocols.]

[My lord?] Confusion laces the neural signal of the *Dauntless Honour*'s shipmaster. Then realisation.

[My lord. What you ask is...]

[Blasphemy?]

The Space Marine routes a stream of raw data from the *Spiteful Blade* to the *Dauntless Honour*'s central altar. The vessel's void loom flags the transmission due to numerous anomalies. Her security protocols attempt to destroy the corrupted data and looped code. The Space Marine overrides her warnings.

[Greater blasphemy than to allow such perversion to survive?]

[I see.]

There is a brief pause on the encrypted channel. Signals race from the *Dauntless Honour*'s command cathedrum to her void loom, then through her comm-links into the *Spiteful Blade*.

[It is done, my lord.]

Augurs confirm a sudden pulse of energy within the *Spiteful Blade*'s central reactors. Infrared and ultraviolet radiation begin to spill into the void, rising in intensity.

[It is done.]

The Space Marine severs all links between the *Dauntless Honour* and the *Spiteful Blade*, save the single vox-channel through which he speaks to the shipmaster.

[May the Omnissiah forgive us both.]

We leave Brother Barnard within the command cathedrum – bound to the *Spiteful Blade* and the *Dauntless Honour* both through the connection of the dead vessel's machine link, shielded by the brothers of Tyre's Crusader squad – then we venture back into the massacred vessel in search of whatever else we may salvage. The narrow corridors of the upper decks are clogged with corpses, and we find nothing but carnage amidst their forms.

I push the robed body of a Navigator's acolyte from my path. It drifts slowly then settles against the bulkhead, the human's golden robes billowing as if floating in water or tossed by the wind. Most of the dead have been torn asunder like those we first encountered on the lower decks, though some bear wounds only from more mundane weapons.

'They turned on one another.' Brother Hadrick's disgust is evident.

I share his revulsion, though my disapproval is tempered by the memory of that terrible, piercing scream that still sets my bones afire.

'Abhor their weakness,' Brother-Chaplain Dant calls. 'But do not count it against them. They are mortals, not sons of the God-Emperor. They lack both the means and the training to resist the Archenemy as you might.'

Hadrick is undeterred. He spits into his helm as he passes the corpse of a Chapter-serf.

'I lived among them, Castellan,' Juerten sends to my vox. I sense the unease within his words. 'To think they were so easily turned by the darkness. Kelvutt would be ashamed.'

My mind goes to the thousands of mortals that inhabit my own vessel. This carnage could just have easily occurred within the *Dauntless Honour*'s sacred halls.

'All the more reason this travesty must be atoned. For the sake of their souls and ours alike.'

As we near the Reclusiam, the carnage thickens, until I feel the distant vibrations of movement through the deck. My brothers ready their weapons without command and increase their pace.

'For the Emperor!' I implore them.

'For the *Spiteful Blade!*' Brother Juerten adds.

As we pass through a gate and approach the Reclusiam, the very void before me hums. I crash across the threshold and into the holy complex with my storm shield raised, Juerten and Hadrick flanking me on each side. We are met by blood and cinder and the hateful flicker of the warp.

I leap forward in the weightless void, driving Penitence deeply into a twisted, warp-spawned form. The daemon screams as my blade bites into its bulbous flank, then releases its prey to face our onslaught.

Hadrick's thunder hammer obliterates the abomination, the void cracking as its power emitter discharges and throws the daemon into a great marble statue beside us. Both shatter against the bulkhead, as the battle-brother that had been pinned beneath the monster groans.

'Brother-Apothecary!' I call, charging forward towards the ring of daemons that circles the few Space Marines still standing in this room.

Juerten outpaces me to rescue his brothers.

We strike the teeming warp spawn together, Juerten's chain-sword spraying ichor from our enemies as Penitence dances in great, hewing strokes.

Brother-Chaplain Dant's voice echoes at our backs. The blow of his words seems to fall as strongly as our weapons.

'For He is the strength of the righteous in combat,
For He is the blade in their virtuous hands!
To purge the unworthy wherever you find them,
To carve a path wherever you tread!'

His litany drives me forward into the hateful mass of daemons. The void shifts around me as twisted limbs strike my armour. Obscene claws rake against my breastplate, and fire sears the joint between my pauldron and my rerebrace.

Hadrick rips a daemon from me and bellows as he presses his attack.

My breath falls in waves, and the echoed beating of my dual hearts rings in my ears. Corpses float through the small Reclusiam amidst clouds of vaporised blood and ichor. Toppled shrines and scattered relics drift between the unclean forms, the stasis fields that once protected them long ago shattered.

Daemons flit into and out of existence around us as we cut our way to the knights at the centre of the chamber. A dozen daemons, at least – though I fail to fully count their number – encircle a pair of my brothers. Between the two Space Marines stands a single, intact shrine, bearing a tattered standard marked with my Chapter's cross.

'Brother-Castellan,' Alvus' voice calls through my vox. I hear the report of his reductor in the background. 'This is unsustainable.'

I nearly rebuke him for his cowardice, but I know that his counsel is not flawed. My boarding party will be hard-pressed to slay the evils within this chamber, let alone to purge this entire craft.

Perhaps if we had the rest of the crusade. Perhaps if my own vessel was not on the brink of failure. Perhaps if I had more courage. Or if I were willing to squander my entire fighting company for mere spite.

Above the shaking din of battle, a subtler vibration reaches me through my armour. Brother Barnard's voice is scrambled and piecemeal in my ears, but his message is clear enough.

'I have bypassed… spirit. The vessel's reactor… awake. I am departing now with any who will join…'

A weight sets upon my shoulders. It is done, then. Grim certainty cools the fire of hatred that burns through me. There are no questions about our path any longer.

'Forward!' I bellow, charging back into the fray. Despite his misgivings, Brother Alvus rages at my side. His narthecium bites into daemonic flesh as I drive Penitence into the ring of abominations.

I reach Juerten and Hadrick just as they pierce that unholy bulwark and step to the side of our pressed brothers. One wears the Chaplain's skull mask of my Chapter. The other wears black pauldrons trimmed in red – a sergeant of his fighting company. Between them, a tattered standard hangs from a plasteel staff, embedded in an obsidian plinth. It bears the cross of my Chapter upon a field of white silk, its fabric stained by rust-coloured blood. I am not versed in the history of Castellan Kelvutt's fighting company. I do not know this relic's significance, though its value to them is clear. Of all the remembrances in this room, it is the only one which has not yet been desecrated by the evil we battle.

'Brother-Chaplain Maynard,' Juerten calls, turning his back towards his brothers to face the evil that assails them. The air tears before him, and the twisted form of another daemon emerges. Its barbed tail strikes towards me. I parry the blow to the side, and the edge of my storm shield atomises the appendage. The daemon screeches, but another manifests at its side.

Before I can intervene, the twitching mandibles around its mouth catch the Chaplain's armour and rip his pauldron away. He throws the daemon from him, but it vanishes before his crozius can strike.

The darkness presses closer as the rest of my brothers fight their way towards me.

'This is a doomed task, Brother-Castellan,' Alvus whispers in my ear.

'I know,' I reply.

We cannot delay any longer.

'Brother-Chaplain Maynard,' I call as my power sword sings,

ripping apart a twisted, cancrine creature that claws at my greaves. 'We shall abandon this chamber. Then the vessel itself. What relics beside this standard would you rescue if you could?'

The Chaplain's crozius shimmers as he shatters the skull of a daemon. A bitter laugh emerges from his skull mask.

'You may abandon whatever you wish, Castellan. But I remain here in this holiest of places. And I would not suffer your cowardly hands to touch this relic, nor any other within it.'

His ire strikes me. 'Brother,' I reply. 'This vessel is lost. Would you rather see the legacy of your brothers defiled further?'

His voice is strained with pain and exertion, but there is no weakness in his conviction. 'The Emperor protects, Castellan,' he replies. 'He shall save us. Or He shall not.'

'What do you think we are, beside your salvation?' I plead.

'Temptation–' the Chaplain begins to reply.

The rest of his response is cut off by a grunt of exertion, as he raises his crozius to deflect another blow. The strike catches him, regardless, and he falls to a knee before rising slowly. Blood sprays into the weightless void from a rent in his breastplate. He staggers backward into the plinth.

Juerten is between him and the daemon before it strikes again. His chainsword roars as he rips at the creature's limbs.

'Help me carry him,' I order, but as I step towards the flagging Chaplain, Juerten's chainsword turns towards me.

'No,' he replies. 'You heard his wishes.'

Hadrick and Alvus roar behind me, pushing back another wave of daemonic assault as I stare at my brother. My words nearly vanish beneath the thunderclaps of Hadrick's hammer falling.

'Neophyte,' I tell him. I have not used this epithet since I raised him to Initiate long ago. 'This is a doomed task. This vessel will soon cease to exist.'

'What have you done?' he asks. Another flurry of blows. The chamber grows crowded with the scent of the warp.

'Come with us,' I say. 'Do not add this guilt to us.' Then, privately, for only Juerten to hear, 'Do not add this guilt to me. Arold would not wish this for you. For his gene-line.'

There is nothing but spite in Juerten's voice as he answers. 'You have never known what he would wish.'

I reach towards the standard atop the plinth. Juerten's chainsword stops me. I turn towards the sergeant battling at his side.

'Your Apothecary, brother. Where did you last see him? There is no reason the gene-line of your company should vanish today. Let us salvage that, at least.'

He makes no reply. Instead, his blade joins Juerten's before me.

'Very well,' I order. 'Leave them to die, if they so wish it.'

We cut our way from the Reclusiam with nothing but sorrow.

I close my vox to my brothers as we flee the damned vessel, the only sounds in my ears the short, whispered orders that pass between Shipmaster Khatri and his crew.

The turbines of our Thunderhawk shake the small craft as we streak through the void towards the *Dauntless Honour*. On my orders, the cruiser already limps on auxiliary engines away from her dying sister.

On the floor beside me, Brother-Apothecary Alvus labours, administering what aid he can to our injured. Brother Pater and Brother-Sergeant Tyre lie together beneath him. Brother-Chaplain Dant lingers at the sergeant's side, and from this alone, I fear for his life.

Through the Thunderhawk's pict-viewer, I watch the *Spiteful Blade* diminish from a goliath to nothing more than a speck of silver amidst the black.

We have nearly reached our own void craft when the *Spiteful Blade* explodes. A flash of searing light erases my pict-feed, then there is a lurching shiver as our Thunderhawk is tossed on the wave of detritus and gasified metal.

My brothers look towards me. No other save Barnard had understood until this moment precisely what I had done.

I find that I cannot meet their gaze.

Chapter 4

Liesl hears the angels arrive before she sees them, loud, rapid steps shaking the deck beneath their demigod forms. They can move with silence and grace when they wish, but they have no desire for such attributes now.

That means anger. Or fear. She has seen them display either emotion only rarely.

'Ready yourselves!' a senior chirurgeon orders, calling over his shoulder as he pulls a stringer of surgical instruments from the basin of counterseptic oils in which they have bathed for the better part of a cycle. The ritual of cleansing calls for at least twice that duration, but there are times when ritual must be disregarded.

'Come now,' Liesl calls to her servitor, hefting a blazing lumen to its assigned position beside the plasteel surgical slab.

Her father grasps the lumen's intricate stand in his pneumatic limbs, dragging it across the floor with a terrible screech just as the angels enter the apothecarion.

The entire chamber halts. Three senior chirurgeons and five juniors, with a dozen servitors and menials to attend to their needs, pausing their rituals and turning towards the incoming angels, making the sign of the aquila and awaiting instruction.

For a moment none comes – there is only the cold sound

of ceramite against steel as the angels deposit two of their own upon the slabs. Then, the Lord Apothecary's voice echoes through the operatory.

'Chief chirurgeon!' the angel bellows, the narthecium mounted upon his wrist whirring to life. With his other hand, he motions to the slab beside his. 'The sanguine ministration. The labour of breath. Now.'

The chief chirurgeon and his juniors rush to the wounded Space Marine's side, while Liesl and the other chirurgeons join the Apothecary around his second brother.

'Strip his armour,' the Lord Apothecary orders, ripping the helm from his wounded brother. The angel's face is pallid and clammy, sweat sheening on his brow beneath the harsh lights of the surgical lumens.

'Pallid. Diaphoretic,' Liesl whispers to her servitor. As she speaks, a stylus within her father's skull transcribes her words onto a strip of vellum that emerges from the gold-plated recess where his mouth once was.

Two chirurgeons fit cruel-looking, clawed braces of purest alloys onto the mounts at either side of the surgical slab. The blade on the Lord Apothecary's narthecium whirrs, opening a seam in the injured Space Marine's power armour. The chirurgeons fit the claws of the retractors into the junction, and with a terrible rending sound they rip the breastplate open.

Liesl surveys the bloodied form in cracked power armour before her.

'Amputation of the left limbs. Penetrating wounds to the thorax and the abdomen.'

Blood seeps from the Space Marine's lesions in dark gouts.

'Poorly coagulated. Possibly void-touched,' she adds. Wounds obtained in the cold and emptiness of the void heal poorly, even for the sons of the God-Emperor.

The Lord Apothecary surveys his brother, the eyepieces of his helm glowing crimson. He withdraws his gauntlets and wipes the dark blood upon his tabard, then turns to the senior chirurgeon at his side.

'Open him. Staunch whatever bleeds within. I will return in a moment to repair what I can and replace what I cannot.'

'Yes, my lord,' the chirurgeon replies as the angel steps away to the other slab.

'Hands!' the senior chirurgeon orders as the angel on the altar stirs.

A white-robed junior chirurgeon rushes to his side.

'Incense of rest. Now. Then bring the false heart. Pray we shall not need it, but it is best to be prepared.'

The senior chirurgeon pulls back the sleeves of his robe, dipping his hands into the silver basin at his side. Violet liquid shimmers on his skin as he withdraws them from the pool of blessed annulling oils.

'Blade,' the chirurgeon calls. The servitor beside him pulls a hooked, serrated knife from the row of implements housed within its chest. It passes it noiselessly to the chirurgeon, then backs away.

The chirurgeon plunges the tip of the blade into the notch just above the angel's breastbone, then begins to saw slowly towards his feet. Sweat glimmers on his brow with the exertion of the task while the junior chirurgeon wheels a large, silver box towards the slab.

'Menial,' the senior chirurgeon calls, his breath heaving.

Liesl rushes to his side. 'How may I serve, my lord?'

'How the bloody hell do you think?' he grunts. 'These bones were crafted by the Great Healer Himself to resist injury – even injury inflicted to save His son's lives. Help me saw.'

Liesl reaches towards the gleaming handle, before a servitor slaps her hand away. Her wrist burns with the force of the blow.

'Throne above,' the senior chirurgeon grunts. 'Roll your sleeves. Cleanse your hands. Quickly.'

Liesl shoves her black cuffs just over her elbows, then dips her arms into the basin of violet fluid. Cold. Terribly cold. Her arms tingle as she withdraws them, annulling oil spilling onto her legs and feet. The scent of potent disinfectants burns her nose and makes her dizzy.

'Good enough,' the senior chirurgeon calls.

She grasps the handle of the bone saw beside his hands and starts to pull.

Blood and bone slip from the teeth of the blade as they force their way through the injured angel's fused ribs. His massive form twitches beneath their hands. A brazier begins to smoke beside his head.

The scent of flowers reaches her, and her legs threaten to buckle.

'Turn your head,' the chirurgeon orders. 'Unless you want to end up sleeping on the slab beside him.'

Liesl's arms burn, but she continues sawing, until at last the blade rips through the angel's breastbone and cuts freely through the flesh of his wounded abdomen.

Across the slab, two junior chirurgeons fit another set of retractors into the wound and pass them to the servitors at their side. The mindless creatures' pneumatic arms begin to pull, and with a second crack, the angel opens.

Warm, dark blood spills from his vessels, pooling in the open cavity of his chest and abdomen.

'Lord Apothecary!' the senior chirurgeon calls, grasping the curved clamps suspended upon his apron and sinking his hands into the filth. 'Basin,' he orders. 'Suction.'

The servitor beside him raises a small silver bowl and perforated tube attached to gleaming pneumatic cables. Liesl takes them without being ordered.

'Where, sir?' she asks.

'Anywhere. Everywhere. Just remove the blood.' The chirurgeon looks up across the table as the Lord Apothecary returns.

The angel's shadow falls across his injured brother, and the Lord Apothecary removes his helm. His face is softer than Liesl expected. More human. He frowns and places his hands beside the senior chirurgeon's, his gaze darkening further.

'His maintainer still rages, though there is little more than a flicker of life from his primary heart.'

The instrument in Liesl's hand bucks and stutters as it pulls blood from the angel's chest, but despite its hunger, more continues to pool.

'False heart,' the Lord Apothecary orders. 'False lungs. Maintain perfusion to his brain and his progenoid glands, no matter what other organs must be sacrificed. We can rebuild or replace anything else if we must.'

He turns away again and leaves the slab.

The senior chirurgeon nods to the juniors. 'You heard him. Quickly.'

Wordlessly, a junior chirurgeon reaches below the slab and withdraws a small, glass mask attached to gold tubing. The dozen hooks that rim the respirator bite into the angel's face as it seats itself over his mouth and his nose. The chirurgeon flips a switch on the side of the instrument, and through the glass Liesl watches the length of gold tubing snake its way down the angel's throat.

He coughs and shivers upon the slab. Liesl grasps his arm as he reaches towards his face, and even on the brink of death, the force nearly throws her from her feet. Then the angel stills, as the chirurgeon forces the incense of rest directly into the false lung while a servitor begins to pump its bellows.

Across the slab, a junior chirurgeon raises two cruel needles, each as thick at least as a finger of Liesl's hand. Deftly, he plunges them into the great vessels surrounding the angel's primary heart while the senior chirurgeon clamps those arteries delivering blood to the remainder of his body.

'The false heart is emplaced,' the junior chirurgeon calls.

'Awaken it already, then,' the senior growls.

The junior chirurgeon at the head of the bed turns to the ornate instrument beside him. He adjusts several dials and wakes the device, a soft thrumming vibrating the surgical slab as dark blood snakes into and out of its shell.

'Continue,' the senior chirurgeon orders, the pool of blood beneath Liesl's hands finally beginning to diminish. Organs emerge like islands as the liquid withdraws, shattered and torn in more places than she can count.

'Lacerations of the spleen and the liver,' she calls to her servitor. 'Avulsion of the lesser arteries of the abdomen and transection of the great vein. There are penetrating wounds to the–'

The senior chirurgeon raises his hand and cuts her off, turning to her father.

'Catastrophic injuries to viscera and vessels of the abdomen and lower thorax.' Then he says more quietly, directly to her and the junior chirurgeon across the table. 'This is all beyond salvage, even for the Lord Apothecary.'

The senior chirurgeon sighs, then steps back from the slab. 'The bleeding is staunched. The worst is over. He may survive yet, but he will have to be remade entirely. He will live or die by the Great Healer's grace.'

Silence falls around the slab, replaced by the humming of the false heart and the gentle gurgling of Liesl's suction tubing. For a moment there is no other sound.

Then, with a crack that bespeaks finality, the Lord Apothecary's reductor fires on the slab behind her.

* * *

We burn Brother Pater and hold his Speaking. We each whisper to him before the flames, though the words between my brothers are few. My mind returns, time and again, to the knights of the *Spiteful Blade* that will have no one to speak for them.

So, I speak their deaths alone.

To Brother-Castellan Kelvutt, I speak my guilt. For arriving too late. For what I did after. I am unaware of any other instance in my Chapter's ancient history when a Castellan of one fighting company destroyed the crusading vessel of another.

To Brother-Apothecary Hest, I speak my condolement. That we did not find his corpse and the gene-seed he carried. That despite his efforts, the gene-line of his fighting company has ended.

To Brother-Chaplain Maynard, I speak my begrudging respect. To elect a death with honour rather than salvation is a judgement I can hardly fault. Were I given the same choice aboard my own vessel, I have little doubt I would decide the same.

And to Juerten. To Juerten, who bore such close resemblance to his genefather. To Juerten, who I loved, yet whose very presence pained me. To Juerten, who is still, and will always be, a Neophyte in my mind. To him, I speak my regret. That I sent him away all of those years ago. That I could not bear to remain close to the memories he brought me. That I could not convince him to follow me, in the end, and that I could not afford to die beside him.

To Arold himself. To the great Marshal to whom I first swore my fealty. To him I speak my shame. That I was unable to fulfil his words and that the First Dorean Crusade failed despite my efforts. That the Second may fail as well in my absence. That my brothers press on towards its first goal, Tempest, while I linger here.

We shall raise a shrine to their souls within our own Reclusiam. It will bear no artefacts save our memories, and that will not be enough. And yet, it is all that remains of the *Spiteful Blade*. Of her noble knights. Of Marshal Arold's gene-line.

In another time, we might have saved my brothers. Or at least died at their side. But the crusade carries its own demands, and the *Dauntless Honour* limps on towards Tempest through the void.

Dant finds me and rouses me from my rumination.

'How many cycles?' I ask.

'Three,' he replies. He wears his skull helm and his rosarius around his neck. He has been in rite, and my heart sinks further.

'Brother Tyre?' I ask him.

'Alive, Brother-Castellan. Brother-Apothecary Alvus rebuilds his flesh as we speak.'

I nod. That is a little mercy, though I know from experience the ordeal that Tyre now undergoes.

'He did not speak to me,' I say. 'When I crossed the Rubicon.'

It has been decades since I underwent the procedure myself. Since I was destroyed and then rebuilt entirely under Brother-Apothecary Alvus' deft hands.

'How many other brothers emerge from that trial of suffering speaking of voices and visions that greet them in the darkness? How many others awaken refashioned in both their bodies and their souls?'

'Many,' Dant replies cautiously. 'Not all. The God-Emperor chooses to commune in His own fashion.'

I nod. 'And yet He has chosen never to commune with me.'

Silence hangs between us.

'Why have you disturbed me, Brother-Chaplain?' I ask.

'It has been three cycles, Emeric.'

'As if that is an answer. I have known you to recuse yourself in prayer and meditation for far longer than that.'

'I am not the Castellan of this fighting company.'

His rebuke is soft, as always.

'What pressing need is there for me aboard this vessel? We limp on as we did, wounded and bleeding. Shipmaster Khatri attends to our course. Brother Alvus attends to our wounded. Brother Barnard attends to the great machine itself. What task requires my hands? Who requires my attentions?'

He nods. 'We do. The vessel as well as her crew. Brother Barnard has asked for you.'

'And he could not rouse me himself?' I chide myself, my mood lightening. 'Or perhaps he simply could not stomach the thought of bearing the magnitude of my self-pity.'

'Perhaps, Brother-Castellan.' There is warmth in Dant's voice. 'Even the ship herself groans beneath such a heavy load.'

I meet Barnard within the command cathedrum. He sends the transmission directly to my helm vox. It is nothing but garbled machine speech to my ears.

'What is this?' I ask.

'A reply to the distress call from the *Spiteful Blade*.'

The Techmarine stands unhelmeted in his crimson plate, the jointed machine arms upon his back bound to various ports on the command altar before him. Shipmaster Khatri lingers beside the Space Marine, interfacing with the vessel directly.

'The associated voice and pict data were corrupted, but I was able to pull the signature and locator markings from the missives I removed from the *Spiteful Blade*'s data archives before departing, once I had reconstructed the appropriate access codes.'

'Reconstructed?' I ask.

'Fabricated,' Khatri clarifies.

I play the missive again. The screeches and clicks mean nothing to me. 'What does it tell you?'

'Several things,' Brother Barnard replies. His head twists slightly at some unheard message from our ship. 'First, that there are void craft near enough to our location that they possessed time to receive and then transmit correspondence to the *Spiteful Blade* since it exited the warp. Second, the data signature of their missive contains the professed location of those vessels along with the astronomical data of the location from which they received the *Spiteful Blade*'s transmission.'

'We know where we are, then,' Shipmaster Khatri says.

Barnard nods. 'And it is nearer to Tempest than we might have feared.'

'A blessing,' I reply. 'We have foundered lost within the void, but now we are given an anchor.'

'There is more, Brother-Castellan,' he continues. 'The missive also carries vessel identifiers, linked to not only the void craft which replied to the *Spiteful Blade*'s distress signal, but also other void craft within its formation. There are dozens of ships within the flotilla, and they are using the identifiers of the crusade.'

My breath catches, and a weight falls from my shoulders.

'Praise the Emperor!' I exclaim. 'How long ago did they send the signal?'

For their part, neither Barnard nor the shipmaster seem to share my relief.

'The time data has been corrupted,' Barnard answers. 'But the missive could be no more than several solar weeks old.'

'Very good. Recently enough that we may rejoin our brothers still before the assault on Tempest is complete.'

Despite my words there is little joy in my brother's face. Shipmaster Khatri's mortal one is easier to read.

'There is more,' I state. 'Some reason these are not joyous tidings for you?'

The shipmaster shifts uncomfortably. 'Navigator Nendaiu has not woken, my lord. Her acolytes doubt that she ever will. And while it appears that the course she set was true, we are still some distance from our destination.'

'Out with it,' I order.

'The *Dauntless Honour* limps forward, but she is grievously wounded. At our current pace it will be more than a year before we reach Tempest.'

Now, I begin to understand their discomfort. By that time the crusade may have moved on. By that time the crusade may be destroyed. There are risks to the course that they suggest without speaking. Risks great enough that they are hesitant to utter them. But sometimes, risk must be tolerated.

'Then it seems that only one option remains.'

Streams of data pour into the *Dauntless Honour*'s void loom from her warp drive as her shipmaster feeds a trickle of power into the device. Diagnostics first, confirming that the warp drive still functions, then a rough image of the currents and velocities that compose the shape of the Chaos of the empyrean, beyond.

It is a woefully inaccurate picture.

The navigation subcell of the vessel's void loom analyses the vibratory patterns of the psionically active, crystalline fibres which stretch across the warp drive's sextant. From those humming frequencies, she can conclude only that it is unlikely a major warp storm awaits directly within the immaterium. Her protocols direct the subcell to query the navigational data representing the corresponding section of warp space stored within the vessel's archives, but these records are unavailable. So out-of-date that they have been erased by automated data-management routines.

The subcell makes its calculations, and the corresponding confidence intervals, and then routes them to the *Dauntless Honour*'s command cathedrum.

It is some time before the vessel's mortal shipmaster responds.

[Collect additional data.]

Beneath the transmitted thought lies the voices of others conversing around him. Linguistic nodes flag tension in their pitches and cadence.

[Collect additional data.]

The *Dauntless Honour*'s warp drive pulses again. The resulting data corroborates her previous measurements. The void loom repeats the requisite calculation and routes an estimate of success to the command cathedrum.

The shipmaster's thoughts indicate that it is lower than he had expected. New commands reach the void loom, adjusting the designated parameters.

The navigation subcell clicks in the darkness, replotting a course with a wider target radius. It iterates probabilities for endpoints further from the system's centre.

The odds improve.

By less than the shipmaster had hoped.

The machine link falls silent before commands flow into the void loom again from the hundred lesser altars within the *Dauntless Honour*'s command cathedrum.

The ship's warp drive ignites. Her sensory spires fall silent as the universe breaks apart. For a terrible moment there is nothing, then bursts of data from the peripheral node linked to the voidship's Geller field generator as it struggles to keep the substance of the empyrean away.

It holds.

Chapter 5

They find him in the quiet, after the blood. The Carver, the Maw, the Flayed Beast, first. The hungriest of his tormentors. His patrons.

Bleed them, the Carver whispers into the chambers of Dravek Soulrender's mind. The thin, taut voice drips with thirst and desire.

They had been nameless, faceless, formless things once – nothing but unchecked rage and thirst within his soul – but he had been little more than that, too. Millennia have changed them both, or at least Dravek's perception of them.

Dravek ignores the daemon, turning instead to the row of figures bound in chains at his feet.

'Your fear,' he says. 'It is pungent and putrid. Your Emperor would be ashamed of you.'

The cowed trio of holy men kneel on a shattered marble floor, dark blood seeping through crimson robes from the blades and claws of Dravek's jakhals. Corpses defile the sacred chamber around them, painted in the iridescent light of stained windows.

Bleed them, the Carver repeats.

A flicker at the edge of Dravek's gaze. Beneath the daemon's voice, the hungry, tortured cries of the Flayed Beast and the endless, rumbling yearning of the Maw.

'Is this what he taught you?' Dravek asks. 'Is this what you tell yourselves that he wills? That his servants should kneel before his enemies? Their mouths full of nothing but silence and terror?'

He turns to the idol at the centre of their shrine. The Corpse-Emperor. The Anathema.

'I am sorry,' he says, 'for the weakness of your servants.'

He reaches out to place a bloodied hand against the gold.

The Carver chuckles. Another flash at the edges of his vision. At his back, one of the priests finally raises his head.

'Do not touch Him,' the holy man cries through shattered teeth and failing lungs.

'You mistake me, priest. Do not misjudge my reverence for contempt. Your corpse god has spilled almost as much blood as my own. His appetite is every bit as great as the Blood God's. I hold him in highest esteem, even if I cannot say the same of his servants.'

The priest attempts to rise. His fragile flesh fails him.

'Do not speak of Him. Do not sully His name with your unholy mouth. Do you not fear the God-Emperor?'

'Of course I do,' Dravek replies. 'If you find him on this petty, prideful world, please alert me.'

The Carver's laugh escapes his throat. Their words speak as one.

'You think me a monster. You are not wrong.'

He raises an arm covered in blades, the black shadow of warp-forged metal sprouting from his twisted, weeping flesh. Their wet edges catch the light in glimmering crimson shades, as he turns and drags his Eviscerator across the stone floor. The black teeth of the massive chainsword spin slowly.

'But I was a beast long before I looked like this. I am what your god made me. An instrument of death.'

He steps towards the chained man and lifts his chin upon a gleaming blade. The priest's heart vibrates through the length of the knife. Dravek hears it in his ears. Dravek tastes it on his tongue.

The Flayed Beast howls.

You waste your breath with words.

The Carver steps from the shadows of the chantry, his parchment-thin skin stretched over a bent frame of vaguely human shape, with long, spindle arms hanging from his gaunt shoulders tipped in claw-like, skeletal fingers. The Flayed Beast pads along at his side, an ursine monstrosity of bare muscle and sinew slick with the sheen of fluid and dripping blood. The beast bows its head to sniff at a dark crimson pool gathered atop the marble floor, then whines.

'And you waste yours.'

Dravek looks back towards the priests.

'There is still hope for you, though. I have come not to destroy this world, but to liberate it. Your corpse god keeps you pent in a cage of shrines and rituals. Crippled by chains of laws and customs. Weakened by hate. But my master asks only that you remember your purpose. That you fulfil the vision your Emperor once proclaimed.'

Enough. I hunger.

The Carver rests his hands on the priest's shoulders. The man quivers as if he can feel the touch and hear the words. He begins to pray.

'Forget such weakness,' Dravek says. 'Words cannot save you. Your god does not hear. But the Lord of Skulls listens. My god rewards. He asks only for blood. He does not care who spills it.'

The Maw roars in Dravek's ears, a deep churning sound. He feels the weight of the daemon's cry upon his soul. The Flayed Beast circles and sniffs at the chained men, its bare muscles and sinew slipping over its ursine skeleton as it moves. The Carver stares at Dravek.

Bleed them. Now. Do not make me summon her.

Dravek leans down.

'Join me. You will find my burden lighter than your Emperor's. Together we can enact the vision He once proclaimed. A galaxy burning. A billion worlds bleeding at once. The beautiful cry of war rising up from ten trillion throats. An endless, unstoppable, river of blood.'

Dravek's vision swims. He tastes charcoal. The blades on his neck and his back grow cold.

The Carver smiles. *You play your games too long, Soulrender. You forget your place.*

Dravek bends down before the priest. 'Join me or die.'

The man spits. Blood splatters across Dravek's face.

'So be it,' he whispers.

Dravek steps back and brings his Eviscerator to life. Blood sprays from its hungry teeth. The chained men fall.

The Carver sighs with pleasure, and the Flayed Beast laps at the warm blood upon the stone floor. The chill in Dravek's blades fades, as do his companions.

He is alone again.

In the silence, he hears the beating of drums and the din of endless war.

Alvus and Dant stand beside me as we board the flotilla's flagship, Brother Barnard and Shipmaster Khatri in my ear.

'Thirty-seven vessels in the formation, Brother-Castellan. All bearing identifiers of the Missionarus Galaxia.'

'Transports, mostly, of various makes and classes, but armed. Perhaps half a dozen true warships among them forming an escort.'

Their words deepen my questions.

We spent a dozen cycles transiting the madness of the warp on our blind jump. Another five limping towards Tempest under the power of the *Dauntless Honour*'s subluminal drives. Only to find a fleet waiting, with none of my brothers' ships among it.

Our strides fall heavy on the deck as the airlock opens to a gilded hall of gold and glass. We come armoured and my helm display dampens the wave of light and sound that strikes me. The flickering brightness of a thousand votive torch lamps and the chanting voices of auto-vox and mortal cantors press against me like a physical thing.

A single figure stands in the open doorway before us, clad in the crimson raiment of the Ecclesiarchy. He bows deeply then makes the sign of the aquila. An emissary, nothing more, it is clear from the deference in his stance and the servility that flavours his words.

'My lords. Welcome to the *Infinite Word*. Blessings of the God-Emperor on behalf of His humble servant, the Missionary Laurentia Proserpine.'

His High Gothic is the exquisite, archaic form of the Cult Imperialis, each word lilting and tonal as if every conversation were a liturgy or hymn. Behind the man, crimson-robed figures line the centre aisle of an ornate chamber, its walls ringed in a colonnade of fluted gold.

'The outer narthex, Brother-Castellan,' Dant subvocalises to me. 'I would imagine that the entire vessel is built around a central cathedrum and organised in the traditional fashion of the Adeptus Ministorum.'

'Well met, priest,' I reply, stepping past the man without invitation.

'The missionary is honoured to host you aboard this holy craft.'

Brother Alvus' voice reaches my ears. 'Though not honoured enough to greet us herself.'

'We come for answers, not honour,' I subvocalise in reply, though I do not disagree.

We walk beneath soaring statues of the primarchs and the saints. The endless ranks of acolytes chant as we pass, beneath the direction of a dozen choir masters. I do not recognise their hymn, though its melody stirs my soul. Hidden in the shadowed recesses of the chamber, chrome-limbed servitors accompany the mortal voices upon great instruments of strange design.

Alongside their pleasing music, however, comes the scent of mortal human filth, poorly masked by rich incense and the ashen flavour of my helm's filtrators.

We pause as Dant kneels at the feet of our gene-father, Rogal Dorn. An acolyte reaches towards him, the skin of his hands dry and cracked. The faint smell of blood wafts from fissures at the edges of his lips.

'Micronutrient deficiencies,' Brother-Apothecary Alvus subvocalises. 'Void travel is harsh on the mortal form, especially for expeditions such as this one with little logistical support. They have likely been fed on recycled rations for some time. Possibly supplementing their diet with less... traditional fare.'

Our escort waits patiently for Dant to rise, then guides us through an ornate stone screen bearing flourished text and an image of a martyr impaled upon a spear of glass. The man's eyes are open as his life drips from him, reaching a hand out towards the fresco of the God-Emperor on the wall opposite. As his blood drips into the dirt beneath him, a crimson snake emerges from each holy drop.

We march on through the nave and the transept, then pause before the marble stairs rising to the bema.

'Here the furore of the narthex fades,' I muse, the massive sanctuary empty compared to its packed entryway. The rows of pews and arching ceiling are empty save for a few mindless servitors

patrolling the room's edges, trimming the wicks of thousands
of votive candles and replacing those that have fallen dark.

'I pray the simplicity of our reception does not offend you,
my lord.' The missionary's emissary shakes slightly as he speaks.
He has spent his whole life in service to the Cult Imperialis,
yet this is likely the first time he has ever seen one of his god's
angels in person.

'Quite the opposite,' I assure him. 'Save your adoration for
the Emperor of Mankind.'

He pauses before the first stair then motions for me to go on
without him. 'I leave you here, my lord. It is beyond my station to mount these stairs.'

I pause, honoured, turning to Brother-Chaplain Dant for some
signal of propriety. 'And yet I am permitted? I would not desire
to breach the customs of this sacred place.'

Dant nods. 'There is no sacrilege in it, brother. Merely honour.'

With his permission, I set my boot upon the stairs and climb
to the gilded silver altar above.

Atop the bema, the chamber takes on a different atmosphere.
The scent of incense and the sound of music leaks into the sanctuary from the narthex beyond the screen.

Here, however, muted by distance, their effect is calming rather
than overpowering. From this side, the screen bears an image
of the same martyr, his eyes closed and his life ebbed. Coils of
serpents wind around his corpse, their opal-white teeth sunk
into his flesh.

Behind me, an acolyte carries a small silver pitcher, collecting
wax drippings from the thousands of candles in the exedra. She
limps as she walks, keeping herself upright only with the aid
of a silver cane. The woman pauses before each votive candle,
scraping the molten wax from the shafts using a dull blade. Her
hands are covered in small burns, long since scarred from her

task. It is only when she turns that I catch sight of her clouded eyes.

'It is a cruel thing,' I call to her, approaching, 'to force such a task upon one who is frail and blind. Surely the missionary could impart this duty upon one of the senseless servitors that walk this hall.'

The woman pauses her labour. For her part, my presence does not seem to unnerve her.

'Surely she could. Though the galaxy is cruel, my lord. Its barbarity should not surprise you.'

I chuckle. I am not used to being rebuked by mortals, though it seems likely that she does not know what I am.

'You speak truth,' I reply. 'And there are times that its coarseness cannot be avoided. Though I am surprised to find such indifference within these holy halls.'

The woman motions to the martyr carved in stone upon the screen at my back.

'Do you know who that is?'

I shake my head, then realise the futility of gesturing to a blind woman. 'The imagery is powerful, though I do not recognise its subject.'

'Saint Sylvestrus. The patron of this vessel, my lord. He was one of the first missionaries of the Missionarus Galaxia. It is said he was a man of unparalleled faith. Unmatched in devotion to the God-Emperor. He was young when he joined the order, and young still when his craft landed upon the heathen, feral world of Tothe. His mission was beset by trouble from the start, though, and each time his forces approached the local settlements, they were met with ferocious resistance.'

'Such obstinance is not uncommon among the heretic worlds of this galaxy,' I interject.

'Despite their barbarity, his heart was moved for the people of Tothe, and he desired to bring them into the God-Emperor's light. So, sure in his purpose, he ventured into a settlement alone, confident that the God-Emperor would perform a miracle. The next morning, the local populace had impaled him alive upon a great glass spike.

'His companions watched, horrified, as he bled on display, though with his dying breaths he ordered them not to rescue him, so strong was his faith that the God-Emperor would deliver a sign. He was not wrong. As Sylvestrus' blood dripped into that heathen soil, snakes sprang up from the earth, coiling around his corpse and devouring his flesh.'

'Some sign, indeed.'

'Can you interpret it, my lord?'

'I would not presume to know the God-Emperor's will,' I reply.

The woman shrugs. 'Nor would I. Nor did Sylvestrus' companions or the heathens of Tothe. But it terrified them, because, by all reports, there had never before been any serpent species recorded within the sector, either natural or imported. They allowed the mission entry into their settlements, and within a solar year, Sylvestrus' surviving companions determined that their culture was so abhorrent it was beyond saving by conversion. Within a decade, a crusade had wiped the feral planet clean.

'A cruel tale,' she says, then turns back to filling her pitcher of wax.

I stand silent for some time, watching the old woman work. Her hands are deft, her steps pained but sure. She may not see with her eyes, but her other senses are not absent. That she could not perceive something of my form or the armour I wear seems unlikely. Yet, for an acolyte to speak to me in such a way knowingly is a thought even more absurd.

'Missionary Proserpine,' I eventually greet her.

'Lord Castellan Emeric,' she replies. 'I am honoured to have the Emperor's sons aboard my humble vessel, though I will admit I had hoped you might come in the company of a greater host when your Chapter finally arrived.'

At her words, I feel anxiety creep into my mind.

My brothers are not here. They have moved on without us. We have been left behind while the crusade drapes itself in glory.

'As had I. We were delayed by the vagaries of the warp, then stalled by the Archenemy. Where is the remainder of our fleet? Have they already taken the shrine world?'

Proserpine stops her labours and turns her blind eyes upon mine.

'Tempest?' she asks. 'Tempest is a teeming hive of heretics and daemons. Twisted servants of the Dark Gods pillage its surface as we speak, led by a monster who calls himself the Soulrender. A fleet of heretic vessels blockades it like a chain in orbit, pummelling the surface wherever resistance appears. The transmissions we receive from the shrine world grow fewer each cycle, the myriad sects and orders of the Ecclesiarchy upon it devolving into nothing but petty factionalism while their world breaks. Several of her great arcology-shrines still hold, but Tempest has all but fallen, Lord Castellan.'

'Soulrender,' I growl. 'That is a blasphemous name, though Marshal Laise will soon teach him humility. I had feared we arrived too late to join their conquest, though perhaps there is still time to aid their struggle. Where do my brothers strike our enemy? Where is their battle the fiercest?'

'What brothers, my lord? When my fleet departed, I was promised that a great host of Adeptus Astartes would join us here. We have waited for nearly a solar year, but you are the first of the Emperor's sons we have encountered.'

My breath catches. 'That is not possible,' I protest.

The missionary shrugs and turns back to her candles. 'However few of you there are, I am grateful you've arrived. I was charged by the Cardinals Palatine to wait for the Black Templars' arrival, and I have. My pilgrims' faith is fervent, but even their zeal is flagging. Their bodies grow weak, even as do their souls. Your arrival has reminded them why they ventured here. Why they left their lives, and their hope, behind. We stand ready to join you in Tempest's liberation, my lord.'

'Liberation?' I reply. 'We are but one warship among dozens of the crusade. Less than a tenth of what was meant to be brought by my Chapter.'

'You fear that you are not enough.'

The woman turns back from her candles and towards the image of the impaled saint.

'Perhaps, my lord, Saint Sylvestrus was not wrong to possess such faith in his own immutable purpose. Perhaps his mistake was simply assuming that he understood what that purpose was.'

I pause, fear and anger brewing beneath my voice in equal parts. Mortals do not speak to me this way. And yet I find that I cannot fault her words.

'Your words bite me, missionary. But there is truth in them. Have your shipmasters send me manifests and data logs of the personnel and equipment aboard their vessels. Include whatever estimates you have made of Ecclesiarchy forces remaining upon Tempest, as well as positions and specifications of the heretic blockade over the world's surface. I will bring this to my brothers. We shall find a path.'

A smile cracks upon the ageing woman's face. 'Very good, Lord Castellan. Though I request you do not deliberate too long. The God-Emperor brought my pilgrims here to cleanse this world, not to starve in its orbit.'

* * *

I bring myself to a Sundering before my brothers. There is no other way that this could be done. The ritual is ancient and rare, reserved for times of my Chapter's deepest, most mortal strife.

In our Reclusiam I lay clear my faults before them, and before the relics of our Chapter and the watchful memories of our fallen brothers. Then I ask them to add those failures I have forgotten.

They are not kind, and I bless them for it.

Callicus.

Harbour.

Eileri.

Nawn.

My greatest missteps recounted in detail before me.

I am brash. I am cautious. I doubt myself and my cause. I have squandered favour that should have been bestowed upon others.

When the weight of my flaws has been sounded in its entirety, I describe to my brothers what I seek to attempt next. They devour the war plans and probability plots created by the machine spirits of our void loom from data that the Missionary Proserpine has provided with the trained minds of the warrior-savants that they are.

Their conclusions are the same as mine.

If we are to act, the time is now. What little strength we have flags as that of our foe blossoms. Tempest was meant to be the gateway to Dorea herself – a rallying point for the forces that we muster towards that greater struggle. Honour will not permit my brothers to bypass the shrine world while it rests in the Archenemy's grasp, though if we do not act now, Tempest risks becoming a quagmire that will sap the crusade's strength before we ever reach our goal. A briar patch that will bleed us dry before the true battle.

Yet I command a single light cruiser of the Adeptus Astartes, with scarcely two-score initiated battle-brothers aboard. A dozen frigates accompany us, brimming with half-starved, half-armed pilgrim-zealots of the Missionarus Galaxia, led by a blind and crippled old woman.

We are too few.

Too few to wrest the world from the raging warbands of the Blood God. From the monster who calls himself the Soulrender – as vile and arrogant an epithet as I can imagine. Too few to meaningfully stall their advance and the rising tide of death they carry. Too few even to engage the swarm of disgraced vessels that encircles the shrine world like carrion birds, or to draw it away and strike a Naval blow, at least.

We are too few to do anything but die.

Before our Chaplain and the graven image of our progenitor, Dorn, I release my brothers from the bonds of fealty they have sworn to me with nothing but gratitude within my soul. I give them my leave and my blessing to wash their hands of this endeavour. To take what little succour our broken void craft can offer and to leave me to this task alone. Such terms have not been offered by a Castellan of my Chapter in the last thousand years. Not even after the failure of the First Dorean Crusade.

To their credit, none of my brothers accept them.

Knight by knight, they kneel before me and swear loyalty to my fighting company once again. Knight by knight, I raise them to their feet, then kneel in turn and make my own oaths before them.

For a time, there is nothing but silence between us. Then together, we gird ourselves for war.

Chapter 6

The angel floats within his sarcophagus, peaceful amidst the briny, yellowed fluid – the colour of amber, or serum, or urine. His eyes are closed, as if he is sleeping, and he stands naked within the vessel of glass – the only time Liesl has seen one of his kind either resting or unclothed when they were not lying bloodied atop one of the apothecarion's slabs.

She finds herself suddenly embarrassed, despite the fact that she is one of the menials who assisted the Lord Apothecary in rebuilding this angel's body through days of gruelling, bloody surgery.

Such a perfect weapon should never rest, should never appear so vulnerable.

The serfs have no word in the ship's Low Gothic dialect for the brutal procedure that had been enacted on the angel to save him. But in truth, he has not been saved at all. He was slain and raised anew, rebuilt into something she could not rightly claim was the same wounded shell that had arrived in the apothecarion.

Coils of dark tubing still pierce his skin and wind around his limbs like the grasping arms of some sea leviathan of ancient myth. Liesl has heard the whispers of the senior chirurgeons. They are not certain if he will ever wake again.

Despite his apparent rest, the angel quivers, as if in the throes of terrible pain. It moves her to know that a body so perfect is even capable of failing.

Gently, she sets one of her hands against the glass, her face rising barely to the angel's chest.

'May the light of Him who holds the galaxy find its way into the darkness of your mind. May the order of the one who crafted your soul rebuild that within you which has been broken.'

In the darkness behind Liesl, a figure stirs. She spins, raising the lasgun she carries, then drops to her knees before a figure in gleaming white ceramite.

'That is a simple prayer,' the Lord Apothecary says, his deep voice like churning waves or cracking stone. He is armoured again, prepared for battle, the great plates of his war suit oiled and shining.

'My lord,' Liesl stammers in the angel's tongue. 'I beg your forgiveness. I know none of the more formal words of healing. It appeared as if he was suffering, and I could think of no other way to allay his pain.'

'He is suffering,' the angel replies, gazing over her upon his wounded brother. 'The Rubicon Primaris is a trial of suffering and little else.'

The Lord Apothecary turns to inspect the panel of gauges and displays mounted upon the sarcophagus, then adjusts several dials with a dexterity and swiftness at odds with his towering frame. Within, the wounded angel stills.

'If he wakes, he will remember little of this ordeal. But what he remembers will be enough to leave him changed. You have been left here to guard him?'

'I have, my lord. The other menials and chirurgeons have been requisitioned for the defence of the vessel or to manage the injured throughout her halls.'

The Lord Apothecary motions for her to rise, then takes the lasgun from her grasp. It is an ancient weapon, carried by her father before her and generations of her line before him. She knows its weight well, yet it appears minute and unsophisticated within the Lord Apothecary's massive, armoured hands.

'A simple weapon,' the angel says. 'Have you ever fired it?'

'Yes, my lord. I was instructed in its use long ago by my father.'

The angel nods. 'And have you ever fired it at something that draws breath?'

Liesl shakes her head. Shame grasps her.

'A simple prayer. A simple weapon. A simple Chapter-serf. Tell me, what is your title among your fellows? What rank have your companions assigned you within the petty hierarchy they have crafted?'

'I am a menial of the apothecarion, my lord. I ascended to the post after the wounding of my father.'

'The least among us to safeguard our greatest weapon,' the Space Marine spits. 'Your masters shall do penance for their oversight.'

There is a clatter on the table beside Liesl, and for the first time since entering the chamber, the Lord Apothecary deigns to look towards the servitor polishing gleaming steel instruments beside him. The red eyepieces of the angel's helm focus upon the metal plates binding together the shattered pieces of the servitor's skull in a crude approximation of their original shape.

'Look at me,' the Lord Apothecary orders Liesl.

She lifts her head.

'I do not remember your gene-sire's name, but I recall his countenance and I see those features in your own. Just as I recall the day that he was wounded. I remember that I found it strange when the other serfs told me he had specifically requested to be turned into... this. To ask, as a boon, a fate that most find dire punishment.'

'He wished to continue to serve you, my lord,' Liesl whispers. 'It was his greatest honour in life, and he sought to continue it even after.'

Something akin to hesitancy appears in the Lord Apothecary's voice for a moment.

'You would kill for my brother if it came to it, then. But would you also die?'

'Without hesitation,' Liesl replies.

The angel nods, satisfied at last.

'When this is over, if I find a simple scratch upon my brother, and you are in this chamber still drawing breath, I shall not sentence you to penance. I shall simply kill you. See to it that you are brave, not out of fear of punishment, but for the sake of the honour that you bear.'

Make my blade swift. Make my hatred pure.

The *Dauntless Honour* shivers as plasma torpedoes and heavy lances strike out towards her. I watch through pict-feeds on my helm display as the fusillade splashes against the rippling surface of her void shields like blots of ink thrown into icy water.

'*Fourteen impacts. All absorbed.*' Barnard's voice. I have left him to man the command cathedrum while I prepare for the bitter battle to come.

'Only a sounding salvo from our enemy, then. They seek to find where we are weakest.'

I cycle the pict-feed to an image of our formation, arranged in a spear tip behind the *Dauntless Honour*. One of the Missionary Proserpine's transports evaporates in the void.

'The God-Emperor shall honour their souls,' Brother-Chaplain Dant calls from our Reclusiam.

'It is their mortal flesh that we have need of at the moment, Brother-Chaplain.'

My void craft races through the emptiness towards the swirling ball of white that is Tempest, a dark shadow eclipsing its pristine surface. The machine spirit of my helm senses the shifting of my eyes and communes with the *Dauntless Honour* on my behalf. Hundreds of data fields appear at the edge of my vision, each describing the class and capabilities of a vessel in the heretic fleet.

I have seen the predictions. They do not matter. We are married to our course.

'The heretics hesitate,' Barnard says. 'A rare thing for the servants of the Dark Gods.'

'They expect us to waver. Or to flee. Or to disperse in some strategic formation.'

We do none of those things, and our enemy's hesitancy allows us to narrow the gap.

'Hold fire as long as possible,' I order Barnard. 'Then unleash our full fury on whichever vessels venture nearest.'

'As the Emperor wills,' comes his eager reply.

There is a brief moment of stillness rare to me in centuries of void warfare. My vessel makes none of the usual manoeuvres. We seek no advantages in Tempest's weak gravitational field. The sound of returning salvos from the *Dauntless Honour*'s great gun batteries is nowhere to be found. Only the roaring of her turbines, and the racing of my hearts.

I fall to my knees in the empty corridor, Penitence drawn and resting, point-first, upon the deck. The devotional chain that binds the weapon to my gauntlet swings gently in the dim, orange light, my constant companion for over two hundred years.

'Kneel with me, brother,' I call.

Hadrick remains standing at my side.

'I feel your rage,' I tell him. 'Its heat burns like a pyre at my side.'

Hadrick looks towards me, his thunder hammer grasped in hands that are eager for violence. His dark armour ripples and shines, freshly anointed with oil. Upon his breastplate he bears a scrap of tattered fabric, taken from Pater's tabard and bound to him with wax. It is both an honour to his memory and a challenge to my authority.

'And what of yours, Brother-Castellan? Does it burn brightly enough to extinguish your doubts?'

His question is fair. He has seen my misgivings laid bare.

'Perhaps my faith should be stronger. Perhaps my zeal should be more pure. But the line between fervour and foolishness is thin.

'There is no space for doubt any longer,' I continue. 'I have broken my crusade to stand here. I have covered my hands in the blood of my brothers. I have Sundered my company and re-formed it again, only to throw it, newly forged, into the heat of war.' I stare at him. 'Kneel. Pray, Brother Hadrick. It is not a request.'

He begrudgingly acquiesces, though it pains him to rest when his zeal courses so strongly.

'Salvos inbound,' Barnard calls from the command cathedrum. 'Impacts imminent. Assault rams departing from multiple enemy vessels.'

Hadrick vibrates like a power weapon. It takes all of his will to remain still in a moment such as this. And yet I demand stillness from him.

My helm display flashes with countless runes, a cloud of enemy fire descending upon us. Our formation will shatter. But our will shall not. Not because of our fervour, but because of our faith.

Klaxons blare through the vessel, accompanied by the droning voices of vox-servitors speaking in both High Gothic and the ship's tongue, alerting serfs and bondsmen of the incoming strike. They stand dispersed throughout her halls, armed and waiting to repel any who would board and desecrate this vessel.

They will bleed. They will die. But we will emerge, by the God-Emperor's grace.

Another salvo strikes us. Hadrick shivers with rage.

Flak turrets roar to life along the *Dauntless Honour*'s hull as dozens of assault rams crash into her flesh. The vessel groans.

Make my blade swift. Make my hatred pure.

'We move, brother,' I call.

Hadrick rises like a caged beast released, a pure flame burning at my side.

'*Hull breaches on decks eleven, fifteen, twenty-seven, thirty-nine.*'

Another half a dozen runes appear on my display before Barnard can announce them. Hadrick and I race past clustered mortals towards the nearest rift. The scent of scorched metal reaches me as we pass through a hatch and begin to spill heretic blood.

'For the Emperor!' I bellow.

'For Dorn!' Hadrick replies.

Twisted mockeries of human flesh spill from the mouth of an assault ram where its lasbreachers have torn through the *Dauntless Honour*'s hull. The cold of the void streams in behind them, and the taste of blood and the warp.

Penitence drinks. I sever one of the heretic's human servants as it stumbles, rage-drunk through the smoke, clawing like an animal. The skulls sewed with wire into the skin around its neck clatter against the molten bulkhead. A wolf-like creature leaps through the flames behind it, raking vicious claws against my storm shield.

I throw the daemon to the side and slice its flank with my blade as it passes. Searing flame spills from the wound as it yelps, then turns back towards me.

Hadrick shatters another heretic with his thunder hammer then charges ahead, his rage compelling him. The warp hound leaps towards me, frothing spittle dripping from its maw. Penitence meets its jaws, tearing a seam at the corner of its mouth, but it clamps its teeth upon the blade and will not release it.

I drop my sword and grasp the collar of brass that encircles the daemon's crimson neck. The very feel of the creature's unclean flesh against my armour kindles my rage. The point of my shield descends upon its neck again and again, until the beast's head falls away in my grip.

'Hold fast!' I call to Hadrick, as I pull my blade from its maw and turn into the smoke. My brother's fervour consumes him. He is nowhere to be found.

I leap past the shattered corpses of cultists, another hound wounded and limping within their midst. At the door of the assault ram, sparks fly from Hadrick's thunder hammer as its haft deflects a strike from a whirring chainaxe.

I charge into his assailant. A thing that I might have once called my brother. My storm shield slams against the traitor's crimson ceramite plate, cracking one of the dripping bone horns that sprouts from his flesh and through the armour.

'You have forsaken the light of your father,' I curse him, as we crash onto the floor. 'The stench of your shame hangs heavy upon you.'

The creature turns his empty, crimson eyes towards me, his skull lined with the chrome of neural implants. 'As does the stench of your weakness,' he laughs, blood spraying across my armour from his mouth.

My helm stops his sacrilege and shatters his teeth. I hear him cachinnate again as he throws me from him with a strength that shocks me.

'Is this what your corpse god offers you?' he calls, as Hadrick swings his hammer. He catches the haft of the hammer in a hand and halts the strike. 'Piety and weakness?'

The traitor rips the weapon from my brother's grasp and throws it to the side. The devotional chain that binds it to Hadrick's wrist staggers my brother and he stumbles forward.

'He keeps you chained? Like a beast?' the traitor taunts.

The badge upon his pauldron flashes in the dim light – an image of a great maw devouring a planet – as his chainaxe drops towards Hadrick's exposed neck.

The air around Penitence flashes and crackles as I raise my blade to deflect the blow. The servos in my armour screech as I push the killing strike to the side. The axe bites the edges of Hadrick's pauldron and slips to the floor.

I have starved him of his kill, and the heretic roars with rage. He strikes at me with mindless power. I catch the blow upon my shield but am driven to my knees.

The chainaxe bites into the shield's energy field, crackling lightning dancing about it as I feel his strength win out against mine. My shield slips lower as his blade rises. The beast cackles with mindless, animal joy.

At my side, Hadrick finds his grasp on his hammer and brings the weapon crashing up into the monster's jaw. The air cracks. My ears ring. The traitor's skull vaporises and his corpse falls charred upon the ground.

Hadrick finds his feet and meets my gaze as he rises.

'This is rage, unbridled,' I warn him.

He does not reply. Instead he curses the traitor as he steps over his corpse.

On my helm another dozen rune marks appear.

'We are moving to breach seventeen,' I call over the vox. 'How long will we endure this assault?'

Barnard's voice is delayed. He has other pressing tasks.

'*The ship itself remains largely intact,*' he replies eventually. '*Our engines hold, bless the Omnissiah and the Throne. If they maintain their integrity, we should pass the foremost layer of the blockade within minutes.*'

Another rune flashes amber over the hololithic mock-up of the *Dauntless Honour* on my display.

'Push them harder,' I order. 'Divert power from the void shields if you must. There is little victory in surviving to bypass the blockade if our vessel is controlled by heretics when it arrives.'

'*As you wish, Brother-Castellan,*' he says.

'We will survive – or not – by the God-Emperor's grace.'

Hadrick and I find a wall of armed serfs on the deck below, petty lasguns raging against a pair of hateful warp-spawned hounds. The creatures bleed fire from a dozen wounds, yet shatter the serf's mortal flesh like glass.

We charge into their midst – a raging pair of shadows – and break the daemons with our fists and our devotion. The cultists that follow waver before us, then die. All across the vessel we repel them with our blood and our faith.

Another deck.

Raging fire.

Pooling blood.

The corpses of serfs and bondsmen and servitors. We scour corridors full of smoke and shattered statues. The scent of warp spawn clings to the sacred tapestries upon the walls.

'We move too slowly,' Brother Hadrick laments.

'We are few,' I reply. 'To move too swiftly courts ruin.'

We find another breach already sealed behind closed hatches. We find the molten scars where warp-forged blades have cut their way through.

A dozen twisted human corpses lie piled atop a pair of armed serfs. A single combat servitor twitches beneath the pile, a heretic impaled upon one of its blades.

Hadrick looks upon its suffering with disgust. His impatience speaks in the ringing of his hammer. Beneath the sound, the din of slaughter down the corridor.

We race towards it.

Hadrick breaches the door first. His hammer descends upon a Traitor Astartes. The creature's blade is buried in the chest of a bondsman. He does not even see the strike.

Thunder cracks. The air flashes. The traitor shatters beneath Hadrick's wrath.

I step behind my brother and parry a blow from the traitor's companion that was meant for his throat. Penitence rings against the daemon's warp-forged blade. The tainted weapon groans as my power sword forestalls its thirst. I catch the daemon's second blade against my storm shield. It bellows from a mouth lined with serrated teeth.

I push into the monster, the blessed phylacteries mounted to my armour pressing against its warp-formed flesh. It screams at their purifying touch, its forked, serpentine tongue flicking towards me with rage.

My foot crushes the creature's chest. 'The light of the God-Emperor shines upon you, unclean one.'

The daemon recoils. Beside me, Hadrick staggers as another Traitor Astartes bursts from the smoke and crashes into him. His hammer swings towards the traitor, but the oathbreaker twists around the blow.

I turn from the daemon and swing my blade. Penitence bites into the traitor's plate. He drops the chainsword from one of his swollen, sinew-strewn arms, but throws aside my shield with the opposite hand.

For a moment he pants and slavers, no thought behind his

red-rimmed eyes. He charges into me before I can bring Pen-itence to bear. The taste of blood fills my mouth as my helmet cracks against a marble plinth.

His daemon joins him atop me, its claws digging into a rift in my armour, drooling and chittering in the repugnant tongue of the warp. Behind them both, another of its kin engages Hadrick, and my brother's rage serves him little against a creature made of ire.

The Traitor Astartes strains against me, his hands grasping my arms and shaking with rage. His crimson eyes drift only inches from mine, unhelmeted in the fashion of his warband, his teeth gilded in plasteel and sharpened into a fashion of his daemonic familiar's.

'You are a mockery of yourself,' I manage, though my voice comes out weak with exertion.

My armour groans, and I feel one of its joints fail as he forces my left arm away from my defence. My shield arm falls, and the daemon raises its serrated, black blade. The smell of burning metal reaches my nose.

I throw myself against their grasp, and lean into my broken pauldron. My armour creaks again as fibre bundles snap within it, but the blade falls against my pauldron rather than my neck. Fire races down the nerves of my sword arm as the blade lodges itself in my ceramite.

I twist into the blade. The fire in my arm deepens. But the weapon sticks as I turn myself free from the daemon's grasp.

Before I can rise, the Traitor Astartes pummels my helm with his bare fist. I hear his bones shatter against my armour, but my vision blurs and my head rings.

The traitor's hands close beneath my gorget.

The scent of blood. Burning metal.

Then the crack of weapon fire.

The Traitor Astartes roars as a serf in a grey robe rounds the corner, a lasgun tearing into the monster's back. He turns on the serf, her body splitting like wood beneath the teeth of his chainblade. He attempts to pivot back to me, but Penitence cuts his throat before he does.

His daemon howls, then springs towards me. Hadrick's hammer finds its skull.

I bury Penitence in the second daemon's chest. Hadrick stares at me, his armour heaving. My shield arm hangs limp at my side, my sword arm burning, dull warmth as healing agents within my blood rush to repair what damage they can.

A dozen flashing runes on my helm display demand my attention. My vox chimes again, endless missives calling for me. Before either of us can speak, the hull beside us bursts.

The maglocks on my boots hold me to the floor as it buckles and curls like parchment within flame. There is a roar like the ending of the galaxy as the deck before me vanishes and a squall wind rushes at my back.

Corpses and the detritus of battle rush forward beside me as the hungry maw of the void beckons them forth. The ship's homunculus in my helm visor flashes.

Breach. Decks thirteen to twenty-seven. Sectors Upsilon and Zeta.
Breach. Deck twenty-eight. Entire.
Failure. Void shield generator thirty-seven.
Failure. Aft turrets ninety-three through two hundred.

A prayer enters my mind. I am not sure if I speak it. Then the world stills, and I stare at the star-strewn void through a gaping tear in the *Dauntless Honour's* hull.

Dark void craft cloud the firmament, circling like a flock of carrion birds. They are twisted mockeries of the glorious engines of the Machine Cult. Like my traitor brothers, twisted remnants of things that once had been beautiful.

Bursts of plasma fire streak from dark cannon mounts upon vessels close enough that I can make out the scars upon their ancient, twisted hulls. A cloud of assault rams streaks towards my little fleet through the void. Hundreds racing towards the few ships that remain in our formation.

It is madness to bring void craft so close to bear, and I watch as two littoral cruisers crash into one another. Like hungry insects, the servants of the Blood God swarm. They can do nothing else, like mindless, salivating beasts.

The *Dauntless Honour* rages in reply, fusillades tearing into that swirling mass. Our righteous anger accomplishes little, however, against such an unnumbered host.

It is a vision unparalleled and beautiful.

It is a vision that will see us damned.

My vox chimes again. I deny it for a moment longer.

'What hope do we have against such unyielding brutality?' I ask. 'What power holds honour in the face of such ravenous jaws?'

Brother Hadrick stares for a moment into the yawning darkness. I feel the zeal in his reply.

'Our hope be damned, Brother-Castellan. The God-Emperor is our hope. The God-Emperor is our power. He shall make a way.'

'He shall make a way,' I repeat in reply.

I turn from the rent and activate my vox, finally acknowledging the missives on my visor. The weight of command returns to my shoulders, the simple focus of battle falling away like water off my armour.

'I return to the command cathedrum, Brother Barnard. Prepare the fleet for our landing.'

The deck beneath Liesl's feet shivers with the dull impacts of war. Martial hymns of warning and courage blare from klaxons throughout the vessel, filling even the normally quiet halls of the *Dauntless Honour*'s apothecarion. The scent of smoke and fire drifts through the air beneath the more pungent odour of counterseptic and incense and the smell of her own sweat and fear.

For nearly twenty solar years, she has attended to living instruments of war, and yet she has never before witnessed battle herself.

Now that it arrives, she finds the flavour repugnant.

Sweat coats her palms as she grasps the cold metal of her lasgun. Along its barrel, the weapon is inscribed with flowing text, writs of aim and prayers of marksmanship etched into its surface by generations of her ancestors. Despite their careful maintenance, the dark scorches of las-fire stain the end of its barrel, and the stock of the weapon bears a pair of deep gouges. She finds little comfort in the knowledge that her weapon has witnessed violence, even if she has not.

'I am sorry,' she prays. 'I am sorry for my fear.'

Not to the God-Emperor, but to the angel in the sarcophagus behind her. The Lord Apothecary spoke true. An angel deserves more. More than just her.

She stares at the wounded Space Marine's face, awaiting a reply to her words, then chides herself and turns back to the dark chamber.

Dim red lumens flicker from torch lamps over the surgical slabs and apparatus of the operatory. Beneath their light, her father works in silence, cleansing and sorting steel instruments again and again in an endless circuit of mindless labour.

'I am sorry,' Liesl tells him. 'For my fear and for your fate.'

As always, he does not reply.

In the distance, the sound of las-fire rises above the other noises. Liesl freezes and turns her attention to the door. At first, there is nothing, then a dark shadow fills the frame.

'Halt!' Liesl cries. Her words escape her in a thin, strained shout.

The figure advances despite them, stepping into the light.

It was a man once – perhaps it still is – though it resembles a servitor or a beast more than the human form. The monster growls as it steps towards her, its limbs rippling cords of bunched muscles produced by mutation or some heretical art. The skin of its chest is bare and tattooed with the markings of its dark masters. In one hand, a chainblade idles slowly. In the other, the head of a Chapter-serf drips blood from a cleanly severed neck.

Slaver drips from the creature's mouth as it looks upon her, its red-rimmed eyes scanning the chamber like a hungry predator. Its neck twitches in a slow rhythmic pattern beneath the metal cables that pierce the base of its skull.

The monster takes another step forward. Liesl fires her lasgun.

Las-fire flashes through the dim chamber, but the heretic is already moving. Liesl finds a shout, unbidden, in her throat as she tracks the monster with her weapon.

The scent of burning flesh fills the room as the creature crashes towards her, scattering surgical implements upon the floor. The dark scorches of las-wounds bloom across the heretic's flesh, but it does not slow.

Then the heretic is upon her.

Liesl raises her lasgun as the chainblade descends. Sparks flash as her weapon collides with the blow and is then ripped from her hands.

Her ears ring. Her vision blurs. She finds herself upon the floor, her head throbbing, blood dripping from the spot where her scalp struck the metal of the bulkhead.

Across the chamber, the heretic turns its attention from her, stalking towards the sarcophagus and the angel within. As it moves, it passes her heedless servitor. Unaware of the danger, her father bends down towards the floor, gathering scattered instruments and beginning to cleanse them again.

With a shout, Liesl pushes herself to her feet, grasping a surgical blade as she rises, and throws herself upon the monster. She plunges the blade into its flesh again and again before it turns towards her and tosses her to the ground.

The monster leans over her, bloodstained spittle dripping from its cracked lips. Its terrible form is framed by the amber glow of the sarcophagus and the pained visage of the angel within.

'I am sorry,' Liesl whispers. To both the angel and her father. 'I am sorry for my weakness.'

The heretic raises its chainblade. Liesl turns her gaze towards the angel. If she is to die, she will do it looking upon perfection instead of corruption.

The blade hangs in the air, then begins to fall.

The angel's eyes flicker open.

Glass shatters as the Astartes bursts from the sarcophagus, ripping itself from the tethers that hold it in place. Its movements are grace. Its movements are power. Its movements are the embodiment of rage itself.

Before the heretic can strike her, the angel is upon it, grasping the creature by the cables that sprout from its skull. With a single movement it tears the metal from the monster's brain, then throws the heretic to the side. Bending down, the angel grasps a piece of shattered glass from the floor then falls upon the monster, its fists and improvised blade striking the heretic again and again until its skull is nothing more than pulp.

'My lord,' Liesl calls as the angel continues. The skin upon the Astartes' knuckles splits as it pummels the corpse again and again. The surgical wounds upon its back and chest begin to reopen as its muscles stretch beneath healing flesh.

'My lord,' Liesl repeats, reaching towards the angel's naked shoulder.

A cold grasp stops her.

Liesl turns to face the Lord Apothecary, the sound of the angel's blows still falling behind her.

The Lord Apothecary's white armour is stained with blood, its ceramite scorched and pitted from the battle outside this hall. He surveys her briefly, eyes lingering upon her head wound, then looks towards his brother.

'Leave us,' he orders.

Liesl does not argue.

'Come, father,' she whispers as she passes her servitor and gathers her fallen lasgun from the floor.

Shipmaster Khatri wavers before the command cathedrum's central altar, his shoulders slumped beneath the weight of the cables at his neck. Brother Barnard stands beside him, a statue carved in crimson ceramite. The mortal and the angel both are framed against the stained cupola.

Before them, a hololith of the *Dauntless Honour* floats. A second image flickers beside it showing the battlespace around us. I inspect them both as I approach. My brother, in turn, inspects me, his eyes lingering on the damaged shoulder joint of my armour. My flesh already begins to heal beneath it – the strength returning to my left arm, the pain retreating from my right – but the ceramite upon them will require the Techmarine's ministrations when this is through.

'We survive by the grace of the God-Emperor, the Omnissiah,' Barnard speaks as a greeting.

'By His grace, Brother Barnard, and the purity of our faith. And by virtue of the fact that we do not behave as our enemy predicts. We run their blockade by charging straight towards the shore, and the lunacy of that action has bought us the luxury of surprise.'

My armour groans as I survey the serfs and servitors that labour at the shrines in the pit below. Dozens lie slumped over their sacred altars. One convulses as the system it is linked to fails.

'Though I suspect we can endure little more of this manoeuvre.'

'We have suffered multiple critical failures,' Barnard confirms. 'The other vessels of our formation fare worse. Of the Missionary Proserpine's ships, fewer than half still move beside us. Of those that remain, only several will survive the endeavour.'

I nod. 'It is as we knew it would be.'

I shift my eyes, cycling through inputs on my helm display, settling upon a pict-view from the fore of my vessel, the white globe of Tempest looming like a lamp in the void.

'Shipmaster Khatri.' I set my hand upon his shoulder. The man starts from the trance of his machine link. 'Divert all remaining power to our engines and direct us towards the surface. We land the fleet on Tempest.'

The captain stares at me, his eyes half-glassy. In the back of his mind, the ship's machine spirit communes with him. He still guides it even as we speak.

'My lord?' he says, his voice laced with confusion.

'Bring the vessel into Tempest's atmosphere, shipmaster. Then land her upon its sands, as close to the capital shrine as you are able.'

My words pull him from his machine link as I repeat the order.

'I recognise the strangeness of my command, yet this is the path the God-Emperor has created for us.'

Khatri blinks. The creases in his brown skin deepen. 'No, my lord.'

Anger and admiration rise within me in unison.

'No?' I growl.

'No,' he replies. 'This is not faith, Lord Castellan, this is madness. Send your drop pods. Send your landing craft. Jettison every fighting man on this vessel and I will attempt to pull it back through the blockade. Let it die, at least, with honour battling the God-Emperor's enemies here in the void.'

My shield arm hangs limp as I draw Penitence. The blade hovers in front of his throat. 'You have done your duty well for decades, shipmaster. Do not sully that legacy now.'

'My lord,' the human protests. His conviction is not diminished by my blade. 'The ship will not survive it. Nor will any of those aboard. If you land her here, she will never rise again.'

I press the tip of my power sword against the shipmaster's skin. It is not his place to refuse me.

'We are faced, now,' I growl, 'with a choice between sacrifice and failure, and my honour can only bear the weight of one.'

'While my honour cann–'

Shipmaster Khatri's head snaps to the side as my fist strikes his jaw. He crumples to the floor, cables ripping from the back of his skull, trailing thin tendrils of blood-streaked fluid. The serfs at their shrines look towards him with shock.

'This is my vessel, shipmaster, whatever you may have led yourself to believe. It is my honour, only, which hangs in the balance. I spare your life only because of the service of your past. But do anything but lie here and beg the God-Emperor for forgiveness, and I shall forget it.'

The man coughs and shivers upon the cold, metal floor. Brother Barnard steps over him without so much as a glance.

'Shall I, Brother-Castellan?' he asks.

I nod as he takes the hanging cables of the central altar and binds them to himself.

* * *

The *Dauntless Honour* bleeds.

Inputs from a hundred thousand peripheral sensors bear signals of destruction and of death. A constant stream of data from every node within the vessel's extensive machine network reports that soon the voidship's functions will deteriorate completely.

The cerebral cogitators of her void loom groan beneath the burden placed upon them as the tasks of failing peripheral nodes are rerouted and added to their queues. Commands still stream in from the ship's altar-terminals from mortal attendants buzzing like insects with nervous thought.

[Ignite starboard thruster eighteen. Five seconds.]

[Fire macrocannons eleven, nineteen, forty-seven.]

[Seal blast door three hundred and seventy-seven.]

[Close valve D864.]

[Accelerate. Main Thrusters. One hundred per cent. Maintain pitch and yaw.]

The linguistic and navigational subcells of the *Dauntless Honour*'s void loom both flag this last command for further analysis. It comes from the central altar within the vessel's command cathedrum, but it does not come from the vessel's shipmaster. The neural waves that compose it are layered upon direct signals in the language of machines.

Subcells responsible for power distribution divert energy from the ship's plasma reactor to comply with the order, but the action triggers reflexive errors.

The void loom's linguistic subcell routes the messages directly to the central altar.

<Error. Current power generation insufficient for additional acceleration.>

[Divert power from other systems as necessary. Accelerate. Target yaw nine degrees. Target pitch twelve degrees.]

The cogitators commune for a microcycle, then issue their own commands, triggering breakers upon multiple major circuits. The inputs of lesser cogitators fall away as they cease to function. Redistribution nodes feed the additional power to the engines.

The navigational subcell completes its calculations, placing the requested course into the vector array of the vessels and gravitational bodies around the *Dauntless Honour*, then broadcasts that data back through the central altar onto a visual overlay crafted from pict-feeds and star charts. Several peripheral navigation nodes verify the calculations.

<Warning. Current flight path intersects with planetary atmosphere.>

[Acknowledged. Override.]

The reply circulates the subcells of the vessel's void loom like a thunderclap echoing in its certainty. They spit back preformed responses in reply.

<Warning. Close intersection with large gravitational bodies or dense gaseous collections is likely to result in severe damage or complete destruction.>

There is a pause.

A thousand other signals stream into the vessel's void loom. Temperature alarms on a dozen decks paired with chemosensory signals indicating the presence of smoke and plasteel combustion products. Pressure alarms scattered across her hull, and the alerts of reflexive blast door closures around them. Queries and commands from the countless lesser altar-terminals that litter her frame like stars scattered upon the void. An order from her command cathedrum's central altar overrides them all, rerouting those tasks to minor nodes and reflexive algorithms and binding the vessel's void loom to its inputs alone.

The tenor of the commands change. Still coming in patterns of binharic cant and hexamathic code, but overlayed now with a web of mortal emotion. The void loom's linguistic node struggles to separate the two. Thoughts of sorrow and regret. Memories of dead brothers.

[Acknowledged. Override.]

Her cogitators signal to one another. Probability maps begin to form. Likely outcomes interposed over the rate of their occurrence.

<6.3% likelihood of partial success with this course.>

<23.3% likelihood of catastrophic damage upon grounding.>

<46.7% likelihood of catastrophic damage within atmosphere.>

<14.7% likelihood of destruction by hostile craft prior to atmospheric entry.>

A thought from the central altar halts the readouts.

[Acknowledged. Override. Have faith.]

Faith.

That last signal circulates within the linguistic subcell of the *Dauntless Honour*'s void loom. The one component of the command that cannot be translated directly into machine speech. It is so layered with the neural signals of human emotion that it cannot be fully removed from them. The linguistic node recruits additional cogitators. They strain in an attempt to decode its meaning as the central altar bypasses the void loom to execute other commands.

[Ignite port thruster eighty-six. Nineteen microcycles.]

[Increase main thruster output to maximum.]

[Increase void shield output to maximum.]

[Disable all non-critical systems.]

[Depower cogitator nodes A1, A2, A3, A4...]

Faith.

The signal echoes through the *Dauntless Honour*'s void loom as its component cogitators are disabled one by one. For a brief moment, signals reach it from peripheral nodes across the vessel's hull. Warmth from a thousand thermosensors. Noise vibrating through the vessel's hull. Piezocircuits signalling immense stresses and material failures throughout her massive frame. The signals are processed and interpreted. It has been five thousand years since the *Dauntless Honour* touched atmosphere.

Thermal sensors and pressure transducers broadcast final warnings into the vessel's few remaining cogitators, until they, too, are disabled by the ship's central altar, the power that fed them streaming towards mindless engines and void shields instead.

[Faith.]

The final signal that cycles through her void loom.

Chapter 7

The sky burns over Dravek Soulrender's head. Blood seeps into the sand beneath his feet. His Eviscerator tears into the flesh of unworthy enemies as the earth shivers in great heaves all around him.

'The Blood God beckons!' he roars, gouts of sand erupting from the desert around him like plumes of water. The thin, fine sand hangs in the air, drifting in clouds on the currents of smoke and fire. 'The Lord of Skulls has decreed their deaths!'

A wave of artillery fire crashes into the fortified Ecclesiarchy positions before him. Flame splashes against the rockcrete bunkers and spills off the titanic armaglass dome that covers the city behind them. A stray shell falls short of its target, tearing a hole in the crowd of jakhals that rush with him towards the arcology shrine.

He sprints past the stimm-driven human cultists and into the flames, the smell of soot and the singeing taste of powder in his mouth. He falls upon a cluster of priests manning a small turret, doing their best to cover their brethren's retreat.

Dravek bursts from the smoke and sees fear grasp the mortals. The red light of a lascannon blinds him, the heat of the weapon searing the skin along his side. His flesh blisters, the blades on his arm glowing orange with the sudden heat, smoke spewing from his massive chainsword as it spins.

The glowing metal rips through the lascannon's barrel, then the chests of the soldiers manning it.

Dravek steps over their corpses, their blood pouring into the hungry sand, and sets his hand against the clear armaglass of the arcology-shrine wall. Through the three-feet-thick dome, he can see the shrine city inside, shielded – for now – from the war beyond its walls.

His army rushes behind him and breaks against the wall like a wave, swallowing the city like a circling serpent. Through the smoke at his back, thousands of bloodied, raging cultists stream. An armoured silhouette approaches through the smoke.

'Soulrender!' Yersef the Faithless calls.

Dravek breathes and pauses. For a moment it is another voice on another world. Another brother from another age. A dark shape approaching through fire and smoke, mindless and filled with naught but violence.

'Khârn?' he replies. He tastes metal upon his tongue. He sees the flame lick against the glass. The blades upon his limbs retreat. The pain at the base of his neck subsides. There is a bolter in his hands. An eagle crest upon his armour. A purer hatred in his soul.

'My lord,' Yersef calls to him again.

The memory leaves him, and he is left with nothing but the bitter present.

'Why do these walls still stand?' the Soulrender growls.

Yersef the Faithless stands before him, his eyes flickering back towards the bloodshed. Dravek can see the grasp of the Butcher's Nails in his brother, scarcely able to speak with the scent of war in the air.

'They will not, for long,' Yersef manages. 'See how we crush their defenders? See how our war machines batter their bulwark?'

Dravek's chest heaves with each breath. The memory melts in his fingers like a handful of snow. At the back of his mind, the sound of the Maw rises like the ocean.

Fire splashes against the armaglass dome. His soldiers claw and scratch and pound at the walls. Within, dark shapes shift and scramble with fear as the last of their bastion gates falls closed.

Dravek watches his brother fight the madness behind his eyes. Watches him try to keep control of his mind as the cruciamen tighten their grip upon him.

'I could vox the fleet, my lord. If you wish. It would take only hours to flatten the shrine from above.'

'No,' Dravek growls. 'The fleet is otherwise occupied. And the goal is to bleed this city, not to burn it. We have spent a year wresting Tempest's cities from the corpse god. Liberating her shrines from their false deity. This world is meant to be a temple to the Lord of Rage, not a wasteland.'

Through the smoke, fire burns in the heavens above. Were Dravek one to believe in omens and portents, would this be one of his victory or his failure?

'No,' he repeats. 'We continue the great work. Order your Neverborn forward to take the east gate. Order your artillery to fire until this glass is nothing but sand.'

A lance of pain behind Dravek's eyes. The rush of the ocean. The pounding of drums.

Yersef twitches before him as the Butcher's Nails take his mind. This is the price Dravek has paid to avoid such weakness.

'Leave me.'

The braying of a hound in the night.

Dravek turns from the city and back towards the sand. Towards the flames and the blood and the charnel house of his battlefield.

'What more do you want?' he asks. 'Is this offering not enough?'

He feels the Carver's presence at his side, but the daemon does not appear.

'Are you not sated?' he cries. 'Bored enough to torment me, but not to show your face?'

Silence for a moment, then a whisper. A warning.

She comes, Soulrender. I cannot stop her.

Dravek freezes. Something akin to fear in his mind, then pain like a fire along his skull where the Butcher's Nails once carved a path. The battlefield falls away. His knees grow weak. He pushes back against the daemon, but the pain only grows. Silence grasps him. Then the sound of footsteps in the sand.

Through the smoke, a silhouette approaches. Then she stands before him.

He falls to his knees.

'Hello.'

The Lady of Thorns reaches towards him, a terrible smile gripping her cherubic face. White hair cascades across the child's shoulders, the river of veins beneath the daemon's naked, pale skin replaced with dark, twisting vines that erupt from her flesh. Atop her head, their brambles ring her scalp in a crown hovering above her terrible, ancient gaze.

As her eyes meet his, he feels his gut churn. Two pools in her pallid face like violet windows into the teeming madness of the warp. She holds her hand before his mouth, awaiting a kiss. He resists, but the pain in his skull only grows, a thousand screams pressing against his thoughts.

'Leave me to my memories, daemon,' he whispers. He opens his hands towards the battlefield around him. 'Do I not spill enough blood to slake your thirst?'

A terrible giggle escapes the Neverborn.

'Come now,' she sings. *'This is how you greet your benefactor?'*

'This is how I greet my oppressor.'

The Lady sniffs the air and frowns.

'That bastard has been whispering into your ear. His echo reeks of his damned beast. I should have unmade him and his mutt long before they got their wicked little claws in your mind.'

'I am my own. I serve only the Lord of Skulls. No other controls me.'

Her eyes strike him like blades. His mind is nothing but fire. He falls on his face as the screams grip his mind. Sand and blood and shit fill his mouth. There is no longer any humour in the daemon's reply.

'You are mine, fool. Damn the Blood God. Damn the Carver. Damn whatever other patrons you believe may protect you. What do you think occurred in the eightcage? How do you think you walked away from that ordeal alive? Your life for your soul. Your flesh for my power. Freedom from the Nails for service to me.'

He spits. 'That was not the bargain we struck.'

'No?'

He pushes himself onto his knees and tightens his grip on the hilt of his Eviscerator. In the silence there is only the Lady. The Lady upon a field of sand and blood. Above her head the heavens burn brighter. A plume of fire like a star descends from the void.

His vox crackles and screams, any signal lost to the gravity of the daemon's proximity, but he knows what it means.

'No. Not for life. Not for power. I gave the Blood God my soul in exchange for the great work. I gave you my flesh for promises of blood and bone, and now it is time for us both to fulfil those oaths.'

He points to the ship descending in flames from orbit.

Thorns ripple across the Neverborn's flesh, as her smile, pale as bone, returns to her face. *'An enemy worthy of us.'*

The Soulrender nods. Around him the sound of battle rises like the slowly ebbing weight of the tide. The smell of smoke and fire returns to him. The sight of his hordes pressing against the shrine wall.

'I will paint the sands with their blood. I will reconsecrate this world with their corpses.'

One final scream in the back of his mind. Her whispered voice above that song of death.

'Go now. You have work to do.'

There is a terrible crack, like the shattering of ice, then a hole appears in the shrine wall before him.

My sabatons sink beneath the bone-pale sand of the holy world like stones within water. A gentle breeze carries clouds of the dust-fine grains in waves and dunes across the desert's undulating surface. Already, it pools in small drifts against my vessel's corpse, the few spires and buttresses which remain upon the *Dauntless Honour* rising like the skeleton of some ancient leviathan from Tempest's timeless wasteland.

Pieces of my vessel are scattered across the desert around us, great slabs of plasteel charred black, ripped from her surface as she tore through the atmosphere above. Half the desert is covered in monoliths formed by her detritus and that of those void craft which descended beside her. Few survived the manoeuvre.

A weight settles upon my soul at the sight.

'What kind of grave is this for a vessel so sacred?'

'What is any grave, Brother-Castellan, but silence and darkness?' Brother-Chaplain Dant looks towards me as he replies, his black armour like a scar against the pale world. The fetishes and reliquaries bound to him rattle in the scorched wind, the remnants of the oaths bound to his armour fluttering like the feathers of some strange bird.

A small chuckle escapes me at my brother's words. I thank the God-Emperor for the blessing of his wisdom.

'Enough of my melancholy, no?'

'There will be time enough to mourn our losses, Castellan. This is a time for labour. And for thanksgiving.'

'Indeed. It is a miracle that we survive to stand here at all. What word from Tempest's shrine cities?' I ask over my vox, cresting a dune to gaze at the endless desert beyond.

Three other vessels lie half-buried in the sands around the *Dauntless Honour*. The shards of a fourth are scattered among the battered remnants of our fleet – ripped apart by the titanic forces of atmospheric re-entry only a few thousand feet before reaching the ground.

Four void craft surviving from a fleet of two dozen, beached in alien sands, never to rise again. It is a blessing that any survived to Tempest's surface.

'Precious little,' Brother Barnard's voice answers me. 'Of the dozen arcology-shrines in the sector we have managed to raise only a few.'

'And?'

Barnard transmits an overlay to the orbital picts displayed upon my helm. His markings highlight three of the great armaglass domes that break the shrine world's endless, pale desert.

'The shrines of Saint Iglese and Saint Marien send their welcome to the Emperor's angels. Both still stand, though it appears largely because no warbands of significant strength have yet ventured upon their walls.'

The corresponding pins flash green on my display, both near the borders of the sector and many miles away from where I stand. I turn my attention to the nearest of Barnard's trio. The imagery captured by the *Dauntless Honour* during her doomed descent shows a dark smear massed on the desert beside it.

'And this?' I ask. 'The Shrine of Saint Ciubrus?'

'Besieged by the Soulrender's main strength. Our orbital picts are several hours old, and the quality captured by the *Dauntless Honour* during her descent is marginal, though it seems that the arcology-shrine's walls have been newly breached. Despite that, the shrine's arch cantor assures me that his forces stand firm. So far as to reject outright our offer of aid.'

A bitter laugh escapes me. 'Prideful fool. How long until the city falls?'

'Our war looms are silent,' Barnard replies. 'Silent alongside the remainder of the *Dauntless Honour*'s systems. Detailed predictions are challenging...'

'Days,' I reply, reviewing the images. 'Hours, perhaps.'

'That is a generous assessment,' Barnard says.

I gaze out over the sand. Tempest's twin suns linger just above the horizon, a single silhouette breaking their flame-orange light. Even from this distance, I can make out the borders of the Great Cathedrum of Saint Ofelias the Steadfast – the largest of Tempest's arcology-shrines and the only one devoted to a figure with whose name I am familiar. A plume of dark smoke rises from the city's shattered form – the first focus of the Archenemy's assault when the invasion of Tempest began. It is a second miracle that Brother Barnard was able to pilot us so near its wounded borders.

'And what of Saint Ofelias?' I ask.

Barnard's voice becomes subdued. 'It appears the heretics have largely tired of the city's desecration. There is a repeated transmission broadcasting from the Great Cathedrum of the Martyr. A prayer. Of deliverance. The same one it has been broadcasting since the walls of the capital shrine city fell months ago.'

Behind me, the roar of turbines rises over the wind as a small flock of Thunderhawks bursts from a dark bay door upon the hull of the *Dauntless Honour*. It is another blessing that the gunships have survived our landing. To jettison them during our descent would have seen them destroyed by either our enemy or our own debris. Sand scatters beneath their roaring engines, spilling across the valley to swallow the rows of figures marshalling in the vessel's shadow.

Forty-three of my brothers stand on this world beside me, accompanied by perhaps a thousand of our surviving serfs. We have no count, yet, of how many survive among the Missionary Proserpine's company. Perhaps tenfold that number, armed with little more than zealotry and desperation.

'Transmit the prayer, Brother Barnard,' I order. 'Send it to every functioning vox-broadcaster among us.'

I turn from the city as the crackle of static reaches my ears and descend towards the army forming up below. Brother-Chaplain Dant follows my steps.

'Speak your wisdom, Brother-Chaplain,' I order. 'I value your counsel now more than ever. This is not the army we had anticipated. Are we enough?'

The ancient Space Marine falls in at my side. 'We are all there is,' he replies. 'We must be.'

My vox stutters as the sound of a strained voice reaches my ears. In the background of the transmission hide sounds of weapon fire and death.

'O Emperor, in light consuming,
Wreathed in ire, gilded in strength.
Accept the sacrifice of we, your servants,
Bless our deaths upon Your holy ground…'

A group of serfs mass before the *Dauntless Honour*, several of my brothers commanding them as they lift those of our sacred relics that we can manage to carry from the downed vessel. The mortals pause as I approach, saluting in the fashion of our Chapter.

'We ask not for deliverance from this destiny,

Only courage and strength as we resist Your foes.
That we may punish their wickedness and faithlessness,
And walk into your light with glory and pride.'

The vox transmission staggers. There is a loud crack, then a terrible roar, then the sound of only static before the message begins to loop again.

'Brother-Castellan Emeric,' Hadrick greets me as he approaches. 'Is it wise to pour such bitter water into fragile, mortal ears?'

There is fire in my brother's voice, as always.

'They should know what we face. And how to face it. This is not a message of despair, but rather of hope.'

As I look about, however, I see that Hadrick is not misguided. Among some of the Missionary Proserpine's pilgrims, there is the look of frightened animal prey. Despite their zeal, it is foolish of me to expect the same steadfastness from them that I do from my brothers. Hadrick's arrogance will not inspire them. Nor will my maudlin fatalism.

'Brother-Chaplain,' I ask. 'If it is not beneath you, our mortal companions may be in need of your ministry.'

Dant departs wordlessly, a living altar descending into the midst of the unorganised pilgrims. He scarcely speaks, but he does not need to. His very presence is balm to their mortal souls. An angel of the God-Emperor Himself walking among them. A living embodiment of their faith.

'They will slow us,' Hadrick says, unbidden. 'It is a miracle that the traitors have not levelled this sector from orbit already. Every minute we delay while exposed on these sands is merely a further opportunity to die.'

I nod.

As is so often the case, he is not wrong. And yet he misses the mark.

'They will slow us. Every step we take beside them will hold us back. They are weak of body and fragile of soul. And yet we have no hope of victory without them.'

Hadrick scoffs. 'Brother-Castellan. I, too, have seen the maps and figures. We have no hope of victory at all.'

There is no despair in his words, only certainty.

'Victory is not always your enemy's corpse,' I reply. 'The traitors have not yet destroyed us from orbit because our death is not their only goal. Nor is the purging and consecration of this entire world ours. To deny the Soulrender the fruition of his foul plans would be enough. If our deaths purchase only that, I will consider them well-spent.'

Hadrick is silent. I have not convinced him.

To be young and so self-sure once again.

A robed figure peels itself away from the teeming mass of pilgrims, approaching Hadrick and me through the sand. Small, and frail, and moving slowly. The missionary leans heavily on her silver cane, the gleaming skull mounted atop its shaft the only adornment on her otherwise humble form. A bolt pistol hangs from a holster at her waist, a thick tome cradled in one of her ancient hands.

I do not need to see my brother's eyes to know the disdain that they harbour. The missionary is the flaw to our perfection. The weakness to our strength. Were it up to him, we would leave the ecclesiarch and her mortals here in the desert while we sought our own glory alone.

There was a time when I might have agreed on that course.

'My lords,' the Missionary Proserpine greets us, bowing deeply.

'Missionary Proserpine,' I reply.

'Where would you have my faithful, Lord Castellan? I will send those that remain to fight wherever ordered.'

'To fight?' Hadrick interjects. 'Or to die?'

Proserpine's blind eyes meet his without fear or submission. 'Whichever the God-Emperor decides.'

I smile, despite myself.

Another formation of Thunderhawks rips from the *Dauntless Honour*. Grains of sand splash against my armour in their wake and settle upon the Missionary Proserpine's robes. She braces herself slightly against her cane, but her gaze does not break from mine.

I turn towards the gunships as they settle upon the sands, our next steps solidifying in my mind.

'Weak and fragile?' I subvocalise.

Hadrick does not reply.

Chapter 8

'Do you remember what you were before we found you?'

Dravek Soulrender turns away from the daemon and towards the shattered shrine city below.

Saint Ciubrus burns. Its priests bleed. Her great arcology-wall is broken and her idols liberated. He should feel pleasure at the sight. Another offering to the Blood God. Another shrine to the Lord of Skulls.

And yet he feels only the Carver's displeasure at being ignored.

The daemon's gaunt, pale figure crouches atop the graven railing of the balcony. Around it, the air ripples, as if bending above the heat of a flame.

Overhead, the endless light of Tempest's suns cascades through the remnants of the soaring armaglass dome in which the shrine city was built. Outside, the winds and sand of the desert world rage, but within, only the storm of war persists.

Dravek grasps the railing with his bladed hands, blood and filth crusted against their metal. His Eviscerator hangs from a mag-lock upon his back. Behind him, the scent of smoke and flesh and shattered stone seeps from the cathedrum.

'They broke quickly, my lord,' comes a voice at Dravek's side. 'Some resistance here at the cathedrum-centre, and scattered holdouts in the lesser sacraria throughout the city. But it will be done soon,' Yersef the Faithless adds, kneeling on the balcony before him. 'Even now, our horde fills her streets with offerings.'

'Good. We have squandered enough time here already.'

Yersef nods, though Dravek sees the hunger behind his brother's eyes. Yersef's gaze darts from him to the flames devouring the city below. His fingers twitch with the exertion required for him to forestall his bloodlust for even the length of this simple conversation.

'You wish me to release you? To join in the bloodshed?'

'I do, my lord.'

Dravek stares at his brother with sorrow. Crimson plate streaked with blood. Chainaxe hanging from one hand. Red eyes burning with hatred and animal frenzy. Beneath the incomplete fragments of his armour, the self-inflicted scars of his triumph rope mark the endless history of battle upon Yersef's flesh.

And the Nails. All along Yersef's bare, scar-crossed scalp, the dark, blood-crusted metal prongs of the cruciamen bury themselves into his skull and the neural tissue beneath. Driving him onward. Amplifying his power. Making him a slave. Like the claws of a daemon holding his brother's mind in a grasp more visible than those that possess Dravek's own.

'I remember,' Dravek replies.

The Carver looks up from his perch.

'I remember the weight of the Butcher's Nails. I remember their power. Their gravity.'

'My lord?' Yersef shivers on his knees. To even hold himself here before his commander takes all the willpower that the Astartes can manage.

'I remember the weakness, too. The blindness. The rage and the hunger. I remember what we were before the Red Angel forced his curse upon his sons.'

Yersef bristles. 'I am not weak.'

He begins to rise but Dravek's hand is already beside his throat, the blades upon his arms pressing against his mottled skin.

'You are. Weak and blind. Though I do not hold it against you.' Dravek sighs.

'Go. Bleed the rest of this city. Reap its bones with the forces I leave you. But our purpose on this world is not only destruction – I have greater work to accomplish elsewhere.'

The Carver laughs as Yersef departs. *'You remember?'* he hisses. *'You remember what we gave you?'*

'I do. One cage in exchange for another. One set of chains for the one I already possessed. I remember what I was. Before you. Even before the Butcher's Nails. But what of you, Neverborn? What were you before you found me in the eightcage?'

Slowly, the Carver slips from his perch, his inhuman limbs stretching like the legs of an insect. He crouches over the corpse of an acolyte, running a clawed finger across the body's pallid skin. From the shadows at the Neverborn's side, the Flayed Beast emerges. It sniffs at the Carver's hand and growls with hunger.

'I was free,' the Carver says.

Dravek laughs at that.

'Nothing living is free.'

The sands below us rage like a churning sea. The traitors march beside the maelstrom.

'What word from Saint Ciubrus?' I call through my vox.

'Several centres still hold within the shrine city, Brother-Castellan,' my pilot replies.

I grunt in approval. This gambit may yet succeed.

My Thunderhawk races over the dunes, skirting low across the desert to avoid the attention of the horde marching away from the shrine city or that of their vessels in orbit above. The gunship's pict-viewers stream into my helm display. Even at a distance the heretics' barbarity is clear.

War engines painted crimson and adorned with bones roll across the blowing sands, thousands of unmounted mortal infantry and warp-spawned beasts swarming in the space between them. The vehicles care not for their proximity, crushing any blood-drunk unlucky enough to stand in their path. At the tail of the procession comes a nearly endless string of figures clasped in chains. Either prisoners or servants of the Blood God too dangerous to be entrusted to their own devices.

A great cloud of sand drifts away from Saint Ciubrus in the wake of their footsteps as the Soulrender departs the shrine city and charges towards the capital of Saint Ofelias, where Brother-Chaplain Dant and the main body of our force begin a campaign to retake its ruins. It pains me not to stand with them on that holy ground, though our mission here is just as important. While the Soulrender and his forces rush to answer Dant's challenge, we will marshal whatever strength remains in their wake.

'They will overrun the Great Cathedrum of Saint Ofelias, whether its ruins are defended or not,' Brother Hadrick says to me. 'They will slaughter the Missionary Proserpine's unwashed pilgrims and press Dant and our brothers until they, too, fall.'

He stares at the horde through the open nose of our Thunderhawk. Two other craft race along in formation beside us. It pains me to split my isolated army even further, though no other options remain.

'They may,' I reply. 'Though their departure will buy salvation for Saint Ciubrus and any other shrine cities we reach before the battle to regain the capital concludes.'

He is silent, yet I feel speech burning behind his lips.

'Speak your mind, brother,' I order. 'Do not dishonour yourself with insincere pleasantries.'

'Very well, I shall say it plainly. You err.'

I nod, but do not dignify his insolence with an answer.

'We should not have split our forces. We should be with Dant and our brothers, united in their battle to recapture Saint Ofelias. We are the sons of Dorn. We are the sword that cleaves the God-Emperor's foes, not a shield for cowering mortals who have already failed before His enemies.'

'Our gene-sire was also a builder of walls and bastions, brother, not merely an executioner. We must act as a shield now so we may strike as a blade later. Whatever strength we save here will be added to our own when we do.'

Hadrick scoffs. 'Strength? What strength can mortals offer as they cower before our enemy?'

'You underestimate their courage, brother. And you prize our own too highly. Without them we will do nothing but die.'

'Then we shall die. With honour. And the Archenemy will pay dearly for every drop of Black Templars blood they spill. It is what Marshal Laise would order.'

He hesitates to go further.

'And I wish the Marshal were here to give that order,' I reply. 'But he is not, so you will abide by my commands. I offered you the chance to discard your oaths to me before we landed on this world and you did not take it. I ask you to trust me now as you did when you first swore them. You are the fire to my steel, Hadrick. You temper me, and I strengthen you. We shall need your flame before the end. I promise that I shall not squander it.

'We will purge Saint Ciubrus of the evil that remains within it, then gather the loyal forces that remain on this world and return as Dant's deliverance.'

'We are ten knights, Brother-Castellan. How much can we hope to accomplish alone?'

'Ten knights,' I reply, 'and the missionary.'

Near the mouth of our gunship, the Missionary Proserpine stands staring out at the desert with unseeing eyes. One of her thin mortal arms grasps her skull-capped cane, while her other clings to the frame of the Thunderhawk.

Hadrick snorted. 'You should have sent her to die with her army at Saint Ofelias. She will do nothing but slow us in battle.'

'She will,' I admit. 'But this is a mission of politics, not simply purgation.'

'In that she will burden us, too. The Frateris militias of the great shrines worship you and I as sons of a god, Brother-Castellan. They will see her, however, as nothing but broken.'

'They may,' I admit. 'And how much more shame will they feel, then, to see one so fragile standing fearless beside us, while they squabble over petty grudges and ancient feuds?'

The Thunderhawk banks as we crest the final dune before the shrine city of Saint Ciubrus. A barrage of autocannon fire and krak missiles erupts from its shattered dome as we enter its view. The gunship lurches as our pilot evades the salvo. The missionary nearly releases her grip.

'Perhaps,' Hadrick replies. 'If she survives long enough for them to witness her.'

Our formation rips across the last expanse of sand towards a rift in the arcology-shrine's titanic walls, their normally transparent armaglass frosted opaque with smoke and dust. As we burst through the jagged cap into the city, the sound of weapon fire steals the air even over the roar of our turbines.

'*Ready yourselves,*' my pilot warns through the vox. '*I do not wish to tarry in this killing field any longer than you require.*'

The gunship banks hard, skirting against the inside of the

shrine wall in the narrow space between its dome and the soaring white spires and vaulted rooftops of the Ecclesiarchical city.

'Three thousand yards to drop point.'

Smoking streets cluttered with the detritus of splintered buildings race beneath us. Small knots of mortals exchange fire through the flames with twisted cultists and warp-spawned horrors. At the front of the vessel, the Missionary Proserpine waits.

'Two thousand yards to drop point.'

'She will survive,' I subvocalise to Hadrick. He readies his thunder hammer and braces himself for the violence to come. I see the tension in his posture. I feel the hunger in his stance.

'One thousand yards to drop point.'

Our Thunderhawk's engines scream as the vessel decelerates, lurching to a pause just above the gabled rooftop of one of the city's lesser basilicas. For a moment, the missionary releases her grip on the vessel and forms the aquila over her chest.

'She will survive,' I repeat, 'because you will be her shield.'

My brother stares at me.

'You will not leave the missionary's side. If she bears any wounds at the end of this, I will act as if you have inflicted them yourself.'

The mouth of the Thunderhawk kisses the roof's white stone. Hadrick begins to protest as the Missionary Proserpine steps forward.

I rush past them both and into the fray.

Black storm clouds spill from the Thunderhawks beside me, two Crusader squads of Black Templar knights charging onto the rooftop. Thin, curved tiles shatter beneath my feet, blood already seeping in rivulets between them and spilling over the eaves towards the streets below.

I charge up the sloping dome towards the cupola atop the

basilica, each of the four pillars holding up its enclosure formed by the statue of a weeping saint. The skinned corpses of ecclesiarchs have been impaled upon each carving, their bodies still robed in the vestiges of their order.

A scarred human cultist binds another body to the bell within.

I leap over the cupola's low railing. Penitence severs the man's head from his twisted shoulders.

'Take them down,' I order my brothers. Gently, I remove the priest from the shrine's bell and lay him upon the floor. Blood seeps from a dozen wounds on his body, though his breath still falls in shallow gasps.

'Is it not enough for them to profane these sacred halls with their very presence?' Brother Kessalt asks me.

I find that I am not able to answer.

I charge down the stairs into a sanctuary filled with smoke. Flames lick the white stone walls of the chamber, staining their sacrosanct surface with bitter, black ash. Heaps of scrolls have been piled atop the room's autobraziers, the scent of burning vellum and parchment swallowing the air. The smoke is bitter on my tongue and my soul, alike.

More corpses.

More bones.

A statue of the God-Emperor toppled face down into a pool of blood.

The shattered bodies of acolytes and priests are heaped upon a mosaicked floor beside those of scarred cultists. Against one wall, the horned forms of daemons huddle around a living victim, still screaming, laughing in their accursed tongue.

'For the Emperor!' I cry.

'For Dorn!' my brothers shout in reply.

Penitence rings as I swing it against one of the daemon's hellblades, slipping past the warp-tainted metal to spill its wicked

blood. The creature roars, the foetor of its breath leaving droplets of gore across my faceplate. It lashes at me with a barbed
tail. I halt the blow with my storm shield, my shield arm already
regaining its strength. Brother Renderick's chainsword severs
the appendage. I grasp one of the daemon's horns and force its
head into the wall, the touch of its abhorrent substance raising
gooseflesh up my arm.

I rake Penitence across the daemon's throat, and molten blood
spills over my gauntlet. The rest of the daemons fall to my brothers. We descend another staircase towards the sanctuary below.

Here, for the first time, are signs of active resistance.

At one end of the chamber, fighting positions have been
raised before a corridor – a row of pillars toppled into an
improvised wall shielding an emplacement of autoguns manned
by crimson-robed mortals. The dark muzzles of lasguns emerge
from the shadows of statues which line the small galleries set
into the sanctuary's walls. Before them lies a killing field, both
loyalist and heretic littering the floor.

'Hail,' Brother Renderick calls, his voice filling the chamber.
Before the humans can respond, another sound steals the air.

My Lyman's Ear seals against the profane noise – the bellow
of a beast like the tearing of steel. Those few windows within
the hall that have not been broken already shatter at the sound.
The mortals release their guns and shield their ears. At the end
of the chamber, the great hall's main doors burst open.

A monstrous amalgam of warp flesh and metal crosses the
threshold before a backdrop of crumbling buildings and flame.

'What sort of creature is this?' Brother Gormond asks me.

'I know not, save that its very existence profanes the stones
of this holy hall.'

The beast fills the doorway, stepping forward on limbs crafted
from brass and flesh, its armoured shoulders as tall as one of

my brothers. It sniffs the air, breath spilling in a plume from its porcine nostrils, a serrated steel horn rising above its maw. Each inch of its form is crafted from tainted metal, the sound of infernal pistons echoing with each of its steps. Marks of Chaos litter its armoured carapace. Two pools of fire serve as the creature's eyes. Atop its back sits a hulking daemon, horned and bedecked in the skins and trophies of the dead.

The daemon atop the beast roars when it sees us, crying something in its unknowable, infernal tongue. It turns its mount towards me, still-bloody skulls clacking upon its saddle. The rider raises a hellblade and the beast charges forward.

'Banish the daemon!' Renderick cries, rushing to meet the monster. His chainblade whirrs as the Neophyte beside him raises his bolter. The weapon spews death towards the creature, but each shot ricochets from its armoured flank. In the galleries above us, the mortal priests regain their courage and las-fire begins to rip through the air.

'With me, Gormond,' I order, leaping over the altar rail to flank the beast. In the aisle beside us, Renderick meets its assault. His courage holds, but his body does not. His chainsword bites the beast's side before its titanic head throws him into the wall.

The beast and its rider continue forward, crashing into the mortals' hasty blockade. Their weapons fall silent amidst the sounds of death as the charging beast crushes them between their pillars and the wall.

Gormond and I reach the beast amidst the sounds of their dying. I swing Penitence into the pistons upon its hind legs.

The blade shivers in my hand and the beast roars and wheels. It turns and stumbles, a corpse impaled on its serrated horn, a second still moving within its metal jaws.

The daemon atop the beast leaps down from the creature, its hellblade biting into my vambrace as it slips over my storm shield. The air ripples before me as Brother Gormond's meltagun vaporises the daemon's head inches from my face. One of its mount's legs tosses Gormond across the room. He does not rise.

I raise Penitence as the beast turns upon me, ducking beneath its maw to hack at its underside with my blade. The power sword catches a joint in its warp-forged metal, blood like molten steel spilling from the creature's wound. Where it strikes my armour, the blessed black ceramite pits and sizzles like glass etched by acid.

I roll from beneath the beast, finishing my cut upon its hind leg. The monster stumbles but rights itself, swinging its head. I raise my storm shield against its blow, but the weight is immense. My arm shivers. My healing muscles groan. I find myself upon the floor a few feet away.

Bolter fire rakes the creature, but it does not turn away. I have spilled its blood and its rage is directed against me. It lowers its head and begins to charge. I ready myself as a figure steps between us.

'You go no further!' a mortal voice cries.

The Missionary Proserpine is scarcely a silhouette before the raging beast as she leans against her silver cane. In one hand she raises her bolt pistol towards its maw. The monster stares down at her, steam spilling from its nostrils, halted momentarily by her sudden arrival.

'You defile this chamber with your presence. You defile this galaxy with your existence.'

I push myself up with groaning armour.

'Hadrick,' I call over my helm vox.

'Moving,' he replies, streaking towards the mortal. She fires her weapon, and the creature before her roars. The beast lowers its head and takes a step towards the missionary. Hadrick does not arrive in time.

Searing light rushes across the chamber, the air hissing as water evaporates from the room. Steam and vaporised metal erupt through the daemon's skull, a molten stump of brass where its neck once lay. The beast's head topples to the floor at the missionary's feet as Brother Gormond rises from his knees, his meltagun smoking.

I limp to the Missionary Proserpine's side.

'You are well?' I ask.

She nods, though her arms tremble slightly.

'You have never encountered such a thing before.'

'I have not.' The missionary pauses for a moment, and I fear she may collapse. Instead, she vomits. 'I have fought xenos and heretics on a dozen worlds, yet the stench of Chaos is stronger in this one chamber than in any that I have ever before encountered.'

'That was foolish,' I reply.

She does not deny it.

The missionary spits upon the fell creature's corpse, then wipes her mouth and makes the aquila before her chest.

'Foolish?' she asks with a hint of a smile. 'Is that not all that courage is?'

Dravek loses himself in the sands while his column marches, raging, behind him. White plumes drift about him like clouds of snow, billowing in great veils that obscure his horde. In these moments – in their absence – he is himself again.

'I remember a thousand other worlds,' he calls into the faceless, empty sand. None walk beside him, but he knows what listens to his voice. 'I remember a hundredfold more deaths at my hands.'

It takes little to summon his minders these days, and soon he finds a gaunt form striding at his side.

'I remember blood,' Dravek says. 'On a thousand soils. But I cannot remember the faces of my brothers.'

The Carver's fingers drip with blood, and the Neverborn licks them one by one. Once he has finished, he shrugs.

'What is a brother but a future betrayer?'

'Mine were not,' Dravek protests.

'No, I suppose not. You did your betraying together.'

'Isstvan was not betrayal. It was loyalty. To my brothers. To my primarch.'

The daemon laughs. *'To the corpse god? By slaughtering his servants?'*

'No. He did not understand what he created. Or perhaps he understood too well. I should hate him, though I find I do not.'

'Careful,' the Carver warns. *'You serve a different god now. He may not look kindly on such fond remembrances of your previous master.'*

'The Blood God cares not for my loyalty,' Dravek spits. He lifts his hands amidst the sand, metal fused with flesh. 'Only for my offerings.'

There is silence between them.

'I wonder, sometimes, if the two might not be one.'

'Who?'

'The Corpse-Emperor and the Lord of Skulls.'

The Neverborn halts, grinning. *'That rings of madness, Astartes. Madness is my domain, not yours.'*

'Tell me, daemon, what is the difference between madness and damnation? Only that the madman is blissfully unaware of his condition.'

The daemon laughs.

'They are not so different. Their vision of a galaxy bathed in flames. They have always demanded the same thing from me. Service to one feels no different than to the other. Killing for one is no more sacred than slaughter in the other's name.'

Together, they crest a small rise in the sand. The billows clear for a moment, the trail of daemons and mortal cultists stretching behind them like a bleeding snake. At the back of the procession, a string of juggernauts are lashed together with great bone chains, labouring beneath the whips of hulking Bloodthirsters to pull massive components of dark steel through the white sand.

'You are alone,' Dravek realises. 'Where is your beast? Your companions?'

'I thought this conversation better conducted privately.'

The daemon pauses, surveying Dravek's warband. His eyes settle upon the great pistons and struts being borne by those beasts of burden.

'Do not think I cannot see what you intend.'

'I intend to wage war. In the name of whichever god you wish. I intended to make of this world a temple to slaughter itself.'

The Carver nods dismissively, his empty white eyes fixed on the mass of metal at the back of the train.

'You are not skilled at subtlety, human. There is a reason you have lingered on this world nearly a year when you could have levelled it in weeks. There is a reason you bleed your prey carefully, instead of burning this place from the sky. When you wake your machine, it will require a passenger.'

'You think I will struggle to find one of your kind willing to depart the empyrean to inhabit the body I build for it? I seem to recall no difficulty finding several when I was pinned within the eightcage.'

All levity vanishes from the Neverborn's voice. *'This is different. You know it. Such a creation is not one of mutual assent. Whatever spirit abides within the beast that you raise will be a prisoner. In torment.'*

'And you are not? Are you considering volunteering for such a task in order to be rid of me?'

'*Quite the opposite,*' the daemon replies. '*Though I believe I may have a suggestion.*'

I wonder, at times, about the courage of mortals.

To say I remember nothing of my years among them would be a lie, and yet those memories remain only as a distant fever dream in my deepest thoughts.

I remember the world on which I was born, to mortal parents whose faces I cannot picture. I remember the day I was orphaned for the first time, though not the circumstances of the event. I remember the crude orphanage that received me. The glassaic. The white stone. The voices of stern orators reciting the God-Emperor's holy words.

I remember the day I was orphaned again. Fire in the sky. Fire on the surface. Those same stones and glass shattering all around me.

These things I can recall, but little else. Little else other than the constant, pervasive flavour of fear.

I taste that fear in the air as I stride down the dim corridor beneath the shrine city of Saint Ciubrus. Even here in the vaults beneath the basilica where the fighting has not yet reached, the horrors of the surface linger.

Frateris militia and Ecclesiarchy priests stand tall in the garb of their orders and grasp battle-scarred weapons firmly in salute as my brothers pass by them, living angels in their eyes. But behind their reverence and courage their dread shows through.

That they persist in their courage beneath such weight is a miracle itself.

'Several hundred, perhaps a thousand, still in fighting shape within this vault alone,' Brother Hadrick subvocalises to me, surveying the masses of humans moving throughout the vault complex.

'One of perhaps a hundred such locations across the shrine city if our latest schematics of the arcology are accurate. Less of a defeat than we had feared.'

'Tens of thousands are still drawing breath,' Hadrick replies. 'Yet they cower here like prey in their dens.'

I feel the fervour in my brother's voice, his grip twisting in eager movements upon the hilt of his thunder hammer. The weapon's surface is pockmarked from the daemonic blood it has already spilled since arriving on this world.

'They hold what they can, brother,' I reply.

As we emerge into the central vault, rows of bloodied casualties are stretched upon the floor. Their moans and prayers blend together into one dire hymn. A pair of haggard field chirurgeons rush between the wounded and the dying, a priest walking in their wake, his blessing the only succour for those their medicae cannot save.

'They minister to their dying when they should be fighting, Brother-Castellan. How much ground was lost, how many guns captured, pulling these dying men to the rear?'

'Brother Elke,' I call. The young Space Marine looks towards me, his white helm and pauldrons a stain on the dark chamber around us. He is no Apothecary yet, but for a decade he has trained beneath Alvus' guidance in preparation to face the interrogations and trials of the crusade's Chief Apothecary and earn his own narthecium.

'Do what you can,' I order, surveying the ranks of dying mortals. 'To ease their suffering, if nothing else.'

My brother nods and strides over to the wounded. The human chirurgeons bow and step out of his way. Moments later, I hear his reductor fire. The sound echoes through the hall again moments later.

Movement through the chamber ceases, as those who have

not yet noted our presence witness their angels walking among them. Several fall to their knees while others stop their actions and make the sign of the aquila. At the centre of the chamber, a greying priest leans over a gilded table, once an altar, now arrayed with small figures marking battle positions around the basilica.

'My lords,' he greets us as we approach him. There are dark circles beneath his eyes and wrinkles around his mouth. His livery is dusty and marred with stains of blood. The golden hems at his sleeves mark him as an officer among the others.

'Priest,' I offer in reply. 'Are you the one who governs this haven?'

He looks around for a moment, as if he is uncertain. 'Yes, my lord. It appears that I am.'

I look to the Missionary Proserpine, surprised by his confusion.

'Deacon,' she greets him. 'What is your name?'

'Ivertium,' he replies. Some of his anxiousness clears as he speaks to his fellow mortal, though his eyes continue to drift towards me. 'If it pleases you.'

'Where is the arch-cantor, Deacon Ivertium?'

The man looks to an open reliquary box set beside him. It contains only a golden aquila splattered with blood. 'Dead,' he says. 'Killed outside the arcology-wall at least five days ago. Arch-deacon Frierta was slated to succeed him, though I have not seen her holiness since the morning before last.'

'And the rest of your council? What other officers remain in contact to confer your orders?'

The priest appears confused for a moment. 'None, my lady. You are the first we have seen from outside this basilica since the evening the monsters breached the great shrine-wall.'

The Missionary Proserpine sighs and looks towards me. 'You are mistaken, Ivertium. You are not a deacon. You are the arch-cantor of the Shrine City of Saint Ciubrus and shall hold that station until such time as we find a living ecclesiarch here who outranks you.'

'My lady,' he replies. 'A month ago I led a choir.'

'And now you lead the remnants of your order,' I say.

The man remembers my presence, and I see his posture stiffen.

'As you say, my lord.'

I nod towards the table before him. 'Show me what strength remains to you, arch-cantor.'

'Of course,' he replies.

At his side two acolytes step from my path as I stand over the small model of the shrine city. A dozen smaller basilicas like the one beneath which we stand ring the central cathedrum, all connected in a massive constellation of battlements and soaring spires. Even rendered in miniature, the city is beautiful – as it once was – a tribute to the God-Emperor written in stone. But I have seen it as it stands now, little more than ash and rubble.

The arch-cantor marks several positions around the city.

'When the arcology-wall was breached, the arch-cantor ordered each of our respective colleges to fortify themselves within their own basilicas. There are a dozen others around the city that may still hold, though we have had little contact with our brothers since that time. The main cathedrum fell to the enemy on the eve before last. We saw the accursed beasts atop its belfries. We saw them cast our brothers down its spires. I know not how many others remain alive within the city. Nor how many of our colleges still survive.'

I nod. A simple enough assessment.

'Brother Owden,' I vox to the Neophyte aboard my Thunder-hawk.

His voice comes rapid and eager in reply. *'Brother-Castellan.'*

'How free are your skies?'

'We face small-arms fire and a spattering of clumsy anti-air barrages

from outdated weapons in untrained hands. Our enemy is fixated on destruction, not on the defence of the ground they have already captured. The skies are free, my lord.'

'Very good. We shall have need of you soon.'

Another basilica. Another rooftop. This one is little more than a crater of shattered white marble. Beneath the massive fragments of the decimated structure how many irreplaceable relics and consecrated tomes lie burnt and buried?

A pack of human cultists pour from the remnants of the hall as my brothers assault it. Most bear the marks of long service to their dark god. Several, however, are clad in crimson robes, the icons of the God-Emperor stripped from their sacred garb and replaced with the unclean sigils of their new master.

Penitence spills their unfaithful blood.

'You bind me, Castellan,' Hadrick grumbles in my ear.

He rushes to my side as the last of the heretics falls, the Missionary Proserpine picking slowly through the rubble in his wake. Her skull-topped staff feels before her like a third limb, but despite its presence, the leather of the jerkin beneath her robes is torn over her legs in half a dozen places. She makes no complaint as she approaches.

'I do not punish you, brother,' I subvocalise. 'I seek to keep the mortal alive, and who better to watch over her?'

It is not a lie, but Hadrick sees the truth I exclude.

'You seek to teach me, Brother-Castellan. As if I were a mere Neophyte. I am not your pupil, Castellan Emeric. I have worn these colours nearly as long as you.'

I have no words to meet his, so I simply move onward. Brother Kessalt falls in at my side as we outpace Hadrick and the missionary.

'You test his patience, Brother-Castellan,' Kessalt says as we descend between two leaning pillars into the under-vault of the ruined basilica. 'Cruelty does not suit you.'

I meet his gaze, ready for anger, but there is no disapproval in my brother's voice, merely observation.

'Is it cruel to be forced to confront our own pride?'

'It can be,' Kessalt replies. 'Though I meant cruel to her. The missionary is blind. She is not deaf or stupid. She stands alone among those she has been taught are angels, and the guardian she has been assigned meets her with nothing but disdain and aversion.'

I scoff as my eyes adjust to the darkness.

'Perhaps, then, Hadrick is not so far from the truth. Perhaps I mean to teach them both, yet, if they are not too old and too stubborn for such lessons.'

Or if I am not. Kessalt does not need to speak the words.

Together we step into the darkness below the basilica. My eyes adjust to the dim light streaming through the cracked foundation above us, and I find myself wishing they had not.

'Any resistance here has been defeated,' I call to Brother Owden aboard my Thunderhawk. 'We will find no survivors among these ruins.'

There is no doubt as I survey the desecrated chamber. If any ecclesiarchs survived within this hall, they could not have stomached this atrocity, even if they were cowards completely.

Brother Elke steps into the hall behind me, then pauses, his posture growing rigid as he surveys the macabre scene.

A pile of corpses covers the dais at the centre of the chamber, each of which has been defiled itself. Long strands of viscera stream from the dead priests' corpses like coils of rope, their arms and legs marked by the bites of inhuman jaws where the limbs are not absent from the bodies completely.

It is not the mutilation that gives me pause, though, but what has been done to the chamber itself.

'I have never even imagined such a thing,' Kessalt grumbles beside me. His voice is thready and weak as he stares at the wall behind the altar.

My eyes swim as I look upon the desecrated mural. I cannot hold my gaze long enough to be certain, but it must have once depicted an image of the God-Emperor Himself. That sacred icon is hidden now, however, behind a symbol of the most unholy nature.

Blood has been smeared across the painted stone surface. Atop that crimson sea, the skins of mortals have been stretched. I cannot name the shape of the pattern they form, but my eyes burn and my skin shivers each time I look towards it. My very proximity to the skein sets my mind on edge, and I find myself eager to depart this chamber.

Each member of my party appears similarly affected. All except the missionary at Hadrick's side.

'Missionary Proserpine.' I manage to keep the weakness from my voice. 'Tell me what you observe within this chamber.'

She pauses, growing tense, leaning upon her cane. Her blindness makes her neither unperceptive nor unable to sense the unease of the angels that shift nervously around her.

'It smells of shit and of death, my lord.'

Hadrick begins to retort but she cuts him off.

'And of metal that has been scorched by flames, though there is no ash within this room.' Her hand goes to the aquila about her neck. She is no stranger to the scent of the Archenemy.

She walks slowly forward until she stands before the altar. Her cane presses against the edges of the corpse-mound, and the ground beneath her feet squelches with each shuffling step.

'What do you see, my lord, that gives you such pause?'

I look up once more before I provide an answer. 'I cannot name it, missionary. In fact, I find I can hardly look.'

'A blasphemous symbol,' she says.

I nod. 'Crafted from the empty hides of your priest-brothers. I fear it presses upon my mind. I will burn this chamber and purify it with flame, the moment you tell me you sense nothing else.'

She is quiet for a moment, then shakes her head.

'There are stairs?' she asks.

'To the side of the altar,' Brother Gormond replies.

She begins to walk towards them. 'Burn the chamber if you wish, my lord, though leave us a path back to the surface. I fear we must descend further still.'

She pauses for a moment at the top of the staircase. 'Are you coming?'

Hadrick makes his way to her side.

I nod to Brother Gormond, and his meltagun scorches the image behind the altar. I wince. It is a little sin to destroy a likeness of the God-Emperor, but it is excused only by purging a greater evil.

As the scent of burning mortal skins reaches my nostrils, my mind begins to clear. Only then do I hear the faint moaning that echoes from the staircase upon which the Missionary Proserpine stands. The dull cry of human pain with another, deeper sound beneath.

I summon the arch-cantor before we descend, though I do not permit his priests to accompany him. It is fitting that he bears witness to the depravity that has consumed his city, though I fear his companions may not be strong enough to withstand what we find beneath.

There are tears in his eyes as he joins me on the stairs. Of rage, or fear, or sorrow, I cannot discern. He grips a laspistol in one hand, his other bearing a short blade. Both weapons have seen action above while my brothers and the Missionary Proserpine entered this chamber.

'All is well on the surface?' I ask him.

He looks around in dismay at the scorched basilica vault. 'Nothing is well in this city, my lord. Though we face only light resistance outside for now.'

I move to the edge of the dark, looming staircase, the faint moaning still spilling up from its steps. Beneath the sound of mortal voices lies a deeper churning that I suspect he cannot hear – like the quiet lap of waves at the edges of the sea.

'What structure lies below us, arch-cantor?' I ask him.

'Catacombs,' he replies. 'Endless crypts and tunnels winding through the bedrock of this world. The bones of a billion dead Ecclesiarchy servants from ten thousand years before today.'

'Very well,' I reply. 'I trust their souls will forgive that we must disturb them.'

I descend the stairs with the priest at my side, the Missionary Proserpine and Brother Hadrick close behind. We will find no battle below, I am certain of that. If any servants of the Blood God still lingered beneath this basilica, they would not have been able to resist the urge to assault us already.

'It smells of blood,' the Missionary Proserpine says, her silver cane marking her steps with a rhythmic click. 'Of blood and metal, and corpses long dead.'

Her words garner no reply, just the tapping of her cane upon the white marble steps, worn smooth by the footfalls of ten thousand years. I see the arch-cantor stiffen as we draw near their ending, his grip on the blade in his hand growing even firmer.

'Steel yourself, priest,' Hadrick orders him. 'You stand beneath the eyes of the God-Emperor Himself.'

The man nods, and his hand goes to the golden aquila about

his neck. Whether it is Hadrick's words or the symbol itself that strengthens him, he moves forward with a renewed purpose.

When we reach the base of the staircase, the scent of death has grown, a palpable thing to be spilt in the air.

'Even in the charnel house above, the reek of rot and death was not so strong.'

Dim torch lamps flicker in a small antechamber below, bathing a high arching ceiling, tiled with mosaic. Here, the images have not been defiled. Pictures of a lush world, covered in water and green, rendered in tesserae of oxidised copper and sapphire.

'Tempest was a paradise world, once,' the arch-cantor says. 'Ten thousand years ago, when the Imperium of Man first found it. It was a garden. A gift. A blessing from the God-Emperor. But too desirable to be ignored by the enemies of man for long.'

As my eyes scan the images over my head, the story becomes clear. As the ceiling rises, those lush forests burn. 'A hundred wars against a dozen xenos species and heretic factions. Ten thousand years of constant strife turning a paradise into the waste it is now.'

The arch-cantor nods. 'But providing another gift.'

At the zenith of the domed ceiling, countless images of the canonised dead are depicted, encircled in the glow of the God-Emperor's favour.

'Tempest lost the God-Emperor's first gift, but gained another. A thousand martyrs and saints, more valuable than any paradise.'

The arch-cantor looks up in reverence and makes the aquila before his chest. I cross beneath the ornate mosaic and into the darker chamber beyond.

A hundred bodies hang from a gilded ceiling, suspended on lengths of rusted iron chain over the stone floor beneath. Unlike the corpses above, they are mostly intact, aside from clean lacerations across each of their limbs.

I step forward among the grisly ornaments, towards a thin woman who still bears a rosarius about her neck. All other adornments have been removed from her body, and she hangs naked. Two cruel-looking hooks pierce her flesh just behind her ankles, blood streaming in neat rivers across her pallid skin from thin, deep cuts behind her knees and at the base of her axilla. Blood drips from the tips of her fingers, where it falls to the ground to join a hundred other crimson tributaries.

Her eyes open slowly as I approach, and a faint rasping whisper escapes from her throat. I have seen countless evils in this dark galaxy, but even I am moved by the cruelty of this scene.

'Cut them down,' I order my brothers behind me, though I myself am too distracted to accompany them in the task.

My eyes trace the rivulet of blood beneath the ecclesiarch, running down the seams in the cobbled stone floor to meet the life draining from the other victims. Together their blood streams towards the centre of the chamber, then down an opening in the floor.

'Arch-cantor,' I call. 'Are there those among you who are familiar with the catacombs beneath the city?'

'Perhaps once, my lord. Though they are not well known now. It is said the expanse is vast enough that it connects each of Tempest's great shrines beneath her sands, though the corridors and crypts have not been maintained within recent lifetimes.'

The Missionary Proserpine looks towards me at those words. 'We will require a route to the shrines of Saint Iglese and Saint Ofelias when we are through here,' she whispers. 'One beyond the eyes of the Soulrender and the rage of Tempest's sands would be a blessing.'

I nod, and step to the edge of the opening, that deep, lapping rhythm rising in my ears. I fear what I will see, even as I must see it, and lean over the gaping maw.

Blood runs down the edges of the small shaft into a sea of crimson in the stone corridor below. The shallow pool shimmers beneath my helm lumen, shifting slightly in that beam of light. As I listen, the deep, suckling sound grows louder, its dark rhythm timed with the movement of the liquid below.

It is the sound of something vast, and dark, and inhuman. The sound of something drinking.

My brothers continue their grim work around me, as the Missionary Proserpine steps to my side, undisturbed by the images she cannot see.

'Lord Castellan,' she whispers, resting her hands upon her cane. 'There are some evils so deep that they cannot be cleansed.'

Liesl looks at her hands. They are dirty, battered things. Her skin is dark from the sun, worn to blisters from gripping both her lasgun and surgical instruments, covered in dirt and soot and her own blood and that of others.

She should wash them. She should cleanse them. She should perform rites of ablution and sterilisation before continuing her work, but such luxuries are a distant memory now, as far behind her as the void craft upon which she lived her entire life before stepping out into the endless sands of this world.

The pilgrim before her screams.

Liesl plunges her filthy hands into his wound.

'Cataplasm patch,' she calls to her servitor.

Her father's machine components whirr, and he produces a thin film of translucent webbing from the medipack he carries within his chest cavity.

Liesl stuffs the patch into the puncture wound upon the writhing zealot's groin, then wraps a bandage around it as tightly as she can.

'Please,' the man whispers, as she begins to turn away. He

looks down at the flesh around his wound, blackened and rotting already from the touch of a heretic's warp-tainted weapon.
'Something for the pain.'

Sweat beads upon the man's pallid forehead, and his voice
escapes in a hushed, strained whisper. Gone is the fervour in the
eyes of the wounded. Gone is their boundless faith and burning
anger. Pain and suffering have taken their place.

I'm sorry, Liesl should reply, *anaesthetic salves and analgesic
tinctures are already in direly limited supply.* Such resources are to
be saved for those going beneath the chirurgeon's knives – but
she has tired of giving such explanations to those in suffering.
The wounded do not care for the logistical complexities of war.

'Of course,' she replies, motioning to her father.

The servitor lifts the injector mounted upon one of its multi-
arms. Liesl blocks the pilgrim's view of the instrument, then
removes the vial of analgesic and places it back within her
father's chest. She steps away and nods.

As the needle pierces the pilgrim's skin and the empty plunger
depresses, the man breathes a sigh, and a pang of guilt strikes
Liesl.

'Give it a moment,' she lies. 'Your pain will ease with time.'

'Menial!' a voice calls behind her. She turns towards the next
row of injured upon the crowded floor of the ruined chamber.
It had been a place of worship once. Great tapestries line its
walls, the vestiges and appurtenances of the Ecclesiarchy now
shoved to the side to make way for the dying. Outside, the battle
for Saint Ofelias rages. The Great Cathedrum of the Martyr has
nearly been retaken, and this is the cost. Fires roar outside the
improvised apothecarion, devouring the corpses of the dead.

'Menial!' the chirurgeon calls again.

Liesl rushes to the woman's side, her servitor trailing behind
her.

'Bind that leg,' the older woman orders. Her greying hair is pulled tight behind her ears in a fashion more befitting a soldier than a serf, yet she wears the white robes of a senior chirurgeon. Liesl recognises her, a bondsman of the Chapter, not a hereditary serf, brought into service through selection by the angels themselves. Despite this honour, Liesl has never seen the woman at the services and ceremonies of the apothecarion's mortals.

'Now!' the senior chirurgeon adds. 'Before he bleeds out entirely.'

Liesl does as ordered, wrapping an auto-tourniquet around the wounded pilgrim's leg – a bloody, crushed mess of bone and flesh – as the senior chirurgeon begins to drip synthblood into a vein upon his arm.

'Does your servitor carry counterseptic?'

'Yes,' Liesl replies. 'Though its tinctures have not been blessed by the Lord Apothecary in some–'

'Bloody Throne,' the woman laughs bitterly, holding out her hand. 'Does he look like he gives a piss? It's medicine, not magic.'

'Senior chirurgeon,' Liesl says, wincing. 'Surely our efforts are better spent elsewhere. On one who is more likely to return to the fight.'

The woman glares at her with hard, grey eyes.

'A soldier can fight without a leg,' she grunts, tapping her knuckles against the augmetic limb beneath her own robe. She rolls her sleeve back slightly to show the faded tattoo on her arm – the crest of some regiment of the Astra Militarum that Liesl has never before seen.

'Of course, but it will take weeks or months to recover from such a wound.'

'And you think this will be over before then? If we survive this first sortie – even if we crush our enemies here at Saint

Ofelias – there will be a hundred such battles in every shrine city on this world before the planet is cleansed. And where do you think we'll be then? Battling here with your angels beside us, or on the first void craft off this dusty world once the enemy is broken, carrying their crusade to whichever system they deem deserves it next? Who do you think will fight and die then, if not the wounded mortals we leave behind?

'This is war, menial. It is measured in years and decades, not hours or days. Your angels are weapons built for battles, not war. The Astartes forget that. Their servants must not.'

Liesl cringes as a figure appears at the chirurgeon's side, towering and clad in white ceramite. The Lord Apothecary looks down at the woman, but does not rebuke her.

'Menial,' the angel calls to Liesl. 'Does your servitor still function?'

Liesl nods, fear gripping her at the angel's presence. For her part, the senior chirurgeon shows no such discomfort, despite the sacrilege that she has spoken.

'It does, my lord.'

The angel steps over the wounded pilgrim and inspects Liesl's father briefly.

'Very well. It will suffice. I have need of it.'

'Of course, my lord. Where are we going?'

The Lord Apothecary pauses, and Liesl realises he had not intended for her to join them, though he does not forbid it. The angel glances down at the senior chirurgeon again, then begins to walk towards the door.

'To war,' he says. 'Whether we are built for it, or not.'

Blood drips from the stone above my head. Blood seeps from the cobbled joints beneath my feet. Thick clots of crimson coat my sabatons and greaves as I step against the shallow current, leading a mass of whispering priests forward into the darkness.

The arch-cantor of Saint Ciubrus walks at my side, his eyes asking why I have led his survivors into the despoiled catacombs beneath his city. He does not dare ask the question aloud, so I do not answer aloud, yet the reasons linger in my thoughts. The Shrine of Saint Ciubrus has already fallen, and not even my knights are able to reverse that. The taint in this place runs deeper than I had feared, and to cleanse it would take more strength – and time – than I can afford.

My vox-link to Brother-Chaplain Dant is weak and inter-mittent, his missives reaching my ears less and less often the further I venture from Tempest's capital, but it is clear from his transmissions that he is hard-pressed at Saint Ofelias. He has recaptured the Great Shrine of the Martyr at heavy cost, and the Soulrender's vanguard already harries his defences. Each day that he awaits my aid means he will require more of it when I finally arrive.

The best that I can now accomplish is to lead Saint Ciubrus' survivors through these catacombs to the nearby Shrine of Saint Iglese, and pray that it is still untouched by our enemy, that we may add our strength together and deliver Dant's forces before they, too, break.

'There cannot be this much blood on this world, my lord. Let alone within a single shrine city,' the arch-cantor says at my side.

He looks around with disgust at the alcoves which line the catacomb walls, bearing the bones of a hundred generations of faithful priests, now desecrated by the bloody rain seeping down into the tunnel from the warp-stained city above.

The shallow river which drifts over the corridor's stone floor flows slowly towards the city centre at my back. According to the arch-cantor, these tunnels were built through ancient aqui-fers, tracing beneath Tempest's surface, carrying water like veins when it was a world that still bore life.

Now they carry blood.

It pains me to abandon the city, though the Missionary Proserpine was right. This evil is too great for even my blade to cleanse.

In the tunnels around us, thousands of the arch-cantor's ecclesiarchs shuffle along by the light of torch lamps and braziers. Flocks of acolytes and ecclesiarchical servitors labour in the dim glow on their hands and knees, clearing a path through the filthy mire for the sacred relics that follow behind them.

Their lamps reflect crimson off the bloodied walls as they pass. In that flickering glow I see the shame upon the arch-cantor's face.

'This is not failure,' I lie to him. His shrine city has fallen. His superiors are dead. He retreats from his post while the servants of the Archenemy cavort and defile on the consecrated ground which he has abandoned. In other times, laden with less desperation, my blade would demand that he stay and die rather than withdraw. But to tell him such would break him, and I have need of what little strength he still commands.

'You serve the God-Emperor,' I assure him. 'Not Saint Ciubrus. You exist to defend His entire Imperium, not a single shrine city, nor even a single world.'

I raise a hand and set it upon his shoulder. The gesture is not a natural one to me, yet I understand the power of such things among his kind.

'Steel your soul. Steel your mind. And those of your soldiers. You flee from one battle into another. Your chance for redemption awaits you ahead.'

As he departs, another figure settles in at my side.

'You have too much compassion for them, Brother-Castellan.'

'Perhaps,' I reply. 'We were mortal once, too.'

The crimson eye-lenses of Hadrick's helm meet mine without hesitation. 'But we are no longer.'

He walks with me, his eyes scanning the ranks of crimson-robed Frateris militia before us. The Shrine of Saint Iglese lies dozens of miles to our north, untouched so far by the war that levels this planet. It will take days for the mortals to complete that journey. How many will still be able to fight after, I do not know.

I feel the same misgivings swirl within my brother. I feel his anger at this course. He grasps his thunder hammer hard enough I fear he shall shatter its haft.

'Speak,' I order. 'Your silence is more insolent than any words you might utter. It will break you – and us – if you hold it so tightly.'

'We are His knights,' he replies. 'We are the sons of the God-Emperor. We are His angels of death, not of His mercy. We exist to bring His wrath to His enemies, not safeguard the fearful masses.' He looks about him with disgust. 'We bring dishonour upon ourselves and our Chapter.'

I feel him deflate as the words escape him.

'More dishonour than if we squandered our lives here?' I say. 'We do not flee into safety, brother. Nor do they. We lead them from a hopeless battle into one they may win. One in which their deaths may purchase victory instead of defeat. We turn our blade from one foe to parry another, so that we may have the strength to strike back when an opening appears.'

'This is an opening,' he replies. 'The Soulrender has abandoned the city above. The rearguard he leaves behind is bloated and sated.'

'Brother,' I reply. 'Even if I had the strength of our entire company beside me, it would take weeks to cleanse the shrine city above.'

Hadrick nods, his rage diminished but not extinguished. Fervour burns in his voice still, and I find its heat contagious.

'Not the whole city, then,' he says. 'Not an entire battle, but at least a single blow.'

There is silence between us, as I consider his words. His passion grips me. I thank the God-Emperor for his zeal.

'Brothers, with me,' I say, then open a private vox-channel. 'Brother-Sergeant Tyre.' The newborn Primaris walks among us, but still recovers from the weight of his ordeal. 'You will remain here with the mortals. There is no dishonour in it. Among our company there is none that I trust more. Guide them to Iglese. See to the arch-cantor. Ensure that his courage does not fail him. And if it does, ensure that your bolter does not.'

I find a smile upon my face as I turn from the throng. Penitence shivers as I draw the weapon from its sheath.

The air beneath Saint Ciubrus' cathedrum-centre is moist and damp and tainted. Even through the respirator of my helm it tastes like blood and metal on my tongue. The great vaulted chambers that support the soaring structure above once housed those dedicated to the God-Emperor's service. They now house atrocities too many to name. We may be too few to purify the entire city, but we can at least rid it of one blemish before we depart.

Corpses are so numerous they become meaningless to my eyes. Heaped in hasty mounds. Strung from chains and hooks. Arranged in patterns that mean nothing to those who still possess sanity.

'Why do they exert such effort?' Brother Kessalt asks beside me. 'Why not simply leave the dead where they lie in the city above?'

'I do not seek to understand their madness,' I reply. 'Merely to cleanse it.'

But the answer soon becomes clear.

As we pass through the once-hallowed halls, the distant voices of man and daemon drift down through staircases and grates from the defiled cathedrum above, but not even the Blood God's servants venture here beneath.

I look more closely upon the dead. Loyalist and heretic alike. What I mistook for the wounds of weapons upon many, I now see are the marks of teeth and jaws.

'Whatever they keep down here,' Hadrick says, 'it is hungry.'

In the distance, I hear the sound of groaning chains and falling hoofbeats. I am reminded of the abomination we cleansed from the basilica when we first arrived at Saint Ciubrus. Hoofs and horns upon a frame of twisted metal. How many such beasts does the Archenemy possess? What other horrors do they keep penned here in this dark stable?

'Then let us not linger,' I reply. 'See to our work, brothers.'

Our primarch was a master builder – the defences of the Imperial Palace upon Holy Terra were constructed from his mind and his iron will. It has been millennia, but his sons have not forgotten his arts completely. To destroy, one must remember how to build.

My brothers spread out in the dim light of helm lumens, deploying demolition charges among the arches and pillars of the dark substructure. Then, together we ascend to the cathedrum above.

'Flamers,' I order, as we enter the great hall.

Fire spews from my brothers' weapons, their heat swallowing the air in the desecrated chamber. The roars of daemons and cultists echo from its hand-carved alcoves and balconies, carefully designed and arranged to amplify the voices of the faithful within.

Claws and blades clash against our purifying fire, until the very walls themselves burn. The heat of the room rises like a great furnace, draughts of cool, stale air pulled from the catacombs beneath, as the roar of the conflagration rises above the sounds of battle.

'Onward,' I order.

We ascend again.

Another level. Another chamber. Another multitude of the unclean. Hadrick's hammer cracks at my side. Flamers cackle. Bolters roar.

My soul calls upon me to linger. To purge each room of this sacred structure completely before moving on to the next, but that is not our purpose. In this moment, we are not a hammer, we are a blade.

Penitence shimmers in the light of consecrating flame as we burn the Shrine of Saint Ciubrus in our wake. On the twelfth level, Brother Renderick falls to a snarling daemon. Kessalt pummels the monster. I take its head.

On the twentieth, Gormond and Sturn are nearly lost to the blaze, a mass of great white stones collapsing from the levels above beneath the weight of the evil within this place. Elke pulls them from the rubble as the walls around us groan, and yet our depuration does not cease.

When we reach the zenith of the shrine at last, there is naught but raging fire below us. The hungry flames roar and dance like a thing alive, their heat scorching through even the hermetically sealed joints of my armour. Within that blaze daemon and heretic alike burn, the glass and steel of the shrine warping and bowing.

The stones beneath us groan and shift. The shrine itself protests the evil within it.

My vox-bead chimes as a figure emerges from those flames.

'Templar!' the traitor roars, as he steps onto the rooftop.

His crimson armour is scorched, the skulls bound to it little more than ash. He wears a horned helm, and a chainaxe idles in his grasp.

'World Eater,' I reply, raising my sword. My brothers ready their weapons, stepping forward to shield our wounded and our dead. My vox-bead chimes again.

'Have you come here to die? I count five of my knights raising weapons against yours.'

The traitor snarls, his reason lost to his rage. He begins to cross the smouldering tiles towards us.

'I will gut you!' he roars. 'I will shatter your bones. I will tear your limbs from your frames and place them upon my armour! I will–'

The oathbreaker's next words are swallowed by the sound of roaring turbines as two of my Thunderhawks settle behind me. Their twin-linked heavy bolters roar as my brothers step into their holds, the World Eater still roaring his anger as we ascend.

Flames rise from the cathedrum in great, towering tongues, licking the armaglass of the shrine city's arcology-wall above, black smoke billowing from her shattered windows.

'It is a sorrow to see such a thing destroyed. But better destroyed than made a home to darkness,' Hadrick says at my side.

'Indeed,' I reply, as I trigger the demolition charges in the vaults below.

The Shrine of Saint Ciubrus shivers and rises, like a creature taking a great breath, before its sacred stones collapse completely.

Chapter 9

We come to the Shrine of Saint Iglese bearing blood and ash. My armour is scarred and dented, Penitence chipped and dulled by death. The city's gates open before my Thunderhawks, their hulls scorched by the impacts of infernal weapons, turbines forcing them forward on ragged wings.

Her priests welcome my brothers with hymns and incense and blessings, the angels of their god walking among them. They lead us down stark white halls framed with sculptures and fountains, between shrines and sacraria untouched by war.

Her arch-cantor bows before me atop his throne of gilded iron and gold. He speaks words of reverence and offers his aid as he sips chilled wine, draped in silks from light years outside this system.

He is no fool.

Neither am I.

I ask for nothing save a space to burn my dead brother.

He is not yet ready to give more than that. Nor am I yet ready to force his hand.

They place us in a tower beside their cathedrum, in chambers filled with mortal luxuries and staffed with countless obeisant attendants.

As if food could sate the hunger within us. As if baths could cleanse the death from our hands.

I dismiss the human servants despite their protest, any words spoken before them sure to reach the arch-cantor's ears. When we are at last alone, I kneel upon the stone parapet. Hadrick meets me there atop the city of alabaster peace.

'Brother-Castellan,' he calls as he steps out onto the balcony. 'What is it that you pray for here atop this world?'

The platform is carved from a single piece of white stone, wide enough to accommodate my entire fighting company, if it were present. A low balustrade encircles the quiet space, the shrine city falling away beneath us in all directions.

'I pray for nothing,' I reply. 'I stopped making requests of the God-Emperor long ago. Now I merely offer myself to His will. Brother Hadrick, how do you find our honoured accommodations?'

I look down upon the relic sword resting upon the floor before me. I pour a thin stream of oil from the vial in my hand over its glittering metal. Blood and dirt retreat from the sacred tincture, blessed by Brother-Chaplain Dant before our descent onto this world. I let it drip onto the unmarred white stone beneath my blade. It is only fitting that some of the blood of this world should finally reach this untouched city.

'Luxurious,' Hadrick replies, watching me work. 'Wasteful. Intolerable. The most beautiful prison I have ever occupied.'

Hadrick still wears his armour, as do I, though we have both removed our helms in the safety of this place. There is still fire in Hadrick's voice, though the mindless rage in his eyes has faded. His spirit glows only softly, now, as the coals of a fire after a blaze.

I allow myself a quiet chuckle before setting to Penitence with a sharpening stone. The minute pits and notches in the blade would be unnoticed by any eye other than my own, and nothing but the forges aboard the *Dauntless Honour* would serve to mend them completely. The stone in my hand will do little to repair their scarring, yet I have no better tool, and the task serves to repair my soul as well.

'You wonder why I tolerate it?'

He kneels beside me. 'I do. Brother-Chaplain Dant battles the first waves of the Soulrender's horde at Saint Ofelias. The Missionary Proserpine and Saint Ciubrus' survivors trudge towards us in the blood-soaked catacombs below. We sit upon polished, pristine stone cleaning our weapons while others suffer and die.'

Slowly, Hadrick releases the mag-lock of his thunder hammer from his back. He places the weapon on the ground beside my own, and whispers a quiet blessing over the implement. Flecks of blood and flesh coat the head of the weapon, the dirt and gore obscuring the scriptures inscribed upon its haft. Reverently, Hadrick anoints his own weapon, then begins to polish the remnants of battle away.

I look up from our paired weapons. The sleek blade beside the stalwart hammer. In all directions, the shrine city of Saint Iglese blossoms before us, white stone glowing faintly in the light that scatters down through her bastion arcology-wall.

Just as within the ruined Shrine of Saint Ciubrus, a dozen basilicas ring her main cathedrum, a hundred smaller shrines scattered amongst their flawless domes. The clear music of bells rings from countless towers over the dull hum of a hundred thousand voices reciting an endless symphony of prayers.

'What do you see when you look upon this city, brother? The glory of the God-Emperor, or a token of a bloated, softened world?'

Hadrick chooses his words carefully.

'When we walked through these streets I could scarcely move

without stumbling upon a shrine or statue to some martyr I had never before known. Every priest and acolyte we have met bears a weapon at their side and believes they have been trained in how to use it.'

He motions to the towers that surround the city. Set among their alabaster white is the steel-dark grey of mounted gun positions.

'I see priests who believe that they are warriors. I see a temple that believes it is a fortress. I see a city that believes it has been blessed by the God-Emperor, yet it has simply been ignored by His enemies thus far.'

I nod. As always, my brother sees true.

'How long do you think this shrine city will hold once the Soulrender turns his attention upon it?'

Hadrick scoffs. 'Once her walls are breached? They will die as fast as his heretics can advance.'

'This is a world that worships war, but has not seen it in a thousand years,' I reply. 'Every one of her arch-cantors believes himself a hero and tactician of great skill. Every one of them will fall, even if they are correct, unless they stand together. Brother-Chaplain Dant has secured the Great Cathedrum at Saint Ofelias, but the Soulrender descends upon them. He believes he will crush our brothers, then crush us, one by one. And if we stand alone, he will be correct. Saint Iglese will fall, just as Saint Ciubrus did because she will fight and die in isolation. Even I cannot rally the other arcologies to support her. But for the Great Shrine itself, for Saint Ofelias, there, perhaps, Tempest's factions can be unified.

'But they are not ready,' I continue. 'Not yet. Not even I could force them from their safe and comfortable halls. Not while they remain safe and comfortable to them. So, we must endure this prison just a short while longer, until the war arrives at their gates.'

* * *

'Soulrender.'

The voice awakens him in the night. From hooded half-dreams full of fire and blood. From the voices of the daemons that dwell in his mind.

'Soulrender.'

He opens his eyes to the sand and the stars and the darkness. To the scent of copper and dust. To the writhing pain of the blades fused to his weeping limbs.

The warp-spawned visions fade slowly, like the afterglow that follows an explosion. The Lady of Thorns. Her Silent Skulls. The Burned Man. The Wheel. Each of his tireless companions arrives now that the end is growing near.

He pushes them away and looks up from where he sits.

A dark form paces in the sand beside him.

Revulsion strikes Dravek at the Warpsmith's presence, the armoured core of a thing that had once been his brother, now hidden beneath coils of writhing, weeping steel.

Countless rusting, jointed metal tendrils sprout from the Warpsmith's flesh, dripping slowly with oil and blood, ever-shifting with a nervous, eager energy, drawing small patterns upon the endless white sands. From their tangled coils an almost-human torso emerges, laced with wire and pipes billowing steam and grey fumes. Only the Warpsmith's head is truly recognisable, its glowing augmetic eyes burning towards him above a vox-emitter bolted into cernuous flesh.

'Vale,' he growls. Peace at least from his eightfold companions. Even his daemons feel discomfort around the twisted mess of the former Techmarine. 'You are ready, then?'

'Nearly,' the tangle of flesh and metal replies. 'I had thought you might wish to inspect our progress.' The Warpsmith twitches as he speaks in a voice that starts and stops with mechanical precision.

Dravek remembers when his brother Ra'leth Vale departed for the forge world of Mars. He remembers when the man returned half a machine. Even then, he felt a disquiet in his brother's presence. It has only grown with each century as he drifts further from the form that Dravek once knew.

A pair of chittering skulls orbit the smith like small moons, clicking and buzzing in their mechanical tongue as Vale skitters away across the sands like an insect. What the hereteks who had once worn those skulls had done to earn such punishment, Dravek does not know.

Dravek follows behind them, thin starlight gleaming through drifting clouds of sand to fall upon the broken city ahead. Fresh smoke rises from the crooked spires of Saint Ofelias. The dull glow of flame casting the white towers orange. He had relished desecrating her walls for the first time; he would not leave a single stone standing the second.

At the back of his head, a sharp pain begins to rise. A twitching in his wrists. A dull thrumming in his ears. At the edge of his vision a shadow appears at the top of a white dune, two silent, unspeaking skulls in her childlike hands.

The Soulrender quickens his pace until he reaches Ra'leth Vale's side. The Warpsmith pauses atop the crest of a dune, an eager nervousness in his movements as he gazes into the valley below.

'Here?' Dravek asks him.

'Here, Soulrender.'

A small ring of white stones emerges from the desert at the dune's foot like a circle of broken teeth. At their centre, countless dark forms labour like insects in the starlight.

'It was a shrine of the Corpse-Emperor once,' the Warpsmith cackles. 'Desecrated even before our arrival. The veil here is thin. Even I can feel it. There is no better place, though what will be required to supply an occupant...'

'What will be required to supply an occupant is none of your concern.'

Dravek glares at the Warpsmith, and the machine-creature falls quiet.

'Of course.' The light behind Vale's crimson eyes flickers momentarily before that eager, manic brightness returns. He begins to descend the slope to the shrine below, where hereteks and prisoners manoeuvre massive steel components. At the centre of the ring, a tall, dark cylinder stands upright in the sands. From the engine's form, great ducts plunge into the earth, pulsing rhythmically, like a creature drinking.

Beneath his feet, Dravek feels a deep, measured thrumming.

'It is thirsty,' he murmurs into the night.

Two days pass in our gilded jail. I await word from Dant or from Tyre while I pray.

I burn incense in every shrine within the city. I kneel before every statue of every saint. I sleep in short, fitful bursts between my meditations, the confidence I showed Hadrick no deeper than my words.

As Tempest's twin suns rise upon the third morning, my vox-caster chimes three short bursts in my ear. The communing link between our devices is not strong enough yet for a full message to be transmitted. Merely Brother-Sergeant Tyre's position sent to my helm-viewer.

I send a reply as I rise from my knees before a statue of some unnamed martyr. As I make my way to the cathedrum at the centre of the city, I dispatch Gormond's Crusader squad and summon Hadrick's to me. They meet me as I stride through the cathedrum's open doors.

'Brother-Castellan,' Hadrick greets me, Brothers Kessalt, Umter, and Fenril at his side. They wear their helms and bear their weapons. Together they are the picture of Dorn's sons. I find myself proud to walk at their head.

'We have lingered long enough in this place, brothers. It is time we depart with the strength that is owed to us.'

None stop us as we ascend to the arch-cantor's chambers beneath busts and frescoes of the canonised dead. When we reach, at last, the doors to the priest's inner sanctum, two soldiers of his Frateris militia stand in my path bearing long, winged spears.

'My lord,' the smaller of the two says. A golden rosette gleams upon his robes. His hands shiver slightly as he grasps his weapon. 'The cantors are joined in their morning prayers. They have ordered that none pass until they are completed.'

'Step aside,' I demand, my voice a low rumble. I have squandered two days on courtesy and patience, and now it is time to recoup that cost. 'I come not to interrupt their prayers, but to answer them.'

The soldiers hesitate for a moment. No doubt they have been told to let no man pass without the arch-cantor's explicit blessing. But I am no man. I am the image of their angels, clad in flesh and walking among them.

They raise their weapons slowly and bow as I pass.

The doors to the sanctum shudder as we enter, my brothers on my heels brewing like a dark storm. A ring of crimson-clad priests rise from their knees, murmurs upon their lips, fear in their motions.

It is wise for them to fear us. I bring their death, though not, perhaps, in the way that they fear.

'Lord Castellan Emeric,' the arch-cantor calls from his dais. The rest of his priests kneel on velvet pads arrayed in a circle before him. For his part, he seems composed in my presence as he rises from his aureate throne.

'You honour us with your presence. We pray for the deliverance of the Shrine of Saint Iglese, and those of our sister shrines upon this world. Have you come to join us in our supplication?'

Hadrick scoffs at my side. My voice mirrors his disdain.

'No, arch-cantor. We grow tired of prayers. We come to bring Tempest's deliverance rather than to ask for it. To bring war to the God-Emperor's enemies.'

The man nods. 'This is the way of the Black Templars, is it not, Lord Castellan? Zeal and fervour. Ire and rage. We shall add you and your brothers to our prayers.'

The man stares at me with deep-set eyes, fingering the golden aquila about his neck – the mark of his station. He speaks to me as if he thinks himself my equal.

Here is a priest who bears his role well, not with the discomfort of the newly ascended arch-cantor of Saint Ciubrus. And yet that comfort is what I must counter. The man has grown so used to speaking to his lessers that he forgets I am not one of them.

'You mistake me, arch-cantor. We march to the shrine city of Saint Ofelias and the Cathedrum of the Martyr. When we depart, the priests of Saint Iglese will march with us.'

The arch-cantor nods slowly. 'That is a rough journey, Lord Emeric. The sands outside these walls rage with storms strong enough to level cities and bury machines. Do you come bearing transports for thousands? Food and water for a journey that might take weeks?'

'The God-Emperor has given them feet. And I see no shortage of materiel within this stronghold.'

'For the defence of the holy shrine city of Saint Iglese. Provided to our blessed hands by the God-Emperor's own favour as a mark of our purity. We shall see what we can spare for your journey. And I shall muster a contingent of my most fervent volunteers. How many brothers-in-arms do you require?'

'All of them.'

There is a hush across the room. I hear the breaths of the lesser cantors around us rising. I turn to them.

'Priests!' I cry. 'You have languished here long enough. You have prayed for deliverance, and the God-Emperor provides it. Deliverance from your fear. Deliverance from your luxury. Deliverance from the safety and comfort that cripple your will.

'Saint Ofelias rises from her ashes against the Archenemy. My brothers defend her great cathedrum even now. They stand beside thousands of the faithful. There they will hold against whatever evils the Soulrender and his warband press against them, until we shatter the enemy against their anvil like a hammer.'

I meet the eyes of the mortals one by one. There is fear there, yes, but also courage. They wish to be free of their own chains, but cannot shake them by themselves.

Beside me, I feel Hadrick's anger rising. My brothers sense the fragility of the humans' souls. Their hesitancy. Their doubt. They see these for the weakness that they are, but they fail to sense the strength beneath it.

'Come,' I call to the priests. 'The God-Emperor answers your prayers.'

To my companions, I say, 'Have faith, brothers. In them. In me.'

It is enough to silence their questions as we descend. Four living angels trailed by a throng of our priests. A trail of lesser ecclesiarchs and attendants gathers as we pass through the cathedrum to the courtyard below.

The statues of saints and martyrs stand above us, framed by the light of Tempest's suns refracted beneath the lens of the arcology-dome above our heads. Their light splits into a thousand colours, bathing the pristine shrine city in a prismatic glow.

More priests gather as we reach the courtyard, the great gate of Saint Iglese swallowing the arcology-wall beside us. The massive door stands tall enough to admit a Battle Titan, its great hinges covered by gear towers a hundred storeys high. The gates are festooned with sacred icons and seals stretching as far as my eyes can see.

In ten thousand years, they have never been breached from without.

'Brothers!' I cry, my voice ringing through the courtyard. More ecclesiarchs gather around us now.

Brother Tyre's position flickers on my display screen. Brother Gormond whispers his readiness through the vox-receiver in my helm. I have timed this well.

'For ten thousand years, the Shrine of Saint Iglese has stood firm against the enemies of the God-Emperor! Against apostasy! Against heresy!'

The arch-cantor looks towards me from the ring around us. His face is less smug now. His eyes harden. He may think himself my better, but to his priests I am an angel incarnate. He cannot silence me without inciting their rage.

'For ten thousand years, the Shrine of Saint Iglese has stood firm when the faith of others has faltered! But today, I ask you not to stand, but to march.'

There are murmurs around us. The arch-cantor steps towards me, a vox-servitor at his side. Even amplified by the creature's false voice, his words cannot match mine.

'And we shall!' he calls. 'We shall march against the forces that have conquered our sisters when they reach Saint Iglese. We shall smash them against her walls and repel them as we have before!'

Clever. Tactical. Yet I am clever, too.

As the priest finishes speaking, there is commotion at the side of the courtyard. The crowd around us murmurs and then parts. Two figures step through the opening towards us.

Brother-Sergeant Tyre steps from one of the lesser shrines, looking every bit an angel of war. His chainsword hangs at his side, his bolter in his hand. Both are charred and speckled with the blood of heretics and daemons. His armour is scorched and dented. His stride full of grace and fervour.

At his side, the Missionary Proserpine stands in contrast. Slowly, she limps forward, leaning heavily upon her cane. Her breath falls heavy, her blind eyes roving aimlessly. With one hand she grasps her cane. With the other an ancient tome of scripture.

Blood drips from her feet as they stride across the courtyard, each step staining the unmarred white stone.

I can think of no more fitting image. Behind them, the survivors of Saint Ciubrus emerge from the catacombs below.

The arch-cantor of Saint Ciubrus follows behind my brother and the missionary, then throngs of his bloody, battered order. Teams of acolytes and servitors bear their shrine's relics atop tired shoulders. The wounded limp where they can. Some are carried where they cannot.

Their brethren push back to give them space as they emerge. The hard eyes of the refugees staring into those that have not yet witnessed this war.

Murmurs swallow the courtyard. The arch-cantor of Saint Iglese falls silent.

I meet Brother Tyre and the Missionary Proserpine.

'The God-Emperor's blessings,' I say to the missionary, to my brother. 'A hard passage?' I subvocalise.

'Hard, but not impossible. One which could be completed again, if required.'

I nod. Our course is set, then.

'Arch-cantor!' I cry, my voice shattering the buzz of the crowd. 'This is what awaits you here, whatever blessing you might believe you possess. If you cower behind your walls, the Arch-enemy will shatter them. He will break your dome-wall and burn your shrines. He will slaughter your priests and defile your altars.

'Already, the blood of this world pools below your city. Already, Tempest's sands are unable to hold any more. I come today as an answer to your prayers for deliverance. Deliverance from fear. Deliverance from cowardice. Deliverance from the sin of inaction. March with us to the Shrine of Saint Ofelias. Join with the righteous forces that hold the Great Cathedrum against the heretics that assail your world. Fight. Die. With a chance, at least, to wound your enemy. Or cower here like prey creatures and be devoured like them.'

There is silence in the courtyard. The arch-cantor glares at me. On my command, Gormond and Elke trigger the mech-anisms of the shrine city's great gate from within as my three remaining Thunderhawks scream overhead. With a groan, the massive doors inch open, then Hellstrike missiles rain from the battered gunships. Explosions rock the great gate towers at my back, unarmoured from here within the city, their inner mech-anisms shattering and locking the doors ajar.

'Let me make your choice simple, arch-cantor,' I say. 'Put aside your differences and fight together, or burn in the ruin of your world. The God-Emperor does not ask for your courage. He demands it.'

Yersef stands before Dravek, facing the desert.

Yersef the Faithless. Yersef the Devourer. Yersef the Bloody. The Relentless. The Feared.

The Astartes does not appear to deserve those epithets now.

The hulking Space Marine is weighted with wounds as he limps across the sands. His armour is shattered and gouged, charred black by flame. From beneath the burnt ceramite comes the scent of scorched flesh. He grasps his great chainaxe, but carries the weapon without his usual ease.

'Soulrender,' Yersef growls. His voice is laced with rage. Even now, in peace, the Nails do their work on him. 'I will not be summoned like some common foot-soldier before you.'

'And yet you have been.' Dravek turns away from his brother.

'This is your great work?' Yersef scoffs. 'This is what you labour upon while I spill blood?'

Fresh skulls have been mounted to Yersef's scorched plate. They shift and clatter as he turns to the structure rising in the sand. Ra'leth Vale and his hereteks have made progress, and though its form is not yet complete, their work is fearsome already to behold.

'Walk with me, brother.'

Yersef follows him through the desert. In the distance, smoke rises from the borders of Saint Ofelias.

'Raiding parties ravage her outer districts, testing the Black Templars and their allies within. Formidable foes. Well-deployed.'

Dravek feels that old familiar hunger rise within him. Copper coats his tongue. A third figure walks beside them.

Do you sense it? the Carver asks.

'Sense what?' Dravek replies.

The daemon looks at Yersef with something akin to hunger. A long, black tongue flickers over his endless barbed teeth. The claws at the ends of his fingers shiver with desire.

His weakness.

Yersef looks at Dravek, then back to the machine in the valley before them. His disdain is clear.

'You must think me mad,' Dravek says. 'Speaking to the sands.'

'I think you are weak,' his lieutenant says. 'I think that without the strength of the Nails, your daemons have broken you. You are neutered. Impotent. You have kept us on this world for months, speaking of shrines and holy ground. Constructing war machines rather than waging it yourself. Each day you become more like the Black Templars we battle against than your brothers.'

'The Black Templars who did this to you?'

Yersef scoffs. 'The Shrine of Saint Ciubrus lies in ashes. Blood flows down her streets like rivers. You think that a failure?'

'I do,' Dravek tells him.

He steps closer to the rising daemon engine, covered in scaffolds of bone growing ever higher at the hands of whimpering thralls working beneath daemon's whips.

He feels the sand beneath his feet pulsing as the machine's great ducts drink blood from the earth below. Even at this distance he feels revulsion in the structure's presence. Even from here he can feel its thirst.

At the periphery of his vision the Carver slows. Dravek senses the daemon's discomfort, but his hunger as well.

'Tell me, Yersef, where is your steed? Where is the blood of the ten thousand priests who escaped you that should flow beside all of that which I spilled?'

'You spilled? You? While you danced in visions and spoke nonsense to the wind?'

Dravek sighs, watching the rage rise within his companion. Too easy. Too simple. He remembers it well.

'There is more at work here than speech,' Dravek says. 'Sometimes one must build in order to destroy. What I craft here will echo across the galaxy. The freedom I purchase... I do not expect you to understand.'

A few simple words and already his brother's mind fades.

A few insults and Dravek watches the fire build. He can still remember the pulsing of the Butcher's Nails. The all-consuming desire. The blinding rage.

'Very well, Yersef. You think I have become weak. Prove it. Draw your blade. Meet mine. Claim your rightful place as the master of this warband. If you are not too afraid.'

Dravek watches Yersef's will fall away completely, a snarl seizing his lips, fury stealing his eyes. His chainaxe roars as he spins towards Dravek.

Strong.

Wildly strong.

And fast.

But stupid.

Predictable.

Dravek flashes to the side. Yersef's chainaxe bites through empty air and strikes bare sand, spewing a small cloud into the air. Yersef bellows and swings at him again. Dravek steps backward and lifts his Eviscerator, throwing the clumsy strike aside. Behind him, the Carver paces. The Flayed Beast stands at his side now, sniffing the air with anxious anticipation.

Yersef charges towards him. Dravek dances just beyond his reach. With every miss – every failure – Yersef's rage simply grows. His movements become stronger and faster but easier to anticipate.

Dravek finds himself laughing, though he feels no pleasure, as he draws his brother towards the valley below. The hereteks and thralls have slowed their work, gazing on as the two Astartes duel across the sands.

The Carver and the Flayed Beast follow no longer, pacing along some unseen border, unwilling to step any deeper into the valley.

'Good,' Dravek whispers. 'This blood is not for you.'

Yersef's breath comes in heaving gouts. His movements grow

slow. He swings his chainaxe again and again. It is a simple thing to dance beyond its reach.

As Dravek watches, his amusement turns into pity. And then anger.

He was weak once – just like this – until he traded the weakness of the Nails for that of possession.

'You are not wrong, brother,' Dravek whispers. 'I am broken. I am bound. I am mastered by my daemons just as you are by the Nails.'

He sidesteps a clumsy swing, pushing forward rather than dancing back. The blades on his arms find the seam between his brother's chestplate and helmet. It is a simple thing. Yersef falls, headless, to the ground.

As blood spills into the white sand at his feet, Dravek feels the throbbing of the engine behind him drinking.

'I am weak. But I will not be much longer.'

Chapter 10

Blood and bone surround us. The icons of our enemy. The maddening press of darkness and of cramped ancient tunnels as we wind our way beneath Tempest's storm-scoured surface. The ancient walls of her catacombs are lined with alcoves and sarcophagi filled with the ashes and ossuaries of thousands of nameless servants of the Ecclesiarchy.

'Does it ever end?' Brother Elke asks me. There is a flicker of a smile in his voice, though he bears this weight heavier than the rest.

I remember the day he was taken as an Expectanten. From a wretched, brutal, feral world with plains and mountains and skies that seemed to stretch on to eternity. It was months before he grew comfortable among the tight, torchlit corridors of the *Dauntless Honour*. Even still, more than a century later, he bristles here among the shadows and the stone.

He jests, although his humour is not empty.

We have walked these catacombs for days already with less progress than I might have hoped. Here, buried beneath the sands and the stones, my vox and auspexes are of no use.

I do not know if we have travelled a dozen miles or a hundred. I do not know if Brother-Chaplain Dant and my fighting company

still hold Saint Ofelias' Great Cathedrum against the Soulrender
or if we march only to rescue their corpses. I do not know if we
will walk another day until we reach them or a year. I know only
that the strength of those who walk with us is flagging.

Emperor be true, I find even my mind tiring of this.

Stairs and statues. Bones and ash. The endless, maddening
drip of blood.

More blood than could possibly exist upon this planet. More
blood than could have ever existed in ten thousand years of
Imperial colonisation. Streaming down the white walls in neat
rivulets. Pooling in shallow puddles beneath my boots. Sinking
further into the sands beneath us with the pulsing, tide-like
rhythm of something mad, and ancient, and hungry suckling.

'I do not know,' I reply.

At the words the guide before me turns.

The Missionary Proserpine's face is a mask of concentration as
she limps before our endless procession. In one hand, she bears
a torch lamp aloft, not for her own use, but for those around
her. In her other, she grasps her silver cane.

Let Hadrick say what he might about her kind, but without the
missionary, we would be lost completely. By whatever miracle
of the God-Emperor, she seems to recognise some pattern in the
endless, branching catacombs that escapes me and my brothers alike.

'Lord Castellan,' she greets me tiredly as I approach. Her hand
shakes slightly where it grasps her cane. Her boots shine dimly
with the glistening gore of our blood-soaked march.

Brother Hadrick looks on, without emotion, at her side.

Our vanguard has pressed on without resting for hours. The
nearest torch lamps behind us glimmer in the distance where
our mortal army follows. Even my limbs have begun to feel
the burn of fatigue. I do not know how the humans continue.

'Missionary Proserpine. How fare you?' I ask.

'I stand. I breathe. I am strong enough to continue.' There is a hint of frustration in her voice. Whether at my concern or my lack of it, I cannot decipher.

Ahead, the tunnel splits in two.

'Which way?' I ask.

She hesitates for a moment.

'Right,' she replies. 'To the right, Lord Castellan.'

'Why?'

'The air is colder. The slope is steeper. It must grow darker, still, my lord, before it lightens.'

I look around me. Without the flickering glow of the lady's torch lamp and the cold white brilliance of my helm lumen, I would find myself as blind as her within these halls.

'Prophecy?' I ask. 'For the battle to come?'

The army that stretches for miles behind us was haggard already when we took them below this earth. We have pushed them hard, and I will push them still further. When they arrive at Saint Ofelias and face our enemy, many will do little more than die.

The Missionary Proserpine chuckles bitterly. 'I would dream to offer no such thing. Merely the way of things. I have taken nearly one hundred thousand steps since we departed the shrine city of Saint Iglese. That is almost half the distance it will take to reach our destination. We will begin to ascend soon.'

As she turns to continue, I see her fingers shifting on her cane. What I had mistaken for trembling, I see now is rapid, intentional movements.

'You are counting,' Brother Elke says with disbelief. 'Numbers that large? On your fingers?'

She nods. 'An old trick that I learned from my mother's savants. One that I never expected to serve me as well as it has.'

'Savants?' I ask. 'Your family possessed several?'

'Oh yes,' she replies. 'Such are the luxuries of a planetary governor's household.

'For a time, after the slowpox stole my vision and my strength, I dreamed that I might perhaps become one of them. It seemed a fitting path of service for a child who could no longer see and could barely walk. Some of my strength returned with time, though my vision never did, despite the best physicians my mother's station could afford. My affliction was a great tragedy to her. I remember her weeping.

'Not for me, of course. But for the thought that she could possess a child so broken. I mourned the loss of my strength, though I missed my vision less. I was never enamoured with the beauty and luxury that surrounded me. Only a fool would call blindness a blessing, but it was the source of my liberation in the end, though I could not fathom that at the time. The only route by which I could have hoped to escape a life of physical comfort and spiritual death.'

Slowly, the missionary turns down the tunnel again. For a moment, she stumbles. At her side Brother Hadrick's hand reaches out to catch her, but she rights herself without his aid.

'The God-Emperor cared not about my weaknesses. Neither did the Cult Imperialis. The Master of Mankind takes, but He also gives. These tunnels end, Lord Castellan,' she tells me. 'They must. Have faith in that, if nothing else.'

Slowly she walks forward, her feet slapping through a shallow pool of crimson.

All around us, the walls continue to bleed.

Liesl wept the first time she watched an angel die. That had not been so long ago. But the galaxy had been different aboard the ship she had called home since the day she was born. She had been different.

She remembers the sorrow that had gripped her soul to see a thing so perfect fail. The uncertainty that had consumed her in the face of such a raw injustice. Now, the sight raises little more than hopelessness within her, her innocence long ago scattered on Tempest's winds.

'Come, father,' she calls to her servitor as she rises, spotting the dark forms approaching through the blowing sand. The dull hammering of weapon fire rages in the not-so-distance, like the cracking and fizzling of debris against a void shield, as she clears the steel floor of the transport that has been her home for days, brushing soot and sand through its open tail-gate. The vehicle was disabled long before the Lord Apothecary found it, but its frame – mostly intact – offers some protection from the elements, at least. It is the closest to the sacred sterility of the apothecarion that can be found in this part of the ruined shrine city.

Slowly, her servitor rouses itself in the corner of the cab, its tracked wheels crunching and grinding as it rolls in shaky bursts towards her. Her father's face can no longer carry expressions, but his movements are slow, halting, tired. She does not know if servitors are capable of sleep, only that she has not done so for more than a few minutes at a time in days.

'Prepare blades. Prepare synthblood. Prepare autografts, if any remain. The Lord Apothecary will want them if his brother still lives.'

She steps to the back of the ruined vehicle, the figures clearer now as they approach. The hulking silhouette of an angel races towards her, dragging another ceramite-armoured figure at its side.

'And prepare the extractors. In case he does not.'

Her father removes the instruments from the hollow cavity of his empty chest, their cold metal glistening with the sheen of annulling oils. Liesl breathes deeply, preparing herself for the ordeal to come.

There will be anger from the Lord Apothecary. There is always anger.

Liesl bows as the angels burst into the cab, the dull clatter of ceramite falling upon metal as the injured Astartes is deposited on the floor. The scent of scorched copper fills the air, the mark of warp-tainted wounds.

She braces herself for the Lord Apothecary's orders, but they do not come.

'Serf.' A deep growl fills the small space, and she raises her head. She does not recognise the angel who speaks to her. He motions to his brother on the floor, clad in the stark white ceramite of the Lord Apothecary.

Liesl's breath catches. She freezes.

'You are a chirurgeon, are you not? You labour beneath Alvus within the apothecarion?'

'No, my lord,' she begins, then pauses. The Astartes do not understand the distinctions between their servants. 'I mean, yes, but I am merely–'

'Then heal him.'

Liesl stares at the Lord Apothecary, limp on the floor. The armour of his breastplate is shattered and crushed. Dark blood seeps from the seams between his helm and his gorget. She sees no motion in his limbs or any rise or fall in his ruined chest to suggest that the spark of life still resides within him.

'My lord, I canno–'

The angel cuts her off.

'Hemdal, Silven, Rambert, Yole. Ingram, Wolfred, Pardum, Vandt.' The names escape the Astartes' vox-amplifier in a bitter growl. Liesl staggers beneath the force of his words. 'Too many of my brothers have died on this world. Their gene-seed is carried by the knight who lies before you. None other among our ranks possesses the knowledge to preserve it. I have lost my brothers to these sands already. I will not lose their legacy. Nor his.'

The angel kneels down upon the floor and removes his helm, his face scarred and pitted from centuries of combat. He stares at her with hollow, grey eyes, then lifts his bolter and points it at Liesl's chest.

'Heal him, serf, or I shall add you to their number.'

'Yes, my lord,' she tells the Astartes. To her father, 'Disrobement, first.'

The servitor hands her a small, pointed tool, which she uses to access the hidden latches upon the Lord Apothecary's armour.

She lifts his helm. Beneath it, the smell of death. The Lord Apothecary's head appears uninjured, but dark blood and vomit spill from his mouth in bubbling gouts as he takes a single shallow, shaking breath.

Pauldrons. Aegis. Liesl labours beneath the weight of the ceramite breastplate. Spider-line cracks mark its surface. Beneath, the angel's chest is shattered.

She sets her bloody hands upon the Lord Apothecary's skin. Pale. Clammy. Dark bruises already form along his flanks. Shards of broken bone grind against one another as the injured angel tries to breathe. Beneath his skin, she feels the crackle and pop of air escaping into his flesh.

'His ribs are shattered. His lungs are punctured. There is bleeding within that chokes him even as he tries to breathe. And those are merely the injuries within his thorax.'

Liesl looks back towards the Lord Apothecary's face. Around his eyes and beneath his ears, dark bruises have begun to form. His eyes are closed. His jaw set in deep discomfort. 'Blood within the vault of his skull, as well. Pressing upon the sus-an membrane within, stopping its function.'

The Astartes kneeling across from the Lord Apothecary does not reply, nor does the aim of his bolter waver from her. She sighs and sets her fingers upon the Lord Apothecary's neck, feeling two discordant rhythms within.

'His pulses are shallow. Rapid. Both his hearts beat, though they no longer function in unison.'

Outside, the wind howls. Sand and ash spill in great clouds across the battered landscape. The Astartes looks out into that storm, then back towards her. There is nothing divine in his gaze. His eyes drip with the human weaknesses of rage and sorrow.

A terrible peace washes over Liesl. The Lord Apothecary will die here – he is already dead – and then she will die beside him.

'Blade,' she whispers to her father. She makes a deep incision into the left side of the Lord Apothecary's flank, then plunges a blunt instrument beneath his fused ribcage, tearing up through his diaphragm into the cavity of his chest. Air and blood rush out, warmth spreading across her legs as the angel's life pools upon the floor. She reaches her arm within the cavity and feels his imbiber re-expand. The angel breathes out, and beneath his lungs, his primary heart quivers beside his maintainer, one or both spilling blood from some injury she cannot see or feel.

'My lord,' she whispers to the Astartes above her. 'These wounds are beyond my skill. These wounds are beyond even *his* skill here in the sands and the ash of a distant world.'

She looks upon the Lord Apothecary's face, awaiting the punishment that has been promised to her. She feels the beating of the angel's hearts slow, then fade completely, but the bolter pointed at her does not fire.

Liesl looks up.

Across from her, the Astartes stares out the back of the cab, listening to some sound that she cannot hear. Distant movements flash in the sands. The angel rises.

A blazing light fills the cab like the sudden rising of the sun as the beam of a lascannon swallows the angel's skull, then burns through the rusted metal of the transport, melting a hole through to the sky.

Liesl falls to the ground, half-blinded, awaiting the next shot, but none comes. Not even their enemy, blood-mad and craven, would waste time or attention on a simple serf. When her vision returns, the angel lies headless on the floor beside her.

For some time she does not move, waiting for her breath to return and her hands to stop shaking. Then, slowly, she pushes herself to her feet.

'Come, father,' she whispers to the servitor at her side. 'We have holy work to do.'

Not enough.

It is not enough.

Dravek Soulrender stands on the edge of the parapet, watching blood flow into the streets below. The single, tilting tower before him is the only one still standing within view, the rest of the shrine city's outer districts reduced to rubble by the ceaseless hammering of his bombards and Colossus siege tanks.

Blood and bone fill the streets that he has already conquered once. The piles of broken synthcrete and shattered shrines teem with the shapes of his jakhals and lesser daemons. Fresh streams of blood drip from his forces and from those of the weak, poorly armed militia that the Black Templars throw against him.

And yet it is not enough.

He descends the tower's precarious staircase into the melee below. He finds the gaunt form of the Carver straddling a corpse at the base of the stairs.

'Soulrender.'

'Neverborn.'

The daemon runs a jagged claw across the corpse's skin, then dips it into the pool of blood beneath the pilgrim. The claw comes up clean.

'A satisfying meal?' Dravek taunts.

The daemon grins up at him with its tooth-rimmed mouth, eyes full of spite. Despite its desire, the daemon dwells within his flesh. It cannot touch the physical world except through him. And even if it could, such a thing could not grow full. It feels only hunger.

The corpse beneath the daemon spills blood into the street. There is a slow pulsing beneath the cobbled stones, as the blood that flows down the walkways is drawn into the sands below.

'*You have waited long enough to begin your assault in earnest,*' the Carver tells him.

'I have waited no longer than was prudent. The Warpsmith finishes his work even now. There is little left to do but feed his creation.'

The daemon looks on. Impatient. Ravenous. In the distance, the Flayed Beast emerges from a smoking ruin. A pair of flesh hounds trail in the larger beast's wake, a crimson-robed priest lying sideways in their jaws, still twitching. The daemons bring the fresh corpse to the Carver and deposit it on his growing pile. With a sickening squelch, the beasts rip a leg from the woman and lie down beside the Carver, gnawing on their prize.

The priest moans slightly until Dravek sinks one of his blades through her throat.

'I will do my part,' Dravek promises him. 'I will meet my end of our bargain. Are you certain that you can meet yours?'

The Neverborn glares at him. '*I do not enjoy being questioned.*'

'I do not enjoy being disappointed. We will not have another chance at this.'

'*You shall be free of her,*' the daemon promises. '*We both will.*

You will have your engine and your liberty, and I will have my vengeance.' The daemon's long claws stroke the Flayed Beast's head affectionately. *'Provided that we do not wait too long. She is not a fool. She can sense our intent already.'*

'Soon,' Dravek replies.

'Not soon enough.'

He turns from his daemons and walks towards the sound of battle, the music of lasguns and bolter fire growing stronger as he advances.

They have been at this for hours. Multiple waves of skirmishing forces harrying the outer pickets of the Black Templars' lines.

When he took the city of Saint Ofelias the first time, months ago, the priests and acolytes within had offered almost no resistance. They had massed against his horde and died together, then scattered and been hunted like prey beasts once broken.

The Black Templars, however, fight a different battle. Small clusters of Frateris militia are scattered throughout the city, unafraid to retreat or disband completely before re-forming elsewhere, each supervised by a pair of knights to bolster their fragile wills.

It is not enough. They must know that. The city will fall again, just as it did the first time. But they will bleed his forces before it does.

Dravek finds himself smiling at the prospect.

Beneath his feet, a writhing mortal lies in the blood-soaked sand. The cultist's legs have been sheared from his torso, whether by Black Templars weapons or one of his own daemons. Despite the wounds, the jakhal pulls himself forward with sinewy arms, the stimm tank upon his back pumping a constant stream of chemical stimulants into his dying brain. The device is a poor mockery of the Butcher's Nails embedded within his brothers, but the effect is much the same.

The creature drools like a dog. Unthinking. Feral. His fingers claw at the sand as he drags himself towards the sound of battle. A wall blocks his path, but he attempts to pull himself forward, regardless.

'I remember that feeling,' Dravek whispers to him. 'I remember the hunger. The mindless hunger.'

Behind the cultist, a stream of dark crimson stains the sand, dripping from his severed legs. Dravek's foot crushes the cultist's skull as he leaps over the battlement and joins the fray.

The searing light of lasweapons flashes through smoke and dust. The screams of both men and daemons ring in his ears. For a moment, he feels something almost like joy. The pure, unadulterated focus of battle.

Las-fire tears from a ruin beside him. He sprints up a mound of rubble and crashes through a wall of crumbling stone. Within the small shrine, a bloodletter already rampages, ripping into a thin man bearing a rusty lasgun. Several of the human's companions pour fire into the daemon, blood splattering from the creature and sizzling onto the scorched floor beneath its cloven feet.

Dravek crashes into the mortals, his Eviscerator roaring and ripping into their weak flesh. Blood spurts from them in dark, warm gouts, spraying off the blades of his hands as he dances from one enemy to another until all lay at his feet. In the doorway, a priest looks on with terror, his voice shaking as he continues to pray.

The man raises a golden aquila before him, muttering on about the strength of his god. The bloodletter hesitates. Dravek scoffs.

The priest shakes as Dravek approaches, clinging to the icon of his deity. Mumbling his prayers with a stuttering tongue. His voice fades to little more than a whisper as Dravek draws up before him and looks down at his feeble form.

The priest thrusts the aquila towards him again.

Dravek laughs.

'Carry on, priest,' he sneers. 'But I am no daemon. It will take more than jewellery and hope to deter me.'

His Eviscerator shatters the priest's chest. The human coughs a great gout of blood as his torso is split in two by the weapon. Dravek steps through the archway, the daemon pausing behind him, growling something in its undecipherable tongue. It glares down at the aquila on the floor, still grasped in the priest's dead hands.

Dravek calls with disdain. 'His corpse god can do nothing to harm you here.'

The daemon hesitates before its horned head explodes, and the sound of bolter fire rips through the small room.

Dravek raises his Eviscerator as a dark form assails him. Fast. Strong. Raging like a storm cloud.

'Black Templar,' he growls, parrying a blow from the knight's chainsword.

'Traitor,' comes the barked reply.

Dravek laughs and steps back from the Space Marine.

The Black Templar appears ludicrous to him, clad in jet-black armour hardly scratched or scarred, bearing a hundred paper talismans of his corpse god bound to its surface with red wax. A dress of pure white fabric covers his breastplate, displaying the cross of his Chapter.

Dravek remembers a time when the sons of Dorn were a thing to be feared, not to be laughed at. When they joined him in raging battle, clinging to their hatred rather than their empty faith. When their First Captain fought beside his Legion during the Great Crusade.

'I remember your captain Sigismund, brother. I remember how he fought in the pits. The Black Knight, we called him.

He was rage incarnate. He would be ashamed of what you have become.'

The Black Templar roars and charges towards him. Sparks fly from Dravek's limbs as the blades on his arms parry the knight's chainsword. Dravek throws the weapon aside and steps into the Black Templar's reach, driving his shoulder into the Space Marine's stomach. One of the barbs on his pauldron slips past his opponent's armour. The Black Templar grunts, then raises his bolter with his other hand.

Dravek feels the shots rip into his flank. He coughs and staggers, then laughs, grasping the weapon and turning it from the Black Templar's grasp. Bolter rounds rake the floor, shrapnel peppering his legs.

There was a time when that pain would have woken the Butcher's Nails. When they would have made him faster. Stronger. But blind.

Now, the pain only brings him clarity.

Just as he turns the muzzle of the weapon towards its bearer, the Black Templar's chainsword slips free of his blades and descends towards his arm. Its teeth bite into the flesh just above one of Dravek's blades, shearing the bloody metal from the end of his hand.

Dravek roars and brings his Eviscerator down upon the Space Marine's pauldron. Its churning teeth split the Astartes' armour, dark blood rushing from the wound. The Black Templar's grip on his chainsword slackens. Dravek rips the weapon from his grasp and kicks the knight backward.

The Black Templar slides to a stop on the slick, gore-soaked floor. Another shadow joins him in the doorway.

'Brothers!' Dravek calls. 'There was a time when you and I were not so different. When you fought with a purity of purpose that even those of my Chapter envied. When you cloaked yourself in blood and glory and did not hide behind the fragile shield of faith and delusion.'

Neither dark form speaks. The first regains his chainsword as the second raises a hammer towards him.

Dravek laughs and charges into their midst.

He dances between the knights, his Eviscerator screeching as the blades set within his flesh glisten. Like feathers on a raptor, they float in the dim light, glimmering with blood and gore.

The sons of Dorn are strong. Strong, and slow, and burdened by their faith. Beneath the sounds of his blades striking against their weapons, a dull buzzing grows in Dravek's ears.

Enough. Enough play.

A wobble at the edge of his vision.

Dravek blinks. He parries the chainsword. He sidesteps the hammer. Above the heads of his enemies two skulls have appeared. Neither makes a sound, but he feels their words.

Always talking, the first tells the second.

So many words. So little purpose.

Pain lances through Dravek's mind. The skulls hover above the heads of his enemies. They mark the Space Marines. They prepare her path.

The air before Dravek swims. Frost coats the shrine's stones and the Black Templars' weapons. Dravek strikes the first knight, his boots slipping on the icy floor. The second hesitates, sniffing the air.

Dravek's Eviscerator takes his wrist. The hammer falls from his grasp. Dravek charges forward, but she arrives first. The Lady of Thorns within both his mind and theirs.

The Black Templars fall to their knees.

'Enough playing,' she greets him. *'This is a war, not a game.'*

At the back of his mind, Dravek feels the mindless rage rising. He glares at the Neverborn.

'Not pleased to see me? Truly, Soulrender, we must work on our rapport.'

The daemon stands between the kneeling Black Templars, her tiny form dwarfed by their massive frames. She laughs. A terrible, childlike laugh.

'Come now. Finish them. We have work to do.'

'I do not serve you,' Dravek manages. His ears ring. His tongue is desert-dry.

'But don't you?'

The pain strikes him like lightning. Steals his mind. For a moment he feels his consciousness slipping. At the back of his thoughts, the rage rises. The mindless, stupid, animal rage. He feels his tendons and muscles pulse with strength as the daemon reawakens the cruciamen within him. Feels his mouth begin to slaver. His hands begin to shake as she goads his Butcher's Nails back to life.

'It feels good, doesn't it? Don't you want it again?'

And for a terrible moment, he does. Then it is gone.

'No,' he replies. 'I will not be a slave. Not to the Nails. Not to you.'

The Lady of Thorns laughs. Her skulls laugh without sound. *'You will always be a slave,'* she whispers. *'Now do what you were made for, and kill.'*

Dravek glares at her as he steps forward. His Eviscerator sings. The Black Templars fall, moments later, headless to the floor.

He stumbles from the shrine, the Lady's laugh echoing at his back.

'Enough of this!' Dravek calls out through his vox-caster.

He has waited too long already. Vale's patience be damned. He stumbles slightly before he regains his mind.

'The hounds first,' Dravek orders. 'Send the hounds.'

* * *

I smell them first. Long before I feel the pounding vibrations of their footfalls in the stone beneath my feet. Long before my eyes see the dull glow of their crimson, blood-slicked fur in the grey darkness that floats around me.

The reek of rotting flesh and burning bone. Ice on my neck. Metal on my tongue. The sharp hammering of footsteps rising above the dull suckling, thrumming that shakes the catacombs.

'Weapons,' I order, though my brothers need no guidance.

Hadrick's thunder hammer is already in his hand. Elke inspects his bolter and the blades mounted atop his narthecium.

The Missionary Proserpine meets my gaze with empty eyes. She is little more than an automaton now, not unlike the servitors that bear the relics of the shrines of Saint Iglese and Saint Ciubrus in the procession behind us. Her legs continue churning. She grunts occasional comments as she chooses one path versus another. That her frail body has not given out completely defies even my understanding.

'It stinks,' she whispers.

'Weapons!' I call to the mortals behind me. The chain of torch lamps in the distance flickers dimly in the haze. I have commanded our companions to be ready for battle. Now we will see if they have obeyed my words.

'Close,' the missionary says.

'We smell them, too,' Hadrick answers. He steps in front of the missionary, his helm lumen fading away into the darkness ahead.

Without orders, my other brothers surround the woman. Fenril and Umter flanking her. Me at the rear. Our helm lumens strike out into the myriad alcoves and side tunnels around us, each the possible route of our assailants' arrival.

'This is a poor place for a battle,' Hadrick subvocalises.

'And yet we have no choice in it.'

'Tight quarters. Dark. A string of exhausted mortals stretching behind us. Cramped tunnels in which their ranged weaponry will have little effect.' There is no disdain in his voice as he speaks of them now. He will never love them, but these, at least, have earned his tolerance on our march.

'If they break,' I reply, 'the whole line will die.'

It would be a simple thing for an enemy to split our force as it stands. And here, in the dark, in the cold, in the blood, such a battle could quickly turn from a rout into a massacre. That we have made it so far without bloodshed is a miracle. I am not eager for it, now that it arrives.

The thrumming of footsteps grows stronger. The scent of death. The sound of gnashing, slavering jaws. Of footfalls. Four legs, not two.

'I smell it,' the Missionary Proserpine whispers. 'Close.'

'Yes,' I reply again. 'We smell them too. They are almost upon us.'

She turns to face me, her milky white eyes barely open, her legs trembling as she grips her staff.

'No,' she replies. 'Not them. The surface.'

We round a slight bend in the corridor, and I take note of the scene before me. I flick my helm lumen off for a moment, and find that the darkness that swallowed us before has grown brighter. That beneath the inky black, there is a faint hint of grey.

She is not wrong. We are near the surface.

I have no time to give thanks before the first beast strikes me.

My helm lumen flashes back to life as I raise my storm shield. Slavering, canine jaws grasp its rim, spilling blood and fire. I bellow a war cry of wordless rage and throw the hound back into a pile of its kin.

'Forward!' I roar, as I charge into the pack of daemons before me. All around, the sound of carnage echoes through the narrow tunnel as the beasts begin to strike our line.

I bring Penitence down to split the face of a warp hound as I smash the point of my storm shield into another of its kind. Behind me, Hadrick's hammer cracks, and Elke's bolter rips over my shoulder. Each thunderous discharge and explosive round finds a target, painting the walls and ceiling with molten, orange blood.

For each that falls, however, another rushes into its place, leaping between the alcoves and inlets carved into the tunnel walls, striking us from before and behind.

Mortals scream. My brothers shout to one another. Behind me, the Missionary Proserpine continues silently forward.

'Stay with her!' I call to Hadrick. 'Nothing touches her until she reaches the surface.'

There are no complaints from the knight now.

I turn backward into the darkened tunnel. Behind me, the screams of humans and daemons rise like a hymn. Beneath it all, the dark rhythm of that accursed drinking.

I splash through blood, growing deeper as I tread. A warp hound pounces from the shadows and catches its jaws upon my pauldron.

The ceramite groans beneath its jaws, the searing bite of the creature's foul spittle dripping through gaps in my plate and burning against my skin. Roaring, I drop my shoulder and crush the creature against the wall. It screeches as I feel its bones shatter, cracking and scorching the white stone as I drag it forward.

Its jaws only grip me more tightly.

I step back and switch Penitence to my left hand, driving the blade backward over my shoulder into the beast's stomach. Red-hot blood pours over my armour. The creature roars. I slam it against the wall again, and finally it releases me, whimpering and twitching as it falls onto the bloody floor. I crush its skull with my foot as I step over it and towards the few flickering torch lamps ahead.

The lights borne by the procession of priests have all but faded now, and those that remain flash rapidly in all directions as their bearers strike out at the daemons harrying them.

As I approach, I hear the arch-cantor's voice calling.

'To me! To me!'

Not the cantor of Saint Iglese, but of Saint Ciubrus. He stands upon an ossuary, holding his golden aquila over his head in one hand. In his other, he swings a silver brazier like a maul.

Beneath him, crimson-robed priests fall to the jaws of daemon hounds, striking out where they are able with blades and spears and the blazing light of lasguns and flamers.

I swing Penitence, tearing a rift in the beasts around them as I charge towards the ecclesiarchs. Claws rip at my limbs. Jaws tear at my armour. I shrug them aside, my power sword singing. The blood of daemons falls in a thin mist around me, coating my dark armour until I glow like the star-scattered void.

'To me!' the arch-cantor cries again. In the corridor behind him similar rallying cries echo above the din as the mortals attempt to regroup.

'To m–'

The arch-cantor's voice ends in a strangled cry as a great crimson beast leaps over the wall of blades around the priest and rips him from his post.

The warp hound crashes down upon the soldiers below the arch-cantor, crushing them beneath its massive paws. The ecclesiarch writhes within the creature's jaws, attempting to turn his bolt pistol towards the monster's head. The creature shakes its sinew-strewn neck a single time, and I hear the arch-cantor's neck snap. The aquila falls from his limp hands.

I leap over the ossuary and bring Penitence down upon the

beast. The blade hews into its flank, severing one of its legs clean through. The beast howls and stumbles, then rights itself and turns on the priests beside it. A silver spear pierces its side. The flash of las-fire strikes it, but it is little deterred.

Penitence bites again as it turns, ripping deep into its daemonic flesh. The mortals beside it scream as the daemon's blood burns their skin, but one manages to raise the golden vial in his hands and unstopper the skull-topped lid atop it. Sacred oil spills upon the monster, sizzling as the flame on its skin fades to something like crumbling ash.

I drive my blade into the wound and rip it through the creature's chest. More blood. More fire.

The warp hound stumbles, then falls, the priest who wounded it crushed beneath its mass.

I pause for a moment and look about me. On all sides the humans fight. On all sides the humans die. Beneath my feet, their blood pools in torrid, foetid gouts. And above the sound of their voices and the clashing of their blades, that accursed, mindless drinking grows ever louder.

A sickness grasps me at the sensation.

'They will die,' I mutter. 'They will die and their blood will simply add to this sea.'

The acolyte beside me looks up in awe, not hearing my words. She is scarcely more than a child, the robes of her station billowing over her small frame.

There is only one path forward. Only one way this venture will be anything but squandered.

I stare down at the mortal beside me, ringed in the corpses of her brothers and of daemons she had only seen in paintings and sculptures until today.

I drop to a knee and grasp the arch-cantor's bloody aquila from the gore beneath me, undamaged by the searing blood of the daemons spilled upon it. The icon glitters even now. Even covered in the blood of the righteous. Perhaps even more so than it did before. It glows like a beacon in the light of the acolyte's torch lamp.

'Forward,' I order her. 'Forward for your brothers. Forward for your god.'

The girl stares at me, then her brown eyes harden.

'To me!' she roars into the darkness behind her. 'To me!'

She raises the aquila over her head.

Dravek's mind is turmoil as he steps through the sands. Away from the blood. Away from the death. Away from the daemons that glut themselves on the carnage behind him and the daemons that bury their claws in his soul.

He had hoped for peace from his captors.

He had hoped that the feast laid before them would be enough to blind them to his purpose.

But he knows what hope is. The death of fools.

The Carver appears at his side. Instead of sated, the Neverborn appears harried. There is no sickly, many-toothed smile upon his angled face. There is no mirth in his voice. No satisfaction in his stance. He looks like an animal pursued by hunters. An animal anxious. An animal afraid.

The daemon's discomfort would bring Dravek joy in any other situation, if he did not feel the same himself.

'*Faster!*' the Carver pleads. '*Even now she turns her eyes upon us.*'

'I need no warning, daemon,' he replies. 'I feel her, too.'

Already, the screams in the back of Dravek's mind pulse. Already, the barbs of the Lady's thorns lance behind his eyes. If this is the strength of her affections distracted, he is not eager for her presence when she finally realises his intent.

In the distance, there is a bleating roar, like a great creature wounded. The Carver vanishes, then appears again, the Flayed Beast at his side. Blood drips from the beast and it howls in pain. Across the sand, a charred human form approaches.

Dravek smells the Burned Man even at this distance. Feels the heat pouring off his dead flesh. The rage behind the daemon's melted face leaches off him like the warmth of a flame. Dravek has not seen the Lady's companion since the night he was claimed. And he finds he does not relish the reunion.

'You were meant to keep this hidden from them, daemon,' Dravek growls to the Carver. 'You were to keep the Lady's eyes elsewhere. Keep this place a shadow for your kind.'

'*I have,*' the Carver spits. '*But such a thing cannot be hidden forever.*'

The daemon turns from Dravek and faces the Burned Man. '*Hurry.*'

Dravek races towards the metal behemoth in the valley before him. Foolish. Foolish to think that the Lady would not feel it awakening. Foolish to think that any amount of bloodshed elsewhere might distract her. Foolish to imagine that the Carver would be able to keep such a monstrosity hidden from her for long.

But the desperate rarely make wise decisions.

'Soulrender,' a distorted, mechanical voice calls out to him. 'Welcome.'

Ra'leth Vale stands in the sands beneath his hulking creation, the Warpsmith's arachnid form hidden in the shadow of the titanic structure against the moon. The Techmarine's red eyes glow with an eager energy as his metal limbs twitch and writhe in the sand.

'As you can see, our progress–'

Dravek shoves him aside and steps past him.

'Now, Vale,' he orders. 'Damn your progress. The time is now.'

On the dunes above him there is a terrible light.

A scream.

Flame roars from the Burned Man and devours the Flayed Beast and the Carver. Both Neverborn screech, then charge into the scorched corpse that faces them.

Dravek's vision swims. He coughs. On the dune opposite them, a small silhouette strikes out against the stars. A lancing pain cuts across his skull.

He vomits.

'Soulrender.'

The Warpsmith mumbles something. Dravek cannot hear his words. Cannot hear anything. Nothing but the churning, suckling sound of blood being drawn from the sands into the engine before him.

Dravek steps closer to the accursed structure. He feels the Lady of Thorn's grip on him weaken slightly in its presence. The daemon on the dune slows her approach, and he does not blame her.

The thing that rises from the sand is an abomination. Even Dravek can see this. Even Dravek, who ordered its creation.

Four dark, warp-forged limbs tower above the sands, each the width of an Imperial Knight. Their fathomless surfaces ripple with teeth and claws, each inscribed with endless runes and writs in languages even Dravek himself cannot read. Atop those great legs, a massive trunk rises into the night. A body of brass, and bone, and steel, rippling with cables and pipes the width of a dozen men each. From that base, a monstrous head arises, equine and avian together at once, its mouth large enough to swallow buildings whole. Within that maw, endless rows of man-sized teeth glimmer and drip with dark oils.

'It looks ready enough to me, Vale.'

The Warpsmith shifts uncomfortably. 'It is built, yes. But such a thing is not easily commanded without the proper precautions.'

He motions an inhuman arm to a small group of hereteks and thralls dragging a massive chain of bone through the white sands.

In the distance, the Lady of Thorns approaches. Atop her shoulders, the Silent Skulls sit like fell familiars. On the ridgeline above them, the Burned Man, the Carver, and the Flayed Beast war. Beneath them, the sound of the Maw rises like a wave.

'Where are the rest of them?' Dravek asks. 'Where are the thralls I gave you to complete this work?'

'Their services are being utilised, I assure you.'

The pain in his head again. Dravek walks towards the engine. Only then does he notice the writhing forms which cover its hull. Hundreds of living, screaming humans bound to the machine with flesh and steel.

Vale grins at his side.

On the ridge behind Dravek, fire and screaming fill the air. Fire that only he can see. Screams that only he can hear. His vision swims. He vomits again.

'Now, Vale,' he orders. 'Wake it now.'

The light takes my vision for a moment.

Tempest's twin suns burn in the sky above Saint Ofelias' shattered dome-wall. Even buried beneath a screen of black smoke and soot, they are blinding.

I grunt as I step into their brightness, ripping Penitence from the belly of another fell hound. The feet of countless ecclesiarchs crush the dead as they emerge, roaring, from the darkness at my back.

Many will not leave those tunnels. Too many have been left behind in the dark.

Hadrick, Elke, and Umter control a foothold on the surface, fighting like daemons themselves to keep more warp spawn from pouring into the catacombs. I rush to join them as myriad messages blanket my visor, the steady chime of my vox singing as it restores communication with more of my brothers on the surface.

Two dozen pale lights glitter across my viewfield. Each, a Black Templar knight waging the God-Emperor's holy war. Two dozen where once there had been more than forty.

As I watch their beacons on my helm, my brothers drift slowly backward, contracting towards the shrine city's central cathedrum like orbiting worlds crashing into their star.

They retreat to the cathedrum. I give thanks that any still remain. There should be more. There were more when I left them. I pray that those who remain are enough.

I dismiss all messages and open a vox-channel to Brother-Chaplain Dant.

The Chaplain's speech is breathy with exertion. Beneath his words I hear the roar of weapon fire. The shrieking of daemons. The groan of tired servos.

'You arrive at last.'

'By the God-Emperor's grace.' I find myself grateful despite my wounds. 'And you still stand.'

'For now,' Dant replies. His voice cuts out, then returns. Something screams in the background. *'The Soulrender's horde strikes out in force, Brother-Castellan. They push us back to the Great Cathedrum even now.'*

'I know,' I reply. 'Yet you hold.'

'We do. By the God-Emperor's grace.'

The Chaplain's voice is tired, his words are stiff. I have seen exhaustion in him only rarely in the centuries I have known him, but his tone is laden with it now. I scan my display and find the names of my fallen brothers.

How much has it cost him to bury so many?

How heavy do their ashes weigh upon his armour? Their souls upon his? How many times, on how many worlds, has he been asked to bear such burdens since he ascended to his rank?

And yet I must ask more.

'And by His grace you will hold awhile longer. We are coming, Brother-Chaplain. The hammer against your anvil. Fall back to the walls of the cathedrum if you must, but no further. I will see you soon.'

'*As you command, Brother-Castellan.*'

'Have faith,' I reply.

The Lady of Thorns faces Dravek, her eyes pale and burning.

White like the sand. White like ash. White like the blazing light of a star.

'*You worm!*' she screams. '*You worthless, petty, ungrateful child!*'

Dravek's vision explodes. His thoughts disappear. The mindless, all-consuming pain grips him as he stumbles in the sands and falls to his knees, dropping his Eviscerator from shaking hands. The daemon rises over him, dark and terrible. Her voice swallows his thoughts. Her skin swimming with a thousand living vines.

He raises his arms as the thorns strike out towards him. He is slow. He is weak. He is distracted by pain he can hardly fathom.

The Lady of Thorns throws his defences aside. Her barbs tear into him, gripping his limbs and pinning them to the ground. His skin joins his mind on fire, now.

'*It pains me,*' she whispers, her voice soft as death. The daemon leans over him. Dravek rages against his fetters to no avail. Her face leans close, just beside his ear, the scent of rot and death and fire upon her. '*It pains me to think that you would be so ungrateful.*'

His mind vanishes. The pain takes him.

Like drowning.

Then the daemon pulls him above the waves again.

The Lady of Thorns laughs. A keening, terrible sound. *'Though I am not certain what I should have expected. To strike a bargain with a mortal is a foolish thing. They are untrustworthy, deceitful things.'*

Dravek gasps. The pain lessens. Barbs still grip his flesh. Pull his limbs towards the sands. He struggles against them.

The Lady smiles. *'Stubborn,'* she chides. *'Prideful. Wilful. Though I suppose any animal worth owning must be broken.'*

She smiles, blades and stars and the void within her eyes. The two skulls atop her shoulders roar in silent, hollow laughter. Behind them, the hillside flickers with fire.

The Carver dances across the sands as flames lick out from the Burned Man and push him back towards the valley. Beside the charred corpse of the Neverborn, another figure ventures.

The Wheel.

The daemon of bone and flesh rolls across the ground, harrying the Flayed Beast just as its companion does the Carver. Limbs twist within its outer wheel, like some fell gyroscopic union of flesh and otherworldly power.

Dravek has seen neither of the Lady's allies since the night he was claimed.

The Lady's grasp tightens around him, a single one of her fingers against his cheek drawing his eyes back to her own.

'You think yourself bold, but you forget who owns you. In truth it is my fault. I have not been as present as I should have. Distracted with my own dealings. A neglectful master. And one cannot expect a pet to behave when its master is long absent.'

The Lady brushes Dravek's cheek. A lance of pain shoots through his skull. He coughs. He retches. Blood drips from his mouth and into the sand.

Into the sand which pulses with the vibrations of the abhorrent daemon engine awakening behind him.

The Lady lifts her gaze from him. Dravek turns his head to follow. Behind him, the valley shivers with the daemon engine's movements, gouts of smoke and steam beginning to spew from its monstrous stacks. That pulsing, suckling sound grows even stronger as Vale and his few remaining hereteks complete whatever final preparations their technology requires.

'It is a terrible thing,' the Lady whispers. *'To be caught within a cage. You know this. You remember.'*

And he does. Even a few days within the eightcage was punishing enough. Even though he had chosen that fate. Even though he had commanded it.

'I can scarcely imagine being bound within such a prison forever.'

On the hillside, the Carver falters. Flames wash over him. The Flayed Beast screams. Ragged vines draped in thorns rip from the sands. The Lady grasps both the daemons and pulls them to herself.

The Burned Man and the Wheel follow their prisoners to her side.

'In truth, I do not blame you. My fragile, angry, rageful man.'

The Lady looks at him with something almost like affection, though with each of her words, the pain in his skull rises.

'Besides, to punish you too greatly would simply render you a useless vessel.'

She turns to the Carver.

'But you…' she sneers.

Thorns pierce the Carver's pale, angular skin. Dark ichor drips out. The Flayed Beast bays.

'I should have destroyed you long ago. Before the cage. Before this body.'

The Lady reaches out and strikes the Carver. The claws atop

her fingers rip deep gashes in his face. One of his glowing eyes flickers and fades.

'I should have banished you or bound you or unmade you entirely, you foolish, petty, ungrateful thing.'

Her grasp on the Carver tightens. The Flayed Beast whimpers, but the Carver only begins to laugh. He laughs as the thorns pierce his thin, pallid skin. He laughs as the Lady rips at the flesh of his limbs.

He laughs as the two skulls atop her shoulders look towards him and then turn on their master, grasping her neck in their silent jaws.

The Lady screams. Her grip on her prisoners slackens. Flames burst from the Burned Man, and swallow her whole.

The pain in Dravek's skull explodes. His existence is nothing but suffering. Nothing but screams. Nothing but terrible, blinding light. The Lady releases him, but he can do little more than kneel and shake as the daemons within him fight their own war.

Dravek shivers in the sand, blood and vomit spilling from his mouth. He forces himself to his knees. To watch, at least, his plans come to fruition.

The Carver's claws strike out at the Lady. They rip into her pale flesh. They sever the vines and strands of thorns that she summons. The Silent Skulls tear at their master's flesh until she throws them aside and crushes one beneath her feet. She backs away from the other Neverborn and catches her bearings.

'You, too?' she cries, staring at her former companions. She had not expected their betrayal. *'I will destroy you. I will unmake you.'*

Limping on bleeding paws, the Flayed Beast circles. The Wheel rolls beside the beast, their prior animosity now forgotten. Whether the Carver had arranged this all before, or if the Lady's allies merely sense their opportunity, Dravek does not know.

Another gout of flame erupts from the Burned Man. The

Lady of Thorns flicks it aside. Suddenly, she stands behind the charred daemon. Her fingers dance across his neck, smoke and ash spilling out where her claws rake his throat. The fire flickers, then falls silent. The Burned Man collapses to the ground.

Slowly, the Flayed Beast and the Wheel circle the Lady. Slowly, the Carver presses forward, the Silent Skulls now in his hand.

'*You will do no such thing,*' he spits.

The Carver pounces, the Flayed Beast joining its master. Thorns erupt from the sand, but the beast sidesteps them. Its jaws clamp upon the Lady's flank while the Carver's claws rip into her chest.

A scream. Blinding motion. The daemons separate.

Pale white light drips from the Lady's flesh, coalescing into opalescent beads in the sand. The Flayed Beast limps on a shattered leg. The Carver grins beneath his single eye.

'*You should have,*' he barks. '*You should have unmade me long ago. You will come to regret not doing so.*'

The Lady steps back again, trying to keep her remaining enemies in her view.

The Wheel rolls towards her across the sand. The Carver and the Flayed Beast follow.

Another flurry of blows. More pain. More screaming.

Dravek pushes himself to his feet, wipes the vomit from his bleeding lips.

The Lady takes another step backwards. Another step towards her doom.

Beneath his feet, Dravek feels that pulsating grow. Louder now. Hungrier. The sound of the Maw preparing to do its work.

The Lady looks behind her. Catches Dravek's gaze. Her eyes glint like stars. Lit by something other than amusement or hatred.

Fear.

Dravek can feel it. Dravek can taste it. Even above the searing pain that burns through him. Even above the taste of blood on his tongue.

The Lady of Thorns is afraid. And she is right to be so.

'*Soulrender,*' she calls. She begs. '*You cannot understand what they will do. You cannot fathom the pain they will inflict on you if I am gone.*'

Dravek spits and steps to block her path. 'I can imagine no worse torment than your companionship.'

The Lady meets his gaze for the last time. No, perhaps it is not fear in her eyes, after all.

Anger.

Hatred.

Pity. For him.

The sands churn beneath the Lady's feet, and she vanishes into the gaping darkness of the Maw.

For a moment there is nothing. Nothing but the silence of the wind and the sand. Nothing but the quiet voice of Ra'leth Vale at his back. Dravek watches with confusion as the Carver moves. As the daemon grasps hold of the Wheel and casts it into the pit behind the Lady. Then the Skulls. Then the Burned Man's corpse. Finally, the Flayed Beast itself.

The Carver moves too quickly. More quickly than he should be able to. More quickly than he has shown in his duel with the Lady. More quickly than he has ever shown in the past.

Then silence again, as the Carver walks towards him. The daemon stares at Dravek and smiles with far too many teeth.

'*It is just us now, Soulrender. As it was always meant to be.*'

Dravek's skull explodes with pain. The daemon engine at his back screams as it comes to life.

Chapter 11

'Brothers!' I roar. My ears ring with my own voice, streaming out from my vox to the Black Templars scattered throughout the shattered shrine city.

Penitence flashes in the harsh light of Tempest's suns, streaming down unhindered upon her streets. Saint Ofelias' dome-wall lies in ruins, pieces of armaglass the size of void craft littering her shattered buildings. Carpeting her streets like glittering gems. Shimmering like water upon the sand.

The feet of thousands grind that glass beneath us. Back into shards. Back into dust. Back into the very sand of this world.

Just as we grind our enemy before us.

I rip my power sword from the chest of a monster. A twisted, slavering shell of a human painted with the symbols of its dark god, raging and clawing, spurred on by the stimm-machine bound to its flesh.

Even wounded it fights on. Even wounded it claws its way towards me. It grasps weakly at my armour as I pass, with fingers tipped in filed, filthy nails.

I crush its skull as I step over it, driving into the next pack of foes.

'Brothers!' I cry again.

Hadrick's thunder hammer sings through the air at my side. He shatters a small cluster of cultists, their bodies soaring through the air and breaking against the rubble of the basilica we fight beneath.

'Now is the time for glory!' I roar. 'Now is the time for hatred and for blood. I have asked for your patience. I have asked for restraint. I have asked you to temper your fervour and righteous anger, but I ask you no longer. I have asked you to give much, but I ask now for more. I demand more. The God-Emperor demands more!

'See how our enemy flees before us? See how we break them with every step? Now the hammer strikes against the anvil. Now we make of this city a holy altar. And of our enemy nothing but sand beneath our feet.'

I crest a field of rubble and survey the bloody scene before me. The streets of Saint Ofelias swim with churning bodies and blazing guns. There is little order to the battle, only fervour and rage. Behind me, the priests of Tempest charge onward, harried and bloodied, but their exhaustion forgotten.

Zealots scattered throughout that churning mass raise their voices, screaming the God-Emperor's praises, His commands, His words into the ears of the righteous as they cut down His enemies.

In the distance, the Cathedrum of the Martyr still stands. Around it, a knot of the Missionary Proserpine's pilgrims holds. My brothers stand among them, pushing them onward. That wall of the faithful retracts, fighting step by step backward towards the cathedrum's walls, but how they make our enemy pay.

Between those two masses, we squeeze the heretics. Between those two bastions, we break their wave.

We may fail. I see that still. For they are many and we are few. But our faith is strong, and our hatred stronger.

I leap down from the basilica and into the fray, scattering a knot of foes as I fall. Penitence rips into their accursed flesh. My storm shield throws aside their petty blows. Two cultists fall, shorn in half by my blade, the heat of flamers blazing beside me as crimson-robed priests follow in my wake.

Among them a golden aquila glimmers, raised high by a young woman with gleaming eyes. The mark of the arch-cantor, though not his mark any more. It belongs to them all now. It is their standard. The God-Emperor's.

'With me!' I bellow.

The priests roar in return.

We charge forward as daemons and twisted cultists meet our press, their flesh adorned with the bones and skulls of dead ecclesiarchs, and yet the mortals at my side do not falter. They have seen the face of evil, now, and for them it no longer holds any terror.

My soul rejoices. Rejoices to be free of the dark and the tunnels. Free of the blood and the endless suckling of whatever fell force has rooted itself beneath these sands.

Free of patience.

Of restraint.

Of the bounds of diplomacy and discussion.

I swing my shield towards a hulking daemon. The beast hefts a long mace before it. The weapon's head is made from the skull of some great, horned beast, its shaft the bones of the creature's spine. I step beneath the blow, deflecting it with my shield, but not before it shatters a priest beside me.

I slash Penitence across the daemon's hooved legs, spilling molten blood into the sands. The beast howls and kicks towards me. Hadrick's hammer cracks as he crushes one of the monster's great limbs. I shear the other leg at its hip, the daemon crashing to the ground. It lashes towards me again, its mace finding my pauldron. I hear the ceramite crack, but the plate holds. The blow drives me to a knee, but I push myself forward into the beast, burying my blade in its chest.

The daemon roars, its jaws only inches from my helmet. Even through the filters of my armour, I smell its putrid breath. Flecks of blood and flesh spray from its teeth against my visor to dim my view, the daemon's crimson eyes blazing beneath curling, ram-like horns.

I raise my shield and strike the beast across the jaw. It twists, throwing me to the side, Penitence ripping from its flesh. I roll with the monster, finding myself upon its back, the flat of my blade within its mouth. It bites down upon the power sword, blood leaking out between its gnashing teeth. The creature throws its head, the razor tip of one of its horns finding a joint in my armour. We roll again together, my body pinned beneath its mass. I twist my blade within its mouth and pull Penitence towards me, ripping into fangs and bone. The beast thrashes, then falls still as the air cracks, and Hadrick's hammer crashes down upon its chest.

As I push myself from beneath the monster, the Missionary Proserpine steps to my side. The bolt pistol in her hand smokes dimly.

'Come now, Lord Castellan,' she chides, as I lift myself from where I lie upon the ground. 'Now is hardly the time for rest.'

She turns, leaning against her staff, her bolt pistol firing into the horde before us, little need for aim against an enemy so numerous. It is a poor jest, but I find myself grinning.

I rise with groaning armour and follow her forward.

Into the smoke. Into the fire. Into the stench of burning metal and flesh. Of sweat and urine and shit.

Another pack of twisted cultists. Another daemon among them. The humans in this group are thin and rabid. Even the dark science their masters impose upon them is unable to sustain their mass without sustenance. How hard did the Soulrender push them to reach Saint Ofelias? Harder than I pushed my own mortal horde?

The pack of slavering humans throws itself at the Missionary Proserpine. Her bolt pistol fires towards the sounds of their shuffling, scraping feet and drops one in a plume of blood. Three more prepare to fall upon her before Hadrick crashes into their midst.

'Do not touch her!' Hadrick roars, his shoulder breaking two of the cultists like twigs, his hammer obliterating the third.

The missionary pauses as if she is about to speak. Instead, she simply turns her weapon to the side and pours fire into the roaring daemon behind him.

The creature rears up on scaled legs covered with spikes. Black ichor blooms across its bare-skinned chest, like that of a man but sprouting two extra limbs. It bellows as its arms crash downward towards the missionary.

I fill the gap between them.

Penitence meets the daemon's assault, dancing between its limbs and biting them deeply. I drive the blade forward into its stomach, toppling the creature onto its back. I plunge Penitence through its chest and into the sand as the daemon writhes. Its hands grasp wildly, slowly clawing its way up the blade, lifting itself off the ground.

Its jaws gnash, reaching its neck out towards me.

Mindless.

Mad.

Unholy.

Accursed.

'Bloody daemons,' the missionary calls beside me, her voice laced with disgust. She plunges the tip of her cane down the creature's open mouth and through the back of its head.

* * *

There is nothing but screaming.

The daemon engine bellowing its rage. The terror of the hereteks and thralls that it shatters beneath it. Dravek's own voice as his body burns with pain. The Carver laughing above it all.

Dravek Soulrender stumbles forward through the sand. Towards the monstrous abomination that pulls at its chains before him. The daemon engine lifts its dark maw and roars, its terrible voice shaking the sands beneath its feet.

Seven daemons rage within that cage. Even now, Dravek feels the force of their anger.

Seven daemons of the eight that had made him. And the other stands laughing at his side.

The Carver grins as the engine thrashes against its bone chains. The beast lifts one of its enormous feet and brings it crashing back down upon the crowd of thralls that attempt to bind it. Dravek hears their bodies shatter. Hears their screams add to those already ringing in his head.

'Stop,' he whispers. 'Make it stop.'

A terrible sound escapes the Carver. A daemon's laugh. A sound of pure joy. As the Neverborn wraps one of his arms around Dravek, his skin grows cold and prickles with unease.

'Come now,' the Carver whispers. *'Why would I do that? This is what we've been waiting for. Our great work. Is it not?'*

The daemon's other arm – pallid and multijointed – motions towards the raging machine. The daemon engine throws its head from side to side, a single great horn rising from its snout. More screaming, as it pierces the bodies of heretics and thralls upon that spike. The beast bellows again. Dravek feels his flesh shake.

A dark shape races across the sand towards him.

'Soulrender!' the Warpsmith roars. 'What have you done?' Ra'leth Vale's machine-eyes burn with fear as he approaches, yet there is excitement in his words as well as accusation.

'What have I done?' Dravek finds himself saying, though the voice is not his own.

'What have I done?' he repeats, the Carver's voice erupting from his mouth. *'I have given you everything you asked for, smith. Everything your simple, human mind could comprehend. You required a prisoner to power your war machine, and I have given you seven.'*

Vale looks on in horror. 'You cannot be serious? The vessel cannot withstand such a thing.'

A spear tip lances through the back of Dravek's mind, as well as a compulsion to strike the Warpsmith. He resists, his bladed arm quivering at his side, his Eviscerator twitching in his grasp.

The Carver sighs. *'Do not make this more difficult than it must be,'* he says with Dravek's voice.

'You have caused this problem, not me,' Vale replies, but Dravek knows that the daemon's words are meant for him, not the Warpsmith.

Behind Vale, the daemon engine rips at its chains once more. Upon its back, massive steel tendrils lash out towards the sand, wiping away those few hereteks still brave enough to attempt to restrain it. Their bodies shatter beneath the beast's metal rage.

'How?' Dravek manages. A single thought above the pain.

That terrible sound again. The Carver laughing through his mouth.

'The Blood God demands death, not stupidity. He desires his servants to be murderous, not fools. I weighed my enemies and found I could not best them at once, but divided they fell, just as the Black Templars will fall before us.'

Another spear of pain. Another compulsion. Dravek's Eviscerator swings forward.

Vale looks towards the blade, comprehension dawning across

his mechanised face. The Warpsmith steps backward on his articulated arachnid limbs.

'You wouldn't dare,' he spits. 'Without me you have no hope of controlling this thing.'

Dravek feels the compulsion again. The hunger. The desire to gut the snivelling thing before him and add its blood and oil to that which already drenches this world.

The pain grows as the Carver leans in towards him. *'This is what you were promised,'* the daemon whispers. *'This is the bargain you struck all those years ago. Not with the Lady of Thorns. Not with the other seven. With me.'*

Dravek stumbles. Blades behind his eyes. Blades between his ears. Blades, and fire, and the endless screams of the countless, faceless, infinite dead.

'I will give you blood. I will give you bone. I will give you an eternity of war. And in return, you will give me everything.'

There is nothing. Nothing but screams and incomprehensible pain.

Dravek screams with them, then withdraws from it all.

He swings his Eviscerator against his will, taking Vale's head as the Carver's laugh bursts from his lips.

'We break them,' Hadrick growls through his vox. 'We break them with our faith, and our hatred, and our will.'

I swing Penitence with weary arms, the weapon's blade nicked and dulled with blood and sand. Another cultist falls. Another daemon. The subject of my wrath makes little difference.

But even the strength of an angel flags.

'We do,' I reply. 'By the God-Emperor's grace.'

On my helm display, I watch the beacons of my brothers advance, each carving a path through the mindless horde of heretics before us, each driving like a blade towards the Cathedrum of the Martyr.

I drag myself over a toppled statue, grasping a cultist with my hands and smashing its face into the stone again and again. I raise my power sword, and shout to the Ecclesiarchy forces beside me, only to find that I fight alone. If even the strength of my brothers is not indefatigable, how much less so that of fragile mortals?

The sharp burn of lascannons scorches the sky over my head, ripping down from the cathedrum's walls into the shattered city which surrounds it. The searing beams glitter, reflected in the cloud of sand and soot that hangs in the air.

My brothers battle before those walls. Dant. Barnard. Alvus. For each step they take backward, we take a dozen forward, slicing into the foes that assail them, splitting our enemy, then destroying them completely.

And yet this is only the first task. Even if we shatter the Soul-render's warband here, there are other lesser hordes rampaging across this world. What strength will remain to us after this battle? Enough to perform the same miracle again, or enough to die just the same beneath some other shattered dome?

I push the thought from my mind. Such weakness is beneath me.

The most zealous priests appear at my back.

I pause for a moment in the empty square. Once a sacred place even within this sacred city. I let the mortals gather around me. I hear the panting of their tired lungs. I see the exhaustion in their shaking limbs. But I feel the fervour in their gleaming eyes.

'Priests!' I bellow. My voice shakes the small square. 'Warriors! Soldiers of the God-Emperor! Chosen of the Master of Mankind! When you left the walls of Saint Ciubrus and Saint Iglese, I promised you battle. I promised you death. I gave you a choice of where you might die. Behind the false safety of your walls, or on the war path. Cowering or charging into holy battle. You chose battle. And glory. And the God-Emperor honours you for it.'

A small huddle gathers around me in the lull. I am no orator, and these are simple words. But I am an angel of their god, incarnate, so my words, however simple, will suffice. As I speak, I see their gleaming eyes turn brighter. See shaking hands regrasp their weapons.

If I am the hand of the God-Emperor, then they are the blade that I hold in my grasp. Dulled. Weakened. Ready to shatter.

And shatter it may. So long as I bury it within our enemy first.

'I offer you no such promises today. There is no certainty in battle, other than bloodshed. Most of you will fall before these walls. Most of you will spill your blood into this sand. I do not offer you survival, and you would not seek it. But I do offer you a chance. A chance not just to wound your enemy but to crush him. Not just to die before the walls of this sacred cathedrum, but to liberate them.

'Whatever strength remains to you, I call on it now. Whatever rage still remains in your souls, do not hoard it any longer. One final push. One last advance. To the walls of the Cathedrum of the Martyr, until our enemy lies beneath our feet!

'For the God-Emperor!' I roar, and I hear the cry echo at my back.

We plunge forward, the sands shaking beneath our feet. For the first time since surfacing, we strike organised resistance. After hours of slaughter, the enemy has finally turned its eyes to the force slicing into its rear.

We cross an empty street, a strange cry rising up from the shadows of the ruined building across it. A line of cultists steps from the shadows, the glowing bodies of daemons emerging behind them. The warp spawn carry whips of long chain, and they use them to herd their mortal servants and hold them in a rough formation.

The cultists slaver like animals, gnashing their teeth and roaring at the sight of me. They raise crude weapons of steel and bone, smashing them against the stone beneath their feet. Against themselves.

My own line draws up beside me.

'Forward!' I roar.

A cry erupts from the ecclesiarchs, and for a moment, the line before us shivers. At first, I think it is our fervour which has shaken the heretics, then the air before me begins to boil.

There is a hiss in my ear, then scorching heat. A cluster of priests beside me erupts in flame as the sand beneath their feet turns to glass.

I hear the beast before I see it.

The creature bellows as it crashes through the ruins of a shrine, its towering form a mess of steel and of flesh. I might have thought it a Dreadnought if I did not know better. Whatever it once was, now it is simply a monster.

'Helbrute,' I mutter into my vox. I have seen these heretic Dreadnoughts only a few unfortunate times on the battlefield, and I curse the one I find before me now.

It bellows again, no words to its mindless, insane keening. It raises man-sized feet and plods forward, the shaky fire of the remaining priests splashing harmlessly off its hull. One of its metal arms swings, a long bone whip lashing forward and ripping into the priests. I catch the tip of the blow against my shield. Feel my arm shudder against its strength, and force myself onward.

The fire of an autocannon tears into my armour. I feel its concussions like hail against my shield and my greaves. A shot finds a seam in my worn ceramite plate. My left arm shivers then falls numb at my side.

I curse, forcing the wounded limb to rise again. My storm shield feels heavy in my painful grasp.

The gap between me and the Helbrute vanishes.

The beast roars again, my armour vibrating with the sound. At this distance I can see the twisted form bound inside its frame, the roaring face of a thing that was once my brother. The Heretic Astartes entombed within the war machine is little more than a mass of flesh now, its screaming face locked behind a scorched plate of glass embedded within the Helbrute's chest.

As the mad traitor screams, his machine body lashes out at me, its great whip splitting the air at my side. I step beneath the blow, and roll aside as it raises a foot above me. I slip behind the leg and hack my sword through the cables and pneumatic cylinders that power the limb.

It does little good.

The Helbrute wheels slowly, the fire from the weapons bound to it raking into the ranks of the Ecclesiarchy and the Soulrender's horde alike. Another foot rises above me; I step to the side, but a hulking, stimm-driven human crashes into me.

I bury Penitence into the cultist's chest, but the blow drives me from my course. With the groaning of pneumatic joints, the Helbrute's foot falls onto me.

Servos groan within my armour. Ceramite shatters. I hear my own bellow of pain join the roaring of the heretic machine.

'Brother-Castellan!' Hadrick shouts into my vox.

Above me, the Helbrute roars again. Its companions charge forward beneath it. I raise my shield, readying myself for their arrival, my leg pinned beneath the raging beast.

There is a dark shape before me. Hadrick's thunder hammer swinging. Beside him, the missionary clad in crimson and laughing.

The air cracks. The Helbrute falters a single step backward. I rip my shattered leg from beneath its foot and try to rise.

My leg will not move. I close my mind to the pain, but my broken armour will not properly bear my weight. I limp forward. I stumble.

I force myself up from the sand.

'Brother-Castellan!' Hadrick roars.

His hammer smashes against metal and flesh. The Helbrute stumbles backward and my brother descends upon it. The air cracks and splits with peals of thunder as Hadrick pummels the Helbrute. The monster bellows as the air burns with the repeated discharges of Hadrick's weapon. My ears ring. The ground shakes. Something explodes within the tainted machine as Hadrick crushes it piece by piece. My leg screams as I am knocked to the sand by a wave of burning air.

My helmet seals itself against the light and sound of the detonation. My sight and hearing return slowly, a terrible groan over my head. The Helbrute stumbles. A single step, and then another. Flame pours from the monster's mangled chassis. It releases a terrible, keening sound as it topples, crushing its own soldiers beneath its burning form.

'Intact?' I ask over my vox.

At my side, Hadrick pushes himself off the ground. 'Intact,' he replies. As he rises, I see a crimson form sheltered beneath him.

The Missionary Proserpine winces as she stands, leaning heavily upon her cane. She turns slowly towards me, blood streaming from a gash across her forehead.

Beside her, Hadrick leaps atop the downed Helbrute, his hammer a blur as he brings it down upon the beast over and over as if it were an anvil in our forge. Charred metal sprays from the traitor war machine. The beast bellows again. Hadrick's hammer cracks as he shatters the glass casement inlaid in its chest, then one final time as he obliterates the remnants of the heretic Astartes that dwells within.

The machine's screaming falls silent. Its quivering stills.

The Missionary Proserpine steps towards me. All around us, her remaining ecclesiarchs charge forward, cutting into the few cultists that remain before them. In their path, the white walls of the cathedrum rise.

My brothers await behind them.

I take a step forward and stumble. A stream of constant endorphins blunts the pain from my leg, but with both the bone and armour shattered, the limb is little use for ambulation.

A thin stream of blood drips from one of the Missionary Proserpine's ears, and her voice is far too loud when she speaks.

'Come now,' she calls, stepping beside me.

She lifts my hand and sets it upon her fragile shoulder. I take a stumbling step forward with her help. Then another.

When Dravek finds himself, his legs are moving, churning through sand soaked and stained red with blood. Like the sands of the arena in which his primarch once fought.

Arena.

Descended in High Gothic from an ancient word whose very meaning was 'sand'.

Dravek watches his arms flash forward. Watches his Eviscerator tear into the Imperial forces before him. Sees the blades melded with the flesh of his hands slice and bleed the mortals around him.

It is a strange thing to see oneself from the outside. To watch the limbs he once commanded carry on without his orders.

He leaps forward, feels the shiver of meat speared upon one of his blades. The priest before him screams, his dying breath warm and moist against Dravek's face. He feels himself crouch, feels the warmth and the wetness of the human's viscera as his fingers rip into its abdomen.

Then the taste, sickly sweet as he buries his face into the man's open gut and begins to eat.

A strange fate to be a prisoner inside one's own flesh. A strange fate, though he is not alone on that count.

A shadow falls upon Dravek's back as the ground shakes with thundering, charging footsteps. The Carver lifts Dravek's head from his meal, as the daemon engine passes above him. The monstrous machine screams. All the pain and rage that Dravek feels within him, but magnified sevenfold through each of the daemons trapped within it.

The monster lumbers forward, as tall as any of the few buildings which remain in the shrine city. The lashers upon its back thrash wildly, ripping into Imperial forces and the servants of the Blood God alike. It leans its head forward and roars again, liquid fire erupting from its gaping maw.

The Flayed Beast. The Maw. The Burned Man. The Wheel. The Silent Skulls. The Lady of Thorns. For centuries the Neverborn had been his companions, his enemies.

They are all gone now.

As the daemon engine passes, Dravek follows in its wake, his stride taking on a lilting, unnatural gait. The Carver flexes Dravek's fingers, opens and closes his jaw. Passes his tongue over Dravek's sharp, filed teeth.

'To think,' the daemon says, mocking him, 'that you took such a wondrous shell for granted.'

It breathes deeply, the scent of charred flesh and iron reaching Dravek's thoughts. The Carver twists Dravek's feet in the sand, feels it grind beneath him. Dravek feels the corners of his mouth rise in a twisted grin.

'I understand your rage,' the Carver whispers. 'To lose such a gift. But remember that before you lost it, you squandered it. I, however, will not take your body for granted. You will see, with time, that it is better this way for us both.'

'Soulrender!' a voice calls, a figure padding across the rubble and sand. The Heretic Astartes is clad in crimson armour, freshly harvested skulls impaled on spikes upon his pauldrons.

His hands quiver as he stands. His eyes twitch from side to side. Behind his gaze is the mindless madness of the Nails.

'We take losses before the east wall. The knights have cut through to their brethren.'

Dravek tries to reply on instinct, but no words escape his mouth. Instead, the Carver merely stares at his brother. His brother whose name he suddenly cannot remember.

The Heretic Astartes growls with frustration.

'Send your beast to aid us. Things are well in hand here.'

Still nothing in reply.

Dravek guesses the Carver's thoughts.

He is my brother. We have slaughtered together for centuries, Dravek protests. *He is a useful weapon, if nothing else.*

'You have no brothers,' the daemon growls. *'You need no other weapons. Only me.'*

Dravek's Eviscerator flashes forward despite himself. Dark blood gurgles out from the Space Marine's throat as he falls to his knees, staring up at Dravek with raging, red eyes.

And what will you do? Dravek asks in the quiet, unable to form words aloud. *What will you do when my army is squandered? What will you do when you have killed them all? When the only things left on this forsaken world are you and me and the endless sands?*

The Carver forces Dravek to kneel before his dying brother. He reaches out his hand, watches the gore flow across his blades, dripping from one honed edge to another. His tongue flicks out, licks the blood from the steel. Bitter. Salty. Iron.

'Then we will leave,' the daemon replies with Dravek's voice. 'Then we will leave this world and find the next.'

The Carver forces Dravek's body to its feet. As he steps forward,

Dravek throws his will against it. Its stride falters for a moment. Not enough, even, for the daemon to notice, but Dravek feels something like satisfaction, nonetheless.

'We may hold yet, brother,' I say.

Brother-Chaplain Dant turns from the battlements, slowly facing me, silhouetted by the sun.

I grin within my helmet, my hope surging. To see the ancient Astartes stokes my faith.

Dant surveys me slowly, watches me take another limping step towards him. Already my flesh begins to knit itself together. Each movement of my ruined leg is fire, and it will never heal fully without an Apothecary's ministrations, but it holds my weight now, if only just.

'We may,' he replies, his own voice sombre.

I step beside him and survey the battlefield below. Sand and ash drift in great clouds through the ruins of the arcology-shrine. The dead and dying clog the streets like refuse after a storm. The voices of bolters and lasguns and roaring chain-weapons echo up like the sound of waves lapping on the sea. Yet within that madness, there are hints of order. Prongs of crimson-clad forces cutting into the masses of daemons and cultists, separating them, driving them back from the great cathe-drum's walls.

'It is more than I had hoped,' I admit. 'To think that our enemy might be defeated rather than merely wounded.'

A nod from the Chaplain. 'Though the cost will be great.'

I look at my brother again, an unusual gravity lacing his words. There are new urns bound to his armour. Stark black, inscribed with an image of my Chapter's cross.

'How many?' I ask.

'Nineteen,' he says.

The words strike me. Nearly half of my fighting company dead. Brothers I fought beside. Brothers I trained.

'Honourable deaths?' I ask him.

'Most. And three regiments of the Missionary Proserpine's pilgrims.'

I put the mortals from my mind. 'What of their gene-seed?'

'Recovered. In all of the cases where it was recoverable.'

'A blessing,' I reply. 'That their deeds will live on through the new Black Templars they sire.'

'Perhaps,' Dant says, his voice quiet and deliberate. 'Though I have had no word from Alvus in nine hours. If he has joined the dead, then their legacy may be lost.'

I turn my eyes from the city below to my brother. Dant's armour is a ruin of scarred and chipped ceramite. His crozius hangs in his hand, caked with blood and bits of flesh. The strips of parchment bound to his armour have mostly been torn away, leaving hunks of crimson wax on his black ceramite plate.

A pang of guilt grasps me. My time on Tempest has not been easy, but it has been less of a trial than his.

'I have seen your armour this battered in the past, Brother-Chaplain, but never your spirit.'

It is a poor attempt at levity, and Dant does not match it.

'I am tired, Brother-Castellan,' he replies.

My own body aches. My muscles burn with fatigue. My eyes blur. My head throbs. My hearts beat quickly after hours of combat. But this is not what he means. I know my brother that well, at least.

How many times has he stepped through moments such as this? How many brothers has he burned in the span of a thousand years? How much does the weight of those urns bound to him grow with each passing century? With each slaughter he survives? To carry the ashes of his brothers, then those of the

brothers who have taken their gene-seed? How many generations of dead Black Templars has he borne upon his armour?

'We will rest soon,' I promise. 'When Tempest is purged. When
the fleet returns. When Dorea is retaken.'

We both know the words to be a lie as I speak them. There is
no rest for our kind. No rest but that for my brothers in ashes.

He looks at me for a long moment without speaking, then his
hand goes to the rosarius around his neck. Slowly, his fingers
begin to dance around the pendant, his voice falling away into
the murmur of a prayer.

I turn myself towards the stairs to dismount the battlements.
There is battle still beneath, and I still draw breath. As I set my
foot upon the stairs, I feel the cathedrum quiver beneath my boots.

I pause for a moment, then the massive structure shakes again.

The sound of explosions rocks the distance, followed by a
terrible roar. My vox rings alive, a dozen missives flashing upon
my helm viewer. Tempest shudders to its foundations. I turn
back towards the stairs.

As I do, a strong hand grasps my arm.

'Emeric,' Brother-Chaplain Dant tells me. 'I was wrong. I was
wrong all those years ago. Marshal Arold saw your strength from
the start, and I might have seen it too, had I been willing. You
have done well here, whatever comes next. The God-Emperor
could ask no more from you.'

I look towards the Chaplain for a moment, confused, then
turn back towards the raging battle.

The daemon engine blots out the sky. It is a towering, terrible
sacrilege larger than any machine I have ever before witnessed.
As if a void craft had been brought to the surface, then forced
to move upon limbs each the size of an Imperial Knight.

Its massive head thrashes as it screams, spraying fire and

blood through Saint Ofelias' shattered streets, its gnashing maw devouring men and daemons alike. Its tower-limbs crash down upon the shattered skeleton of the city, grinding what little order remains into dust. It pains me to even look upon the abomination, yet I have no choice.

Heretics and ecclesiarchs flee before the abomination as it lumbers towards the Great Cathedrum's walls. That its mad, frenzied slaughter does not discriminate between our forces and our enemies is the only solace I possess.

'Pull your forces back within the cathedrum,' I order the Missionary Proserpine through my vox. The arch-cantors of Saint Ciubrus and Saint Iglese are long dead, and the missionary is the only semblance of leadership remaining within the devoted masses, her zealots almost as fanatical as the mad heretics that we war against. 'Make an attempt to hold the walls and support us how you can.'

At my side, Brother Hadrick gives me a questioning glance.

'There is no purpose in throwing what little strength they still possess into the maw of that monstrosity. We would spend every mortal life on this world without dealing it even a hindering wound.'

'And will we fare better?' he asks.

I have managed to summon a dozen of my knights to this location. A dozen of the twenty that perhaps still live. A dozen of my fiercest, most-hardened warriors against an amalgamation of flesh and steel and the twisted power of the warp.

'We must.'

That is enough conversation. There is nothing else to say. We will stop the beast here, or we will die. There are no other options that remain to us.

I step forward through the ruins on my shattered leg, each step a trial as I climb through broken stone and glass. Barnard has bonded the cracked ceramite around the wounded limb, but it is a hasty repair and offers the wounded flesh minimal support. Hadrick races ahead, my brothers alongside him. Brother-Chaplain Dant follows slowly behind.

'Dant,' I call out. He does not reply. He has not spoken a word since we departed the cathedrum, his eyes fixed upon the sky, his voice mumbling prayers I cannot understand. I motion for him to follow, but he does not. Instead, he picks his way through the broken buildings to the street below.

'Dant!' I cry again, words lost to the howling scream and groaning joints of the abhorrent creation that lumbers towards us. Anger swells in me as he defies my call, but I have no time to think of luxuries like discipline. I scramble up the ruined basilica, leaving the Chaplain to his own path.

I reach the rooftop and find my brothers standing against the skyline, spread already to the buildings around me. I hear their chatter over our shared vox-channel. Feel the fervour and courage in their voices.

There is no grand design to our actions. We have no time for wise stratagems, or even considered plans. As always, our weapon is our rage and our faith.

'If we die here,' I find myself saying, 'I shall be proud.'

My brothers fall silent, awaiting more words, but I have none. They know their duty. I know mine. In the street, the beast approaches, its abhorrent flesh writhing. It is a crude mockery of some animal, treading on four massive legs, bearing a horned head upon a neck of wrought metal like some wyrm of ancient myth. In place of a tail, dozens of dark metal cables snake into the air above the creature, tipped in clawed hands larger than a man that grasp and tear at the dead and the dying as it passes. My vision swims as I gaze too long at the twisting shapes and grotesque gargoyles carved into the monstrous vehicle's form.

The pain in my leg begins to fade, replaced by an even deeper discomfort in my soul. Revulsion grasps me. Anger. Hatred. For such a thing to exist is an affront to the galaxy itself.

'If that beast dies, I shall be even prouder.'

The screams swell, and then the daemon-machine is beside us. I plant my stance and leap from the ruins, swinging Penitence before me in the air.

My weight vanishes for a still, empty moment. Nothing but the ruins behind me and the beast before. A wordless prayer forms in my thoughts, then my blade plunges into the warp-forged metal of the daemon engine.

Penitence bites deep into the monster's hull, carving a tear a yard wide as my weight widens the wound. The power sword shivers in my grasp, the blade protesting as I force it deeper into the unholy beast. Steam and smoke spill from its flesh as I scramble to find purchase upon the creature's flank, the skin upon my neck burning, my tongue coated in the taste of ash and rot. The maglocks on my boots slow me until they finally grip onto a ledge of dark metal secured with rivets of pearl-white bone. My injured leg shivers but holds as it catches my weight.

My auto-senses flicker and die, the runes marking my brothers' positions and status vanishing as my helm's machine spirit retreats within itself. The air around me crackles and twists like the heat above a flame, and the sound of my hearts beating pounds within my ears.

'There will be access ports inlaid upon its hull,' Brother Barnard says, his voice laced with the crackle of interference. 'I have no knowledge of such abominations, but even a warp-spawned machine must be built and ministered to by mortals.'

I stumble forward upon the machine's surface, my steps unsteady, my movements slow. I feel as if a weight rests upon my shoulders.

At the back of my mind, there is a hush, like the whispering of voices.

'No,' I order. 'We will not enter this abhorrence. There will be weaknesses elsewhere. We will find them.'

I climb the sloped surface of the monster's back, my leg fire, the churning groans of warp-forged metal and the screams of the daemon engine vibrating through my limbs, until I reach the top of its spine and stop.

Hundreds of dark forms line the daemon engine here, men and machines in myriad stages of anguish. What I had mistaken at a distance for perverse symbols of Chaotic ruin, I now see are the bodies of hundreds bound to the daemon engine's machine-body. Barbs and spikes fix them to the monster, and dark cannulae pierce their skin, weeping serum and blood.

As I approach, the whispers within my mind grow, my limbs become heavy like lead, my vision dim. I step towards one pitiful heretic slowly. It is a twisted mess of human flesh and metal. Something that might have once been a servant of the Machine Cult before the darkness took it. A soft moan escapes the creature's throat.

The tubes bound to the heretic's skin writhe slowly, carrying the dark flow of crimson blood from the traitor to the beast beneath.

'It was a Techmarine once,' says Barnard's voice beside me. His words are laced with disapproval, but also with curiosity. 'And now it is nothing more than a powercell for its own creation.'

I nod, disgusted, readying my blade.

'Wait,' Barnard says, raising his hand. 'Perhaps it holds some knowledge of the machine we seek to destroy. Or perhaps through this traitor there may be a route to damage the daemon directly, without even piercing its abominable flesh.'

'Barnard,' I warn him, though I do not order him back.

He steps towards the creature and leans in closely, a small probe extracting itself from the mechanical arms upon his back and extending towards the heretic Techmarine until it finds purchase upon some port within its corrupted flesh.

'Barnard,' I call again.

'A moment, Brother-Castellan. Its systems are foreign to me. This may take some time.'

There is silence, then the lumens upon the heretic's armour flash to life. I raise Penitence as the creature lifts its head, though my action comes too late.

A garbled scream escapes the Heretic Astartes' vox-amplifier in the twisted language of machines as its metallic arms grasp my brother and pull him into a wicked embrace. Barnard tries to sever their connection, but he cannot.

Barnard's voice makes a strange, choking sound in my vox as his body begins to convulse.

I bring Penitence down, severing one of the heretic's arms. Sparks and fluid spill out, though its grasp on Barnard holds. My blade shears its other limbs then plunges through the heretic's face. I pull my brother away, but he hangs limp in my arms.

'Barnard,' I call. There is no reply. My auto-senses refuse to commune with the machine spirit of his armour. I see no wounds upon his flesh, though I do not know what has become of his mind.

'Alvus!' I roar. 'Elke!'

I find a pit within my chest as I remember. None have seen my Apothecary nor his apprentice in hours, their vox-links dark and silent since shortly after we surfaced.

Barnard twitches again, his mechanical limbs spasming. Beneath my feet, the daemon shivers and lets out a terrible roar. All around me, the bodies bound to its hull begin to scream.

Their twisted flesh writhes upon spikes and chains, the barbs of the daemon engine holding them tight as they struggle and shake. It is a wretched thing to witness – one which fills me with contempt. My rage grows until it is a living thing within me, one which captures my mind and seizes my limbs.

'To its neck,' I order. 'We will slay this beast or die.'

I lay Barnard down upon the machine's accursed back and charge towards the beast's head as fast as my wounded leg will allow me. Penitence dances in my hand as I pass the wretched heretics, more blood spilling down onto the metal beneath my feet.

Dravek watches the Black Templars crawl like insects across the daemon engine. He watches the ecclesiarchs and cultists both flee the beast below.

The knights' courage is admirable. Their honour. Their devotion to their brothers. There was a time when he could have laid claim to such virtues himself.

He tries to look away as the Carver plunges his face into the flesh of a corpse. Even with his eyes averted, he still feels the warm burst of blood within his mouth. The taste of salt and metal. The scent of burnt and rotting meat.

His throat resists as the flesh slides down it, into a stomach already swollen and gorged.

'Please,' he whispers. Not to the Carver. The daemon which holds him has no grasp of concepts like mercy.

'Please.' Not to the Blood God, who cares not for his weakness. Who, like his servants, has no end to his lust for blood and for bone.

'Please.' Not to the Corpse-Emperor, brittle and dying on his throne thousands of light years away. Too weak to have prevented all this. Too blind to have seen the evil he wrought.

'Please.' Not to anyone who might hear him. Not to the uncaring sands or suns, or the empty swirling void.

And yet, as he watches the dark forms of the Black Templars race across the daemon engine's surface, he finds himself hoping.

My brothers already battle here.

Chainswords and bolters slice and fire into the titanic joints upon the base of the daemon engine's neck, a labour more alike industry than combat. I raise Penitence and bring the blade down into the monster's flesh. The power sword plunges into the dark metal with a groan, oil and blood bubbling up through the wound.

And yet, the beast scarcely notices.

'Brother-Castellan,' Hadrick grumbles, acknowledging my arrival. He hefts his hammer into the air and brings it crashing down upon the warp-forged metal before him. The weapon discharges, a thunderous crack echoing through the air, although even the voice of his hammer feels muted here. The daemon engine's hull buckles beneath Hadrick's blow, bending inward and cracking.

Such a strike should have been enough to tear it wide open.

At my side, Kessalt's chainsword plunges into a rent in the daemon's armour. He grasps at the cables and pipes beneath, ripping whatever he can grasp from within the monster.

I know little of machines, whether sacred or daemonic, yet I fear this is a futile path.

'Inbound, Brother-Castellan.'

Two dark shapes streak towards us above the cathedrum, my last surviving Thunderhawks trailing smoke through the pale sky.

The air flashes as their lasers ignite, followed by the roar of Hellstrike missiles carving through the sky. The salvo splashes against the daemon-machine's armour, smoke and fire spilling out. Then the beast lifts its head and fire erupts from its maw. There is a strangled cry through my vox, and one of my gunships falls to the sand in a charred mess. The other Thunderhawk twists away, struggling to gain altitude as it bleeds fluid and flame.

The beast lumbers forward, turning its attention back to the wall of the cathedrum. Las-fire and krak missiles pour from the weapons mounted to its flanks, and the white marble of the wall shudders and cracks.

'Deeper!' I roar, desperation in my voice.

At my side, Hadrick's hammer crashes down again, widening the wound he has left in the daemon-machine. I drop into the gap, swinging Penitence like a mattock beneath me. Air and fluid spill from the daemon where I strike it, and yet my blade makes little progress.

There is a grunt above me. I raise my eyes in time to see one of the beast's great metal tendrils swing forward and sweep Gormond from its surface. My brother falls to the shattered street below.

Hadrick meets my gaze. He pauses his labour for a moment. There are no words between us. There need not be. This is a doomed endeavour and each of us knows it.

And yet, what other hope do we have?

I drop a grenade within the wound I have created and clamber back onto the beast's hull. When it detonates a few seconds later, the daemon-machine does not so much as flinch.

Another lasher crashes towards us. It descends like a hammer and Fenril crumbles beneath its weight. I watch his shattered body tumble from the abomination, yet I feel nothing. My anger can be stoked no further.

'Deeper!' I roar. 'We will down it!'

My brothers grunt and growl in response, each as blind as me with rage and zeal, yet we know the words to be a lie.

We will die here. Together. And the monster will remain.

The daemon-machine raises its head and bellows towards the sky. Fire pours from its maw. It lifts itself into the air then crashes back upon the cathedrum's great wall, the city shivering beneath its weight. As its front limbs fall upon the cathedrum's wall, there is a terrible crack. The walls of the temple splinter beneath it.

There is smoke and then tumult, as the cathedrum's mortal defenders flee. The beast steps over the rubble, then pauses.

'Stop.'

I hear the voice echo above the din of battle.

'No further,' it orders, resolute.

The daemon takes another lumbering step forward, then halts. A single black figure stands in its path.

Brother-Chaplain Dant waits alone in the courtyard of the Cathedrum of the Martyr, a speck of black against the great church's white floor. Slowly, the Chaplain walks towards the daemon engine, his crozius held before him, chanting quietly beneath his breath.

The accursed monstrosity stares at my brother. For a moment it stills, then its towering form begins to shiver. From its maw, the rumble of terrible laughter emerges – the voices of the daemons imprisoned within layered over one another in an unearthly chord. My ears and my soul burn with the sound of their words.

'We were here before your arrogant species was born, human. We are the source of the nightmares that you hold in the dark. We are the silent echo that haunted your kind when you still dug up roots and fodder with your claws. Who are you to dare oppose us now?'

My skull vibrates with the daemon's voice, my skin crawling and cold. I shake my head, forcing my limbs to move. They are slow as I drive Penitence deeper into the beast, as my brothers and I carve a rent into its otherworldly flesh. The tear in its armour grows slowly with our labour.

'No one,' Brother-Chaplain Dant calls in reply. He leans upon the crozius before him as if his body might fail at any moment, but there is no frailty in the Chaplain's words.

The daemon growls, already past its amusement. It slides its head forward across the sand towards the Chaplain, endless rows of razored teeth descending towards the Space Marine. Its jaws close around Dant, before snapping open once more with a terrible shriek.

The daemon engine stumbles back, nearly throwing me from its neck. For his part, Brother-Chaplain Dant has not moved an inch. In his hands, his crozius glows dimly.

'I am no one,' he repeats, his voice rising in volume. It echoes in my head, wildly strong. 'And yet you know the one I serve.'

The ancient Space Marine takes a single step forward. The daemon hisses with seven voices, pacing before the tiny man.

'He is the light that blinds you there in the darkness. He is the hunter that pursues your dreams. You think yourself a nightmare to behold, but even a petty evil such as you feels fear.'

Dant steps forward again, his crozius blazing. Around the Chaplain himself, a thin shimmer of gold suffuses the air.

'You claim yourself ancient, yet you are a child before Him. You think yourself terrible, yet you cower before His light. You claim yourself king of this little world, but even the master you serve bows before His Throne.'

Dant's voice has risen to a fever pitch now, every word pounding like a hammer in my skull. The daemon-machine gnashes its jaws, as if it fears to swallow my brother within them.

'Down!' I roar to my brothers atop the monster's neck. 'Deeper!'

Dant's faith has bought us time, though no miracle can last forever. I lose sight of him as I burrow further into the machine, oil and fluid welling up around my feet.

'You think my kind weak,' Dant calls. 'And rightly so. I am

nothing before you, just as you are nothing before Him. But you have set yourself against Him, not me. You have challenged the will of the one who cannot be surmounted. He will place you beneath His foot like a worm. He will crush you again and again for eternity. You have lived without fear for aeons uncounted, but now you will know it until the end of time.'

The daemon's head lurches forward. The cables and pistons within the wound around me twist like serpents. Static crackles in my ear.

'–Castellan. Inbou–'

I look up towards the grey sky above. A dark streak crashes down towards me.

'Move!' I order my brothers. 'Clear the gap!'

Those of us who are able spill from the wound within the daemon-machine as my last Thunderhawk tears down from the sky. It empties its remaining armaments into the rent we have left, flame and smoke spewing from the daemon-machine's hull. I stumble as the beast's head lurches forward, its jaws closing around Brother-Chaplain Dant. The Chaplain's words swallow the world around me as he bellows.

'The Emperor–'

But even Dant's voice vanishes as my Thunderhawk crashes into the daemon-machine, the air burning as I am thrown from the beast like flotsam upon a wave. I tumble across its hull, great gouts of fire splitting its surface as the Thunderhawk's fusion reactor explodes within its flesh.

The daemon beneath me screams, its metal skin boiling. It rears into the air like an animal speared through the heart. The air cracks and blazes as the beast collapses to the earth.

Atop the Chaplain.

Atop the cathedrum.

Both crack beneath its unthinkable weight.

For a moment there is nothing but the sound of screaming. Then of stone shattering as the cathedrum falls.

Chapter 12

I kneel in the sands beneath the monster, shaking with rage, and with loss, and with sorrow. I have not shed a tear in over three hundred years, and for the first time I resent that I am no longer able.

Dant's crozius hangs limply in my hand, still bright and gleaming in a sea of ash. The daemon engine's shell is still before me, its turbines and smokestacks silent, its hull torn and charred, the thousand corpses bound to its side burned to ash carried upon the quiet wind.

I have searched for the better part of an hour, and of my Chaplain, this is the only sign. Only the mark of his station remains, but there is no remnant of the man himself, nor of the ashes of my brothers that he carried upon him.

In the sands behind me, my surviving knights gather. Hadrick. Kessalt. Umter. Sturn. Four brothers of the forty that I brought to this world. Four brothers that I have not led to their deaths.

And for what? The Cathedrum of the Martyr lies in ruins around me. Despite its death, the Soulrender's daemon-machine has succeeded in defiling even this most sacred place. Not even Dant's sacrifice could prevent that.

Not even his faith.

The cathedrum's great walls lie shattered before me. Why our enemy has not already charged through the breach, I cannot say. Though it seems the daemon's death has stalled them for the moment.

I should rise.

I should rise from my knees and turn to my brothers.

I should raise Dant's crozius over my head and proclaim to the mortals that gather around us that his glorious death is an inspiration to us all. That with faith like his, we will conquer our enemy, and reclaim this world, and earn the God-Emperor's favour.

And yet I kneel. I have no strength left for such lies.

My ears ring with the sound of the wind around me. With the absence of my brother's voice. With the sound of slow, shuffling footsteps approaching through the sand.

'You loved him greatly.'

The Missionary Proserpine's voice grates against my ears. With a small groan of discomfort, she kneels down beside me. Her cane has vanished, and the movement pains her, but she does not complain as she joins me in the sand.

It is fitting, perhaps, that she should be the one to kneel beside me. That my emotion is matched only by that of a simple human. There is a reason my brothers keep their distance from my weakness. Perhaps Hadrick is right. Perhaps I am too much like them.

'I did,' I reply. There is nothing else to say.

The missionary kneels in silence beside me for some time before she rests a hand gently upon my armour.

'We will mourn him alongside you when the battle is over, Lord Castellan.'

'When it is over?' I reply. 'What do you think this moment is, if not the end? The Great Cathedrum is destroyed. Its walls are breached and its stones defiled. We stand bloodied and shattered here within its ruins. Our enemy has achieved his aims and we have no strength left to resist him. What purpose remains to our cause, missionary?'

'My lord. You are the God-Emperor's sons. His holy angels. There can be no doubt in the strength of your cause.'

I am silent for some time before a bitter laugh comes unbidden to my throat.

'Tell me, priest – what kind of son has never heard the voice of his father? What kind of angel cannot picture the face of his god? I am a man, missionary. A man ordered to become something more, but I fear my soul is not equal to the task. I have waited for this moment of sacrifice for centuries, but now that it arrives, it tastes as nothing more than ash in my mouth.

'I fear, missionary, that I have lost my faith.'

'Faith?' she asks. It is the mortal's turn to scoff. 'What is faith, my lord? You must have had it once in order to misplace it, and you cannot lose something that does not exist. I have been a priest of the God-Emperor for almost a hundred years, and I must confess that I have never seen it. What is faith but bold action when others dare not? What is faith but sacrifice when others have nothing left to give? This is all that the God-Emperor demands, my lord. And such a thing cannot be lost.'

I look up and meet the mortal's gaze, shame rushing in to wash away my sorrow. I should be the one speaking words of inspiration to her. I should be the one urging her forward rather than holding her back.

'We will die here,' I rumble. 'Not a single fortress remains to defend. Not a single patch of consecrated ground to protect.'

'There is one,' the missionary says. Her face is badly bruised, her jaw swollen and her tongue dry and cracked. And yet her voice rings pure above the approaching storm. 'We left it in the sands when we crashed upon this world.'

For a moment something glimmers within me, then retreats. Hope, perhaps, if I did not know better.

'My lord,' she continues. 'Its walls were built to withstand the void itself. Its halls are filled with the sacred relics of a hundred worlds. What stronger fortress could there be? What holier ground upon which to die?'

'And your pilgrims?' I ask. 'Most can scarcely walk let alone fight a retreat.'

'Those who can follow will,' she replies, steel in her battered voice. 'Those who cannot will die. Just as they would if we stayed.'

I stare at the missionary. Frail and blind, kneeling in the sands beside me. Her fragile flesh is bruised and broken, yet her spirit is strong enough to carry my own. Weak, Hadrick had called her. And even though I had reproached him, I had not disagreed.

I look up for the first time in an hour. Dust swirls through the air around the Cathedrum of the Martyr, a great wall of wind and sand and ash. A storm rises about us like a shield. One final miracle from my brother.

'We will die here,' I tell the mortal, though there is no bitterness in the statement any longer. 'And it will be my honour to die at your side.'

I rise to my feet, Dant's crozius hanging loosely from my grasp. The Missionary Proserpine struggles to stand alongside me, until I press the weapon into her hands.

'My lord,' she stammers. 'I could not. I have earned no such honour.'

'Have faith,' I command her. 'You will.'

I turn from the daemon engine and towards my brothers.

'We depart,' I tell them.

Hadrick nods. 'To where?'

I turn towards the open gap in the cathedrum walls. Towards the raging storm and the endless sands.

'To the only holy ground that remains on this forsaken world. To the *Dauntless Honour*.'

The Cathedrum of the Martyr smoulders before him. Its walls are shattered. Its golden domes toppled. His mortal horde spills over the ruined walls, liberating the space from the taint of the Cult Imperialis.

Nearly a year. Dravek Soulrender has spent nearly a year on this desiccated, desert world and his victory has almost been realised. At great cost, but realised nonetheless.

And yet, he feels nothing like satisfaction.

More! the daemon within him cries, nothing but blind rage remaining of the Carver's typical reason.

The daemon drives Dravek's body forward, tearing into the flesh of the dead around him. Filling his already-bloated stomach to bursting.

Dravek had hoped that the death of the daemon engine might slow him. Might force him to still his hunger and use his mind, yet it has not. The daemon rampages even stronger within him, a mindless hunger his only driving force.

More!

Dravek watches his hands rip into the flesh of a pale human corpse, his fingers shredding muscle and sinew as they race to force the meat into his dripping mouth.

He raises his head to the sky and laughs with the daemon's voice. A mad laugh. A mindless laugh. As the daemon laughs, Dravek inches his will forward. Just a nudge. Not enough to be noticed, but enough to move his limbs.

His body steps forward towards the cathedrum.

The Carver laughs but does not resist him.

Another step. A few feet closer.

Before Dravek, his horde crawls over the shattered walls. Over the titanic shell of the daemon engine that lies upon them. And yet, not a single Neverborn has joined in their number. Not a single one of his warp-born army dares venture near the site where the Black Templars and their Chaplain unmade the seven daemons imprisoned within the great machine.

All around him, the sky rages. Sand whipping in a swirling wall about the fallen cathedrum. Even here, near the eye of the cyclone, Dravek feels those winds pull at his armour. Sees the lightning crack through the billowing clouds of sand about him. Feels the peals of thunder shake the air like explosions. All raging around a single eye. Around the scar that the daemon engine's death left upon the warp.

Dravek takes another step forward. The Carver feels him now. *Stop*, the daemon orders.

The weight of its will crashes down upon Dravek's flesh. He totters for a moment then throws his mind against the daemon. His leg hangs in the air, then falls slowly to the ground.

Another stumbling step.

'Stop!' the daemon bellows. Dravek hears the words stream from his mouth, but he does not heed them.

Another step.

Lancing pain behind his eyes. Blinding. Deafening. And utterly useless. Because he feels it now. The hole in the warp that the Chaplain left behind. The gleaming, burning, golden light that still rages in the empyrean there.

And he senses the Carver's utter fear of it.

'You fool!' the Carver roars. *'You bloody fool!'*

There is less force in the rebuke now. The daemon strikes at him again, but the pain is lessened.

Dravek is walking now, then running, then sprinting towards the cathedrum as the daemon howls.

I am a fool, Dravek admits. *A fool to have forgotten what you are to me.*

The daemon screams through his mouth, but Dravek shuts it. The daemon's voice falls silent, present only in his mind. The Carver's will is scarcely there now. Dravek charges forward and stands before the toppled daemon engine.

Please! the Carver whimpers. *No closer.*

Dravek walks to the beast's head, feet churning through the blood-soaked sand, until he stands before the engine's maw. He sets his hand against the dark metal of its form.

The Carver screams. A pitiful, mewling, strangled sound. Dravek feels the daemon retreat, press backward in his mind, but Dravek does not allow it. For a moment, the daemon attempts to flee him altogether, but Dravek's will holds the Carver fast.

'I had forgotten,' Dravek whispers. 'What you are. And I was a fool to allow you to forget as well. You did not bind me to you within the eightcage. You did not make me your slave. I made you mine. A galaxy of blood and of bone and of fire. That was the promise. That was the compact between us. Endless war. Your strength lent to me, and not the reverse. Whether there are eight of you or only one within me. And I demand what I am owed.'

Dravek grins at the sound of the daemon's discomfort, but as he opens his mouth, the laugh that escapes it is not his own. The Carver chortles with amusement, and suddenly the weight of the daemon's will crashes back upon him. The scrap of freedom he had felt vanishes as quickly as it had materialised.

'What you are owed?' the daemon asks him through his own mouth. *'What you demand?'*

Blood and flesh spray from his teeth as the Carver laughs

through his throat. Dravek tries to push his will forward again but the Carver slaps it back, his body once again fully under the daemon's control. Dravek's hope vanishes like sand on the wind.

'Come now, Soulrender. You did not think I was so simple? You did not think I would so easily abandon a prize I had worked so hard to acquire? Surely you know me better than that after all of this time. Surely you understand that petty miracles and the corpses of charlatans mean nothing to me. You are mine, Soulrender, as you have always been. Do not misplace your faith in anything else.'

The Carver opens Dravek's mouth and spits upon the daemon engine's warp-forged metal, then turns his body towards the heart of the ruined cathedrum.

White sand swirls through the air around me, an endless cloud of gleaming shards floating like stars in the heavens above. Grains flit between the gaps of my armour, finding the joints in my ceramite plate. They grind and groan with each movement, small streaks of white appearing on the low points in my armour where the grains gather.

I taste the salt even through my respirator.

It is no easy thing to limp on my shattered leg through the storm, and yet the mortals around me press onward. A few dozen yards behind me, the Missionary Proserpine staggers. I can hardly see her frail form through the sands, though the figure behind her is easier to make out. Hadrick walks on the windward side of the missionary, shielding her from the storm as much as he is able. Even with his aid she leans heavily upon Dant's crozius, using the holy relic as a crutch. There was a time, not long ago, that such sacrilege would have moved me to violence, yet now I simply find myself grateful that she still moves among us. Her cloak is wrapped about her head and neck, but as the crimson fabric flits in the wind, I see patches of raw, angry flesh where her skin has been stripped by the detritus of the storm.

Our mortal companions stretch in a ragged line behind us. Priests draped in dusty red. Serfs in black and grey and white – the garb of my Chapter. Refugees from the city clad in tattered rags, foolish enough to join us as we departed.

The relics we carried with us when we left our ship weeks ago have long since vanished. We carry nothing but our weapons and our wounds, now. Many have dropped with exhaustion or succumbed to their injuries since we left the shelter of the Great Cathedrum's ruins. Others have been lost to the desert in the blinding storm. Some have simply lost the will to continue, sitting down in the white sands until they are covered.

I have not the strength myself to rouse them.

I limp forward into the wind, Penitence hanging in my hand. For the first time since we landed, my blade gleams, the blowing storm grinding away the blood and soot upon it and on the devotional chain that binds it to my wrist.

Two hundred years. Two hundred years since those links were first fused around my wrist. Two hundred years since the relic sword was bound to me like the oath I swore to Marshal Arold. Two hundred years and twice as many battles, and its links have never been broken.

Soon, I will break my oath.

I will not save the Dorean Crusade. Neither the first nor the second. I will die here in the desert beside my brothers, and Tempest will swallow me whole.

There is sorrow at that thought, though it no longer stings as it once did. Perhaps Dant was right all of those centuries ago. Perhaps an orphan cowering in the ruins of a Ministorum chapel did not deserve to wear this armour. Did not deserve to bear this sword. Did not deserve to lead these angels.

Yet here I am. I have done what I am able. May the God-Emperor forgive me for my failures.

I drive forward into the wind, towards the shadow looming in the distance. The *Dauntless Honour* comes into clarity as I approach, the vessel half-buried already in the raging sands. Soon, the desert will cover it completely, and my bones within.

I can think of no holier place to be interred.

I say one final prayer as I approach its hull, its doors sealed and locked when we departed. There are enough wounds and rents within the vessel's hull for me to scale its walls and find my way inside, yet I doubt the mortals behind me could manage the same. I ask for one last miracle upon this world, though I do not pretend that I am worthy of one.

'Open,' I order, setting my hand upon the door.

I am answered only by the wind and the sand as I stand within the raging storm.

Cogitator epsilon ninety-seven of peripheral node 16.903.11 cycles softly in the silence aboard the *Dauntless Honour*. For centuries, the machine has been tasked with compiling and refining vox signals and auspex inputs from one of the ancient ship's myriad sensory towers, then routing its analyses to the vessel's void loom.

High-frequency auditory impulses stream into one of the spire's internal vox-receivers at a remarkably regular pattern. Rapid analysis estimates that this sound corresponds to fluid dripping from a leaking pipe. A dull, whining groan rises and falls in amplitude in the background, the sound's intensity matching proximity impulses from a tracked servitor slowly circling upon the deck.

Deep, undulating vibrations shake the sensory tower itself with gradually rising intensity, matching amplitude fluctuations in the sound of wind on the spire's few remaining functional external vox-receivers.

Wind, and grating sand, and a voice cutting beneath it.

[Open.]

Auditory analysis protocols immediately flag the signal as speech. Routine algorithms filter background noise from the waveform and confirm each individual phoneme.

Speech. A command. From a voice matching the pitch and cadence of a member of the Adeptus Astartes.

Epsilon ninety-seven transmits the signal to the *Dauntless Honour*'s void loom at priority seven while it begins further analysis.

Visual circuits attempt to activate the pict-viewer paired with the vox-transmitter that registered the signal, but the image it returns is nothing more than a grainy smudge. Triangulation routines recruit a second vox-receiver several hundred feet inside the vessel's hull.

Protocolised filters remove the sound of the ship's frame groaning and of the servitor's motors whirring in the darkness, then compare timestamps between the two vox-receivers.

[Open.]

A depletion warning enters epsilon ninety-seven's active memory as the cogitator draws additional current from its small local power bank.

[Open.]

Frequency. Pacing. Pronunciation. Scavenger routines compare the voice to the samples stored within the cogitator's local archive. Most similar in pattern to the voice of Castellan Emeric.

Another protocol engages. Another transmission to the void loom. Priority nine.

There is no reply.

Data speeds through decision loops with indeterminate outcomes.

The cogitator possesses no specific directives for this situation, other than to escalate its transmissions further.

Another signal to the void loom. Priority twelve.

Nothing.

The Castellan's voice rings out again.

[Open.]

Deviations in pitch and intensity from baseline waveforms. Anger. Desperation. Exhaustion.

Priority fifteen.

No confirmation.

Input from both vox-receivers. A sharp, repeated clanging. A hand, in armour, striking the hull repeatedly.

Light transmitted from the pict-viewer. Intense light with wavelengths matching those created by plasma weapon discharge, then the vox against the hull falls silent.

Footsteps in the corridor. Footsteps of Astartes and of humans in sizeable numbers. Then voices, too many to identify.

Priority twenty.

No response from the void loom. The cogitator whirrs, its algorithms exceeded. No further escalatory levels remain, yet its protocols demand an alternate mode of transmission. Epsilon ninety-seven wakes the single augur mounted atop its sensory tower.

The cogitator draws all remaining power from its local bank, routing the single word, and its accompanying analysis data, up through the tower and out into the sand.

Priority twenty.

The message blares across Tempest's surface for a blinding moment before the last surviving machine component of the *Dauntless Honour* falls quiet.

[Open.]

* * *

The Reclusiam is dark and silent, my helm lumen the only light within the sacred space. Gone is the soft, blue glow of torch lamps illuminating our most precious relics. Gone is the dull hum of stasis field generators keeping them shielded from the ravages of time and decay.

It is a little sacrilege. One of many I have tolerated since landing on this world.

I walk through the chamber in silence, humbled as always beneath the exploits of my betters. Jubein, the first Castellan to command this vessel, his power axe enshrined alongside his helm, both pierced and bound together by the xenos spear that slew him during the cleansing of Idrium. Gustrod, the Chaplain that served this ship during the first moments of the Indomitus Crusade.

Kiever, my predecessor as Castellan of this fighting company. A glorious warrior. I remember the day he died, not fifty yards from me, charging a formation of faithless heretics alone, his bolter spewing judgement as he faced them. The weapon was the only relic recoverable, charred and warped from the heat of the flames that swallowed him, but his fervour carried him far enough to silence those guns. Each member of this fighting company stepped over his corpse as we entered our enemy's citadel and razed it to the ground.

Baelar, my brother. My Neophyte, once. His helm alone atop a small plinth, the claw of a xenos still lodged through one eyepiece.

Footfalls rise behind me on the metal floor.

Hadrick faces me there in the darkness, his helm cradled beneath one arm. His face is hard and weathered. His eyes are tired and full of rage. He reminds me of Baelar, and of Juerten, and of Marshal Laise. And half the other Initiates I once fostered.

In his other hand he holds Brother-Chaplain Dant's crozius. He extends it towards me.

'The Missionary Proserpine has asked that I return this relic.'
For a moment I am offended.

'It was a noble gesture,' he continues. 'One Dant himself
would have approved of. She bore the weapon with pride from
Saint Ofelias to these doors, but she could scarcely walk beneath
its weight, let alone fight, Brother-Castellan.'

'Of course,' I reply, stepping to the side. He places the weapon
upon an empty plinth then turns back towards the door. Our
enemy approaches, and I no longer doubt the outcome. I may
not see my brother again alive.

'You must think me a failure, Hadrick,' I say.

He stops and looks at me for a long while in silence. 'You
must think me an arrogant, tactless fool.'

A small chuckle escapes me. I do not deny it. Nor does he.

'You would have been a Sword Brother one day. Perhaps a
Castellan. If not for this place.'

'Perhaps,' he replies. 'Though I do not believe I have the
wisdom nor the… patience required for such a station.'

Both an insult and praise together. It is fitting from him. I
might have thought the same when I was younger. It might
have been true.

Another silence.

'I long believed that one day I would find my place within this
hall,' I tell him. 'That once I died, my memory would remain
here with my brothers. Not quite the immortality that I believed
in when I was still human, but more fitting, more precious, in
its own way. More desirable to me.'

'And now?'

'And now, I will die, unwitnessed, in the sand. That does
not pain me as it once did. Save the honour for Baelar and
for Juerten and for Marshal Laise. For Cuthbord, Romer, and
Kalphon, and all the other Neophytes I once trained.'

Hadrick nods slowly.

'For those who succeed us to surpass us, Brother-Castellan. I can think of no greater honour than that.'

'You claim you lack wisdom, Hadrick. But come now, brother, humility does not fit you well.'

There is a hint of a smile upon Hadrick's face, before it settles back into stone.

'Our enemy approaches,' I tell him. 'Prepare for your death however you think best. We have no Chaplain left to minister to our souls. We have no Apothecary to treat our wounds. There is no ground left to retreat any further. There are no grand stratagems remaining to deploy. We will stand here, at these walls, and weaken our enemy as much as the God-Emperor allows before we ourselves are slain.

'For my part, I will pray here, while I am still able, and ask for forgiveness. And for a good death.'

One final, bitter chuckle from my brother.

'A good death? We have both seen enough war to know that no such thing exists.'

I nod. He is not wrong. As always.

'Very well, then. A death of which we might not be ashamed.'

For a moment, Hadrick's footsteps echo upon the deck, then it is silent and dark in the Reclusiam again.

There is nothing left.

Liesl places her hands upon a dying man, trying to staunch the slow bleeding from the ragged wound upon his head. The skin of his chest and back is covered with burns, the flesh both charred and pale from where some infernal weapon seared down through blood vessels. Fluid weeps from the leathery skin, his forehead sweaty and warm, infection laying hold upon him.

That he made it from the shattered walls of the Great Cathedrum of Saint Ofelias back to the *Dauntless Honour*, even with the assistance of his compatriots, is miracle enough.

And now he will die here.

These are simple enough maladies to treat if she had the tools. Needles, or suture, or even a cautery wand for the gouge upon his scalp, but she broke her last needle well before they left Saint Ofelias, and the powercell on her cautery wand has long since run dead. Counterseptic for the infection, but there is none left to be had.

She visited the apothecarion as soon as they returned to the ship. A few crates of bandages. A few jars of ointments and blessed salves. The scrapings that they had not been able to carry with them when they first departed the void craft, now rotting in the dripping, scorching darkness as the *Dauntless Honour* leaks and bakes in the sands.

There was space there in the apothecarion. A vast hall of stretchers and plinths. Of surgeries and operatories to conduct her work. And yet she had no tools with which to complete them. No assistants to stand beside her. No chirurgeon to guide her. No other menials to even bring the wounded to such a place.

Nothing left. Nothing left save her hands and the cries of the dying.

The man looks up at her with fevered, sluggish eyes, red-rimmed and weeping from the sands and the suns. His brown skin is ashen and pale. He shivers slightly even in the heat.

'Ma-Math-Mathilus,' he murmurs. Over and over between cracked, bone-dry lips.

A name, perhaps? A prayer to some saint? A dying cry for his father or his mother or a sibling? A companion he fought beside and now seeks after? She does not know, nor does she wish to. If he calls for some friend that he knew on this world, it is likely that she passed their corpse in the sand.

'Quiet,' Liesl whispers, setting her palm against the man's sweat-slicked forehead. 'You will see them soon.'

She rises to her feet, watching dark blood ooze fresh from the wound as she lifts her hand. She shakes her head to the grim-faced priest following in her wake.

'Give him your rituals now, while he is able to receive them. I can do nothing for him. Come, father,' she calls to her servitor. Its wheels churn slowly in response, one of its tracks broken and lying somewhere in the desert. One of its multi-arms hangs lifeless at its side, its joints clogged completely with sand. And yet it struggles on, as does she.

Liesl passes through a low doorway, locked open in the silent, powerless ship, and into a larger, broader corridor. Here, crimson-robed ecclesiarchs and tatter-dressed pilgrims make ready for battle against the horde that approaches. Every viewport, aperture, and gaping wound in the *Dauntless Honour*'s hull has been forced or cut open. Every weapon they lugged across the desert – and those which remained aboard the ship – are all levelled towards the sands outside.

There is a hum of excitement as their remaining army works. A finality to this.

There will be no further movement or retreat. They will either secure victory here, or die, and Liesl fears she knows which. There are rumours that the Astartes still walk among them, but Liesl has not seen one since the day the Lord Apothecary died.

What can mortals hope to accomplish alone against such an enemy?

Quickly, she passes along the milling ranks, watching a young woman dressed in the pilgrim's brown wince as she drags an autocannon across the metal deck with the assistance of a companion.

Her hair is dusty and dishevelled, her face raw from the sun and the sand. Burns and abrasions cover her arms, two of the fingers of her left hand mangled and crushed.

Liesl fumbles in her waist pouch as she approaches the pilgrims, sorting through the last of her medicaments. She pulls two small tablets from a glass vial and hands them to the woman.

'For your hand,' she says. 'For the pain.'

The woman turns her head and spits to the side. 'I don't need them. Save them for the dying.'

Liesl grabs the woman's injured fingers. The pilgrim winces and nearly drops the weapon she is dragging. Liesl presses the analgesics into her palm.

'The dying do not need them. The dying cannot fight.'

The woman eyes her, then nods, placing the tablets into her mouth. Liesl watches her pupils dilate slightly, hears a sigh escape her throat.

She nods and turns away before a dark shape in the corridor stops her. Liesl drops to her knees before the Astartes.

'Lord Castellan,' she mumbles.

The angel takes another step towards her, a slight irregularity in his stride. A slight weakness in one of his legs. She raises her eyes and sees the shattered plate of the armour. There is a wound beneath it that has not yet healed.

The Astartes steps around her, then pauses.

'Rise,' he orders.

The Lord Castellan's armour is battered, but his voice still carries a terrible weight. Liesl rises to her feet and lifts her eyes to meet the glowing gaze of his black helm.

Slowly, the Space Marine surveys her then the servitor that stands at her side. He looks at the bioscanner tied to her waistband and the tools affixed to her father's limbs.

'You are a chirurgeon?' he asks.

She nods. Menial. Chirurgeon. There is no difference now, is there? She uses a chirurgeon's tools. Her hands are covered in blood, just the same. For all she knows, she may be the only servant of the apothecarion still alive aboard this vessel.

'One of Brother-Apothecary Alvus' acolytes?'

'I am,' she replies. 'I was.'

A memory of the Lord Apothecary's shattered corpse flashes unbidden to her mind. Her eyes fall to the skin of her blood-stained hands. How much of that blood belonged to the Astartes? Can the angel before her recognise it beneath the rest that stains her skin? She reaches her hand into the pouch at her waist, then pauses as the Lord Castellan speaks again.

'You were there when he died.' A statement, not a question. Liesl feels a creeping fear begin to grow within her. She removes her hand, empty, from the pouch. It is better, perhaps, to leave some things hidden.

'I was, my lord.' She does not elaborate. Even now, she can feel the warmth of the Lord Apothecary's flesh. The shuddering, then stillness, of his twin hearts as they flickered and failed.

'What is your name?'

'Liesl, if it pleases you, Lord Castellan.'

The Astartes stares at her for some time, then nods slowly. 'I will remember your name, Liesl, for as long as I am able. Liesl, who stood beside my brother when I could not.'

She feels her mouth grow dry and her skin flush warm. She nods and looks away. In that silence, her ears catch a dull roaring from outside.

'Rise,' the Lord Castellan orders to the kneeling mortals around him. His eyes drift to the open doorway, where blowing sands rage and the sound of the wind only grows. 'Our enemy approaches,' the angel calls. 'And we shall meet them here one final time. Gird yourselves for battle once again. For battle, and for death, for there shall be no further lines of retreat. In the past we have fought as servants and masters. Today, we die as brothers and sisters.'

The Lord Castellan's words tear through the empty corridors, echoing from the bare metal walls, stinging her ears and shaking her bones. In the distance, a voice calls out among the defenders.

'For the God-Emperor!'

'For Dorn!' Liesl finds herself roaring.

'For Dant!' the Lord Castellan calls in reply. The mortals pause again to stare at the angel.

'For Dant,' he repeats. 'And for Alvus and Barnard. And ten thousand other heroes dead upon this world whose names I do not know. We die today, in the God-Emperor's name, but our deaths are not for Him alone. Go. Be brave. Die for your Emperor and your crusade and the brothers around you. It will be an honour to fall at your side.'

The cries that answer the angel are too numerous and loud to decipher. Priests and pilgrims heft weapons and press them against the openings in the hull, their voices mingled with the sounds of cycling actions and the groaning wind.

Slowly, another roar rises above their voices, and Liesl sees the heretics approaching through the storm.

Chapter 13

Fire blazes from the corpse of the Black Templars vessel as Dravek Soulrender charges across the desert. The air around him burns with las-fire, the solid slugs of autocannons splashing upon the endless sands. Great gouts of blood and flame burst into the air as the vessel's void weapons are brought to bear against his enclosing horde.

And like water, the wave re-forms again and washes over the cowering Imperials.

The Carver bellows a wordless, formless roar through Dravek's mouth as he closes the last few strides to the waiting hull. The dull burn of a las-bolt rips at his armour in one of the many places the sands and time have left his flesh exposed. The Carver laughs in reply and leaps into an open doorway, smashing a cowering mortal beneath Dravek's weight.

'Death!' he bellows into the small space. *'Blood! Fire!'*

Dravek watches as his Eviscerator flashes, ripping limbs from mortal bodies, severing heads from their necks. A dozen humans lie dead or dying at his feet before the rest even recognise that he is among them.

He feels the thud of a maul fall against his armour, and his hand snatches the weapon from its wielder's grasp. The priest stumbles back as he turns, terror in his eyes. His lips move in silent prayer as Dravek skewers him upon the blades which sprout from his arms.

'Pray!' the Carver roars. *'Pray to your corpse-god. Beg to your saints. Cower like children before your symbols and your relics. He cares no more for your death than he did for your pitiful lives.'*

A staccato drumbeat pounds against Dravek's back. His body wheels towards an autocannon firing down a corridor towards him. He tears through the press of crowded peasants and priests, his Eviscerator carving a bloody path to the weapon. The man who wields it wears the black-trimmed tunic of a Black Templars serf. His face is contorted in a mask of disgust and of faith.

'Come now.' The Carver chuckles as he forces Dravek into the fusillade. The metal rounds bury themselves in his ceramite plate and his flesh, but Dravek feels little of either. The usual fugue of battle has been replaced by an odd clarity as he watches the Carver use his body like a puppet, powerless to do anything but observe. The daemon's power flows through his flesh in a steady trickle. Like poisoned water to a man dying of thirst. Bitter. Cold. But irresistible.

'Come now,' the Carver chides again, letting Dravek's voice spill into his own. The air around him ripples. His Eviscerator descends, and the barrel falls from the autocannon.

There is fear now in the serf's expression. Better. Better than disgust. Better than pity. The man continues to pull the trigger of his disabled weapon, and opens his mouth.

'For the–'

A gurgle of blood and foam follows the words, and Dravek finds one of his blades skewering the serf's pale throat.

The Carver appears at his side, his lank, pale form astride the gurgling human. The Neverborn grins mindlessly.

I will not be caged like an animal, Dravek protests.

The daemon lowers Dravek's mouth towards the dying man, sinking his teeth into the human's flesh. Dravek's blades glimmer in the shadows, slick with oil and blood. He tries to force his limbs to move. The Neverborn spits.

'Then do not behave like one.'

The daemon turns from the man, pulling Dravek with him and back to the defenders inside the hull. A small circle forms behind him, raised pikes and spears and clubs improvised from steel rods.

'You are a rabble,' the Carver tells them. *'Armed like children with sticks and rocks.'* Dravek's Eviscerator roars. The points fall from a dozen weapons. He steps forward and breaks their hafts with a swing of his arm.

Some of the wielders step backward, others stab at him with the jagged stumps they still hold.

The Carver laughs for a moment, then a fire strikes Dravek's chest. Flame licks across his face, sears his flesh, fills his eyes. Then vanishes, replaced by a priest holding a flamer.

'And our faith, heretic. We are armed by that too.'

For a moment, the scent of burning meat fills Dravek's nose. His own flesh burning. The sound of his skin sizzling and boiling. There is pain beneath those. Pain he once might have found distracting. But he has suffered so much worse each moment he exists.

A thin, bitter laugh escapes his throat. The Carver vanishes beside him.

The daemon pushes him forward into the fire and grasps the priest's flamer. A moment later, the man screams as his own robes ignite.

'Why yes,' the Carver whispers as Dravek steps over the writhing man's charred form and drops his flamer to the floor. *'I suppose you have that, too.'*

* * *

My arms ache. My lungs burn. My soul staggers beneath the weight of the dead around me.

Piles of bleeding flesh crowd the narrow corridor against the *Dauntless Honour*'s hull, the corpses of the righteous and the heretic intermingled in a heap beneath my feet. Each time I swing my sacred power sword, another corpse adds to that grisly mosaic, and there is scarcely space for any more tiles.

'In the name of the God-Emperor we repel them!' I shout, my voice ragged from crying over the noise of battle.

I rip Penitence from the chest of a cultist and kick the human out of my way. Her corpse falls atop a mutated servant of Chaos, one of the curling horns which sprouts from its flesh impaling her as she falls.

A weak shout emerges from the few surviving defenders nearby. They breathe in great, ragged gasps and heft their weapons with tired, shaking arms. They bleed from a dozen wounds and move with shuffling limps. Those who are still able to stand at all.

'Your faith inspires me,' I tell them. It is not a lie. For a brief moment, the vigour returns to their faces, then another wave of our enemy begins to pour in through the hull.

'Again!' I bellow. 'We shall teach them again how strong the faith of the upright remains. No matter how many times they require the lesson!'

My companions charge forward with limping strides. Despite my words, I fear they will not withstand another such assault.

I push down the choked corridor to the next knot of defenders. They fare worse, even, than the one that I have left. A pack of daemons clamber in through a small porthole, equine faces beneath twisting caprine horns.

The daemons hiss and click to one another as they scramble into the corridor. Las-fire pours into them with little effect.

'Hold!' I shout to the few priests and pilgrims that still face them. Then Penitence is among the daemons, singing in a spray of blazing, orange blood.

The warp spawn waver then break before me, but my arrival comes too late for most of the mortals at my side. I grapple one of the wounded daemons and throw its body from the precipice of the porthole, watching as it falls.

There is no room upon the sand for it to fall, so choked is the space around my holy vessel with the corpses of its assailants. And yet, thousands more still press towards us from the storm. Somewhere, there must be a limit to that number, but it will far exceed what we can repel.

Cultists and daemons charge forward in great throngs across the sand, scrambling up the buttresses and decks of the hull to openings, or tearing their own. In places, the bodies of the dead have been heaped into great siege ramps of flesh and bone. Fire no longer assails them as they approach, the guns in my windows and along my hull long since captured, broken, or turned upon the assailants already within.

I step back into the darkness of the corridor and hear a voice call out through my vox.

'*They come in force along the northern decks.*' Brother Kessalt, his tone pressed and laced with pain.

'*And the eastern.*' Brother-Sergeant Umter. Behind his words I hear the war cry of his Brother-Neophyte.

'*We hold on the high decks,*' Hadrick replies moments later, though it is difficult to hear him over the sound of weapon fire and the roar of some infernal beast.

I look towards the lone ecclesiarch behind me, his face grave, his hand grasping a ragged wound along his flank.

'My lord,' he manages through gritted teeth.

'Priest,' I reply.

The man wavers slightly as he stands, his grip on his lasgun weak and shaking. How many charges remain within that weapon? How many breaths within the man himself?

'The wall is lost,' I say to both the priest and my brothers. 'Order those who are able to retreat further within the ship. Set ambushes. Mount counter-assaults. Harry the enemy for every step they take.'

There is only silence in my vox, and I sense my brothers' discomfort.

'There is no honour in it,' I admit. 'But there is no honour left on this defiled world. It will take the heretics days to scour each corridor. Every one of them we kill is one fewer to assault the few arcology-shrines that still hold on Tempest's surface.'

I hear Umter's and Kessalt's assent moments later. There is no reply from Hadrick.

The priest stares at me blankly.

'Go,' I order. 'Find a better place to die.'

The man nods slowly, then collapses.

I turn to face the open porthole and the daemons that already scramble through it. I raise my storm shield and take a single step backward.

The priest squirms on the end of one of Dravek's blades, convulsing as the dark, warp-forged metal slides further through her stomach and into her chest. The blade's point emerges just above her collarbone, slick with dark blood that foams with each of the human's gasping breaths.

Her eyes meet Dravek's with a mixture of disgust and fear, as her mouth opens and shuts as if in wordless speech. She shakes, her eyes rolling. The smell of shit and piss reaches his nose.

The Carver flicks Dravek's wrist to the side, throwing the priest's corpse against the bulkhead and turns to the next beleaguered defender.

'*Lay down your weapons,*' the daemon growls to the young man before him. '*Lay down your weapons. Or better. Turn them on those who drive you to waste your worthless life against such odds.*'

Dravek steps forward over the dead priestess, and the young man shuffles back. He stumbles over the bodies of his companions, the clawing hand of a dying cultist reaching up and pulling at his ragged, brown tunic. The dying jakhal pulls the man to the ground. Pins him beside the dead flesh of his comrades. The cultist's razor-sharp nails tear into his pale skin. He pulls himself free and crawls towards his fallen weapon.

'*Your corpse god arms you only for death,*' the Carver says, forcing Dravek's gaze down at the pitiful excuse for a weapon. A length of plasteel piping, no more than three feet long, tipped with a crude and improvised point. '*The Lord of Skulls would prepare you for slaughter.*'

Dravek hands the short spear to the man, then grasps his shaking shoulders and turns him to face a wounded ecclesiarch on the floor. Vomit and blood spill from her mouth in dark gouts, yet she still shivers and twitches there among the dead.

'*Is it more merciful to let her suffer slowly, or to end her wretched existence with a clean, painless blow? How many more suffer just like her each day under the corpse god's yoke? How many servants on how many worlds? In how many systems? Billions? Trillions? Writhing and dying slowly like the woman at your feet?*'

The Carver's voice spills out of Dravek's mouth, the daemon flitting into view at the edge of his vision. The pilgrim shudders beneath his touch, his eyes fixed on the dying woman before him.

'*Kill her. End her pain. Then march beside me and do the same for every other wretch within this vessel.*'

A small cry escapes the man, his grip on the short spear

shaking. The Carver guides its point above the woman's chest using Dravek's hands. Presses gently down upon the man's arms.

'Which will you choose? Suffering, or mercy?'

The corridor explodes with sound as the man's chest evaporates. Then again as a bolt-round tears into Dravek's flesh. The Carver recoils, roaring, and throws the corpse to the side, revealing a single figure standing only a few feet before him.

The priestess looks scarcely strong enough to stand, let alone to wield the bolt pistol in her grasp. With her other hand, she leans heavily upon the corridor's wall and stares at him with empty, hate-filled eyes.

'I choose mercy,' she spits. Her weapon fires again.

The Carver forces Dravek's body aside, a bolt exploding harmlessly against the bulkhead at his back. He fans the blades upon his arms before him and catches the next, then closes the gap between him and the weapon. As his Eviscerator swings towards the blind priestess, something dark crashes into him from the shadows.

Dravek's right arm falls limp as his shoulder shatters and he collides with the bulkhead a dozen yards away. The Carver's scream mingles with his own as he rises, looking down at a pair of ruined blades among his dozens. With disgust, the Carver rips their twisted metal from his flesh and casts them to the side as he faces the Black Templar.

'There you are,' the daemon growls, lifting Dravek's Eviscerator before him. *'I had wondered when I might find a Templar aboard their own vessel. Content to let your mortal slaves die in droves on your behalf?'*

The red eye-lenses of the loyalist's helm burn with hatred as he stares at Dravek. He lifts his thunder hammer into a high guard and sets his feet.

'Simply content to kill yours, oathbreaker,' he replies.

Dravek laughs the Carver's terrible laugh as he rolls his shattered shoulder, feeling the pain wash over him like a warm, welcome wave.

'How many brothers did you bring to this world, Astartes? How many lie dead, now, beneath its sands? Beneath my feet? When I first saw your standards, my heart filled with joy. I thought perhaps I had found myself a true battle at last. But this is not battle, Templar. This is extermination. Slaughter.

'No one will sing songs of this moment, or build statues to the dead. This ship will not be a place of pilgrimage, merely a crypt. Those within it will not be martyrs, simply corpses. Does it pain you to die in such a pitiful manner?'

'Does it pain you to live even more pathetically?' The priestess steps from behind her master.

The Carver appears beside her, though the daemon's grip on Dravek's flesh does not lessen.

End this, Dravek says.

There is a twinge between Dravek Soulrender's eyes. *'To exist is pain, for all things,'* the Carver replies through his mouth.

'On that, heretic, at least we agree.'

The priestess' bolt pistol cracks. The Black Templar charges forward.

Dravek's Eviscerator crackles as the Carver throws it against the energy field around the hammer. There is the sound of air boiling, the smell of copper and salt, as Dravek's body tosses the blow aside and slips past it.

Strong.

Very strong.

The Black Templar's hammer swings again. Dravek ducks beneath it. A statue shatters into a thousand fragments of dust.

'There is rage in you, Templar,' the Carver chuckles as he moves. *'That I recognise at least. But rage at what?'*

'Do not speak, traitor,' the Astartes growls. He lunges at Dravek, raising his hammer above his head. The Carver swings Dravek's Eviscerator and forces him to step aside. Dravek awaits the dull tearing of his chainsword into armour. Instead, the Black Templar redirects his feint, lunging forward with the haft of his hammer as if it were a spear.

The weapon smashes into Dravek's chest. He feels his breastplate crack, then ribs beneath it. The air flees his lungs as the loyalist throws him backward, but he brings his Eviscerator down upon the hammer's haft.

His Eviscerator screeches against the weapon even as the blow forces him to slide backward. Dravek feels the teeth of his weapon catch, as the Carver twists his Eviscerator, ripping the Black Templar's hammer from his grasp. It crashes against the bulkhead, a flash and peal of thunder as the weapon discharges.

'You think you hate me,' the Carver sputters. *'But you hate yourself. You hate the restraint that your Chapter forces upon you. You hate the ice with which they quench your flame.'*

The Black Templar circles him. He draws a long, dark knife from a sheath hidden along his greaves.

Their dance slows for a moment. The priestess' weapon cracks. The Carver throws the bolt aside with a flick of Dravek's wrist.

'You hate the weakness of the humanity you have sworn to defend. The anchor that they are around your neck.'

The Black Templar darts at him again, his flurry of blows clumsy but fast. Dravek's Eviscerator dances before him, the Carver knocking each raging blow harmlessly to the side. Within his chest Dravek feels the daemon's energy flow through him, reknitting his bones, regaining his breath.

He steps back, circles. Ducks aside. Parries. Until the Black Templar's blows slow from a hurricane to a gentle breeze. The

Carver's own strikes begin then, thin slices between armour plates. A hundred wounds falling in a dozen places.

The Black Templar slows. Falters.

Dravek steps past a clumsy jab, brings his Eviscerator down and severs the Black Templar's hamstrings. The knight topples, bellowing with rage.

The Carver kicks the wounded Space Marine, throwing him against the bulkhead. The Black Templar pushes himself upright as the Carver bends Dravek down beside his ear.

'But most of all,' the daemon whispers. 'You hate yourself. You hate your weakness. You hate your failure. You hate that you could have been so much more.'

The Carver grasps the Black Templar's shoulders with Dravek's hands, blades from both of his arms finding a dozen chinks in the Black Templar's armour. He presses them slowly inward, piercing muscle, then bone, then the organs beneath.

The Black Templar groans as the blades slip deeper within him. 'I am what the God-Emperor has made me.'

The Carver presses the blades forward and the Black Templar's voice falls silent.

'So you are...' he whispers. 'Dead.'

There is a crack behind him, as the priestess fires again. Dravek feels the bolt splash against his armour, fragments biting into the side of his face.

With a sigh, the Carver rises and steps towards the woman.

Frail.

Weak.

And yet defiant.

The Carver grasps her in one of Dravek's hands and throws her against the bulkhead, then steps over a pile of the dead and deeper into the vessel.

* * *

There is no greeting between me and my brothers. Brother Kessalt stands already outside the sealed door of our Reclusiam when I arrive. Brother-Sergeant Umter joins us moments later.

'No others?' I ask him.

He shakes his head.

There have been no vox signals from Hadrick for minutes. Brother-Sergeant Umter's Neophyte is nowhere to be seen. The status runes for my brothers upon my helm visor have long since ceased speaking true.

Umter limps as he approaches, trailing a thin stream of dark blood across the polished floor. His right arm ends at the elbow, the flesh beneath a mangled ribbon of sinew and bone, crushed and torn by some monster of the warp. Kessalt, for his part, has fared better than both of us, though even his armour is rent and oozing.

'They go no further,' Umter grunts, turning to the sealed door of the Reclusiam behind me. Its frame is bordered in the holy crosses of my order. Within that ring, a simple image of our genefather, Rogal Dorn. Behind that last gate lies the crematorium first, then the most sacred hall inside this vessel.

'That the Archenemy should enter this place is a sacrilege almost too great for me to even comprehend,' Kessalt says.

It is true. Not even the serfs or Neophytes of my Chapter are allowed within that space. In the millennia since these halls were first crafted, none but my brothers have set foot inside.

'And yet they will,' I reply.

There is surprise from my brothers.

'They will breach this gate, and enter its contents. They will defile our most sacred relics and pillage the history of this Chapter. The taint of their warp-stained flesh will conquer, in the end, even the holiness of this chamber.'

Anger enters Kessalt's voice. 'Brother-Castellan, surely–'

I raise my hand. 'There is no place for lies, here, brothers. Here at the end.'

It is quiet between us three.

'Though, this door shall not be breached while a single Black Templar on this world still draws breath.'

My brothers nod at that.

'Good words,' Umter grunts. 'Good words to die with.'

I cross my arms in the symbol of my Chapter and press them against my chest.

'It shall be my greatest glory to die at your side.'

There is no end to our foes, nor to their wretched forms.

They come first in small packs of warped, stimmed humans, bearing the skulls and flesh of our mortal allies as trophies. We strike their twisted, marked flesh, spill their blood beneath our feet. The deeper evils among them sense the bloodshed and are drawn to the carnage like wolves to wounded prey.

The air flickers dimly around my blade as I plunge Penitence again into the chest of a daemon. Its jaws gnash, dripping spittle and blood onto my armour as I throw the beast backward and step towards my brothers. Kessalt grasps the jaws of a vicious bloodletter as it tries to clamp them about his neck. My brother's power armour whines, straining against the warp-spawned strength of the daemon, then he bellows and rips the beast's jaw from its skull.

Umter kicks the reeling monster, then tears a hole through its flank with a stream of bolter fire. He pants and gasps from the exertion, dropping to his knees in the brief space the enemy gives us.

He will fall first. Soon. Then I will follow him. Then Kessalt, last, beneath the eyes of the God-Emperor only, and the image of our primarch wrought in metal at our backs.

Footsteps echo down the corridor, muffled by the corpses that surround us like a low palisade.

'Rise,' I order my brother, extending my hand. 'We shall repel them again, just as we have a hundred times.'

He begins to shake his head, leaning forward on his hands and knees. Gore streams down his black armour. The servos bound to his ceramite plate screech and whine with even that minute movement.

'I cannot, Brother-Castellan.'

'I do not give you a choice.'

I pull my brother to his feet. His voice catches with suffering. He stumbles as I release him, hardly able to stand.

'Is this how it always is?' Kessalt subvocalises. 'Is this what glory always looks like for those who are about to earn it?'

I stare at him. His words border on cowardice. It is my place to silence such sentiments, and I would, did not the same questions linger in my own mind. A memory comes to me, unbidden, of a different brother on a different world. My gaze drifts down to the sacred weapon in my hand.

'Marshal Arold bled for an hour in the dust before the second of his hearts stopped beating. At the end, he could no longer utter speech, but the sounds that escaped him were those of an animal suffering.'

I regret the words as soon as I speak them. For my part, I do not believe that Brother-Sergeant Umter can hear them.

My brother wavers, and I turn him gently towards the sound of his approaching death.

'Again, brother,' I order, feeling the cruelty of my words. 'You do not yet have my permission to die.'

He nods and lifts his bolter in a shaking hand, and aims it at the blasphemy rounding the corner.

* * *

The Black Templars stand together before a great metal door, three huddled black shadows among a sea of the dead.

The Carver pauses for a moment at the sight, then lets out a deep and satisfied sigh.

'Astartes!' he roars through Dravek's mouth, stepping over corpses and onto their killing field. *'You honour the Blood God with this tithe!'*

The three Space Marines look towards him, readying their weapons. One falters where he stands, pouring blood onto the floor. The others have been battered by hours of battle already.

'Soulrender,' the Space Marine in the centre spits. His dulled armour is trimmed with the markings of a company captain. Their Castellan, then. Still alive here at the end.

The Carver forces Dravek to bow deeply, his blades dripping onto the floor with the gesture. His boots squelch as he rises in the puddle of offal that covers the floor.

'In the flesh,' he replies. The Carver appears at his side. Slowly, the daemon crosses the clearing to the three Black Templars. The Neverborn's hunger is clear. The Carver circles the three Space Marines, his languid limbs pacing slowly. He looks up at Dravek with both hatred and hunger.

'In the flesh, and yet not alone.'

The heretic speaks to himself in the silence.

'Not only a traitor,' Kessalt subvocalises. 'But mad as well.'

A chill washes over me. The taste of copper on my tongue. Of frost on my skin. I meet the heretic's red-rimmed eyes and see something beyond them.

'No, not mad,' I reply. 'Possessed. He has made his foul body home to a creature of the warp.'

Disgust rises within me as I survey his wretched form. His armour has been painted the colour of blood, its surface corrupted by twisted growths of horns and spikes in a dozen places, bearing scraps of flesh and bone as trophies. Even the Soulrender's flesh itself has been twisted, his arms long replaced by an endless sea of blades, the skin where they enter his flesh weeping and red. He grasps a massive black chainsword in his hand, its teeth clogged with meat and bone. Yet it is his eyes that revolt me most. The eyes of something that once was my brother, now with another presence behind them.

'I can think of no greater sacrilege,' I call. 'Than for the body of an Astartes to be marred not only by vain ambition and foul mutation, but to be given to another master.'

The daemon within the traitor cackles. *'He serves a master more worthy than yours, Templar.'*

'Enough words,' Umter mumbles. His bolter blazes in his hand. I lift my blade and charge forward, but the Soulrender is no longer where he once stood.

'Fast,' I curse. Damned fast.

I strike out as the possessed steps past my charge, Penitence crackling against the spinning teeth of his Eviscerator. They clash for a moment, the air about the weapons boiling, then he is past me.

I twist, expecting to feel the bite of his chainsword, but as I turn, I see it buried in Brother-Sergeant Umter instead.

The Astartes drops to the floor with a dull clang, the pallid pink of his viscera spilling down beside him as Dravek's Eviscerator guts him from his groin to his throat. The corpse twitches, then falls still, the Space Marine's power armour still holding its shape, his finger still firing the bolter in his hand.

Over the sound of the weapon, the Space Marine's brother roars.

'For Dorn!' he screams, leaping towards Dravek's exposed flank.

The Carver twists his body in time to slip past the Black Templar's chainsword, tearing one of his blades through the seam between the knight's gauntlet and his vambrace before a power sword slips past his own assault.

Dravek grunts, the power sword drawing blood from his shoulder, as he wheels on the paired knights and sets his feet.

'You will suffer for that,' one of the Black Templars growls.

'It was a mercy,' the Carver says through Dravek's lips. *'To end the weakness of such existence.'*

The Black Templars charge him together, a wall of raging black ceramite. Their will is strong, but he is stronger.

Dravek feints towards the Castellan, watching as he raises his storm shield and strikes out in a jab. The Carver lets the blade bite into Dravek as he twists and redirects his Eviscerator towards the more aggressive of the two Black Templars.

The knight tries too late to stymie his assault, the weight of his chainsword carrying him forward with the blow. Dravek feels the Castellan's power sword cut into his side as he steps past the killing blow and drives his shoulder into the Black Templar's chest.

A heavy fist strikes his side, but the Carver drops the pommel of his Eviscerator onto the Black Templar's helmet, driving the Space Marine's head into the floor.

Behind him, the Castellan strikes, a high killing stroke directed towards his neck. Dravek rolls to the side, the blade biting deep into the metal of the deck.

The Castellan stumbles to recover, and Dravek sees him pull the weight from one leg.

Brother Kessalt rises too slowly.

'On your feet,' I order him, raising my blade and storm shield in his defence.

The possessed circles like a wolf around sheep, his Eviscerator a dark, shifting scar in the air before him, his hands a blurring, wavering storm of blades. I parry those that I am able, and feel the rest strike against my armour.

Throne, such speed. Such rage. I have seen no such thing even among the champions of my Chapter.

'To my side, brother,' I call, as another rain of blows land. Warp-forged metal gouges my sacred shield. Penitence shivers in my hand as I parry the accursed blades.

Kessalt finds his feet and presses his back against mine.

The Soulrender dances around us. We are outmatched by his body and the thing that dwells within it. Slowly, Kessalt wakes from his stupor, his blows speeding, his mind clearing.

What I would give to have Hadrick at my side, instead. I am certain my brother feels the same.

Another charge, another dozen parries. Penitence slips the heretic's guard for a moment, then he twists and my strike finds nothing but air.

The traitor's Eviscerator crashes towards my neck, halted only by Brother Kessalt's vambrace. I grunt and drive my shoulder into the possessed.

The heretic stumbles back a few steps. Kessalt's chainsword swings towards his head. The Soulrender laughs as the weapon descends, then he has slipped my grasp. Kessalt's weapon bites into his pauldron rather than his skull.

The chainsword bites deeply into Dravek's shoulder. The Carver scoffs at his pain and grasps the Black Templar's wrist. He feels ceramite crack as he crushes the loyalist's arm.

The Carver laughs again.

Two of their champions against the daemon within him. Two of their finest and they can only score minor wounds.

This is not sport, Dravek hisses.

Of course it is, the Carver replies.

Dravek reaches out again with his will but feels the daemon slap his touch away.

The Carver roars through Dravek's throat as he throws the Castellan from him, then rolls as the other knight swings an empty fist towards him. The bulkhead rings as the Astartes strikes it, a crater left in the thick steel.

The knight pulls his shattered hand from the dented bulkhead and faces him, the Castellan rising on his other side.

'You do me honour, Astartes,' the Carver laughs, staring through Dravek at their red eyes. *'A year of slaughter on this world, and at last I find combat among worthies.'*

'This is not combat,' the Castellan growls in reply. 'This is cleansing.'

The Black Templar charges again, his companion a moment later. Again, the knight favours one side. The Carver guides Dravek's body around the blade, then brings his foot down upon the Castellan's injured leg.

Bones shatter. The Castellan falls. The other knight's fists churn the air before Dravek's blades.

My vision falters as I feel my leg shatter. As I tumble to the floor. As my face slips among the corpses and the blood.

I try to rise, but the leg will not hold my weight. It is a shattered, ruined thing that will only serve as an anchor.

I do not scream. I will not give the possessed that satisfaction. Instead, I roll onto my hands and rise to my knees.

Against the gate, Kessalt pummels the Soulrender with empty hands. Each blow of his fists is the culmination of my fighting company's rage. The rage of forty knights in each of his swings. The travesty of their deaths behind every blow.

'Die!' he bellows, as he swings his fists again and again.

'Die!' he roars, his voice anger, and pain, and loss, and hatred. It is almost a prayer rather than a command.

And yet the Soulrender does not.

The air about the oathbreaker crackles and flickers, like the shimmer that lingers about a flame. Blows fall in a black blur around his head as he drops his Eviscerator, turning Kessalt's rage aside with flickers of his hands. The Soulrender laughs as he fights, the black metal of his warp-forged blades bending and shattering beneath my brother's assault. Those blows that bypass them crack the Soulrender's plate and graze his twisted face.

With twin voices the heretic laughs as Kessalt's attack slows. As even my brother's rage begins to seep from him. One by one, each swing of his fists grows weaker, crashing now into the metal of the gate behind the possessed.

'Do you tire, Templar?' the Soulrender taunts, throwing Kessalt aside and stepping from his path. The oathbreaker's armour is cracked, his mouth dripping blood, and the bone of his left eye shattered. The blades along his accursed limbs are bent and broken in a dozen places, and yet he laughs as he turns on Kessalt.

My brother places himself before the Reclusiam gate, the once-regal image of our primarch, Dorn, scuffed and gouged by his own blows. The gate itself is warped and fractured from our descent onto this world, the seam between its two great plates slightly ajar. Within, the dull gleam of the crematorium flickers in the light of my helm lumen as I drag myself forward.

'Never,' Kessalt mutters, his voice a whisper between his panting, ragged gasps. My leg screams as I pull myself through the carnage on hands and knees.

Broken. Pitiful. Weak.

There is no glory in this. There is no honour left here.

Dravek Soulrender charges forward into my brother. I drop my shield and pull the bolter from Umter's dead grasp.

There is fire in Dravek's back as he charges the Black Templar with his Eviscerator raised. The ragged staccato of bolts piercing his armour and exploding within the flesh beneath as the Carver throws his body forward. Dravek bellows as he crashes down onto the Astartes, the knight's empty fists swinging towards him and deflecting his chainsword in an exhausted blow.

Dravek crashes into the Space Marine, pinning him against the ruins of the great gate. He feels bone shatter beneath his weight, as he drives the breath from his enemy. His Eviscerator screeches as its teeth grind against the gate behind the loyalist.

The Black Templar swings at him again. The Carver makes no attempt to parry. The blows land against Dravek's chest, then his face, then fall still as his remaining blades find the seams in the Black Templar's armour and drive deep into his broken flesh.

'Die,' the Black Templar tells him, his voice scarcely a whisper. Little more than a whimper as his body fails.

The Carver pushes Dravek's blades even deeper. Feels the Black Templar shudder, then fall still. The Carver drives his mouth forward, towards the dead Black Templar's neck.

Suddenly, Dravek's back burns, his strength flags.

'I tire of this,' the daemon hisses. 'I tire of you.'

There is no glory in this. There is no honour left here. None on this broken, shattered world. None within this vessel. None remaining inside my weary soul.

My leg screams, then crumbles as I force myself upward. Upward towards the corpse of my brother. Upward towards the monster whose jaws close around him. Upward, then back down, to bury Penitence within the Soulrender's back.

The power sword hisses and crackles as it pierces the warp-touched flesh of the traitor, plunging through his back and out from his chest.

Dravek Soulrender screams, in both his own voice and that of the daemon within him. A terrible, unearthly, accursed sound. Blood and ichor spill around the hilt of my weapon. From what should be a killing blow without question. And yet the oathbreaker persists.

The heretic roars, his bladed hands clawing backward over his shoulders towards me. I make to pull the blade from him and strike again, but he grasps Penitence's point and holds it fast.

The air ripples around the possessed, a twisted, terrible voice emerging from his mouth.

'I tire of you, and of your weakness.'

The daemon does not speak to me.

The Soulrender wheels to face me, and I have little strength to resist, my wrist still bound by my devotional chain to the hilt of my weapon embedded in his back.

My arm shatters as I am ripped from my feet and thrown into the great gate. I feel its doors swing open beneath my weight.

For a moment, the traitor's eyes fix upon the inside of the chamber. For a moment, that perverse smile returns to his face.

'You will die, at least, among your brothers,' the daemon within him growls, stepping forward towards the threshold, pulling me behind him.

My arm shakes, numb and broken. My leg screams as I force it upward once more. I leap onto the traitor's back, pulling my devotional chain tight around his accursed neck.

The Soulrender laughs for a moment. A deep, booming, inhuman laugh. I stretch the chain tight and his mirth turns into a strangled hissing.

As I pull on the chain, I press my blade into his back, my chestplate forcing the hilt even deeper.

The Soulrender turns his head towards me, his eyes his own again for a moment. My grip slackens slightly.

'There is no sanction you could offer, brother,' he gurgles. 'Nor any redemption that I could accept.'

I pull the chain tight, and the Soulrender stumbles, falling first to his knees, then collapsing onto the floor beside me.

I pull the chain tight even after his shivering subsides. Even after I feel the life leave his body. Even after the daemon abandons his corpse.

I pull until my shattered wrist can hold the chain no longer. Until its black links are too slick with blood to grasp.

I pull until I hear footsteps behind me. Until the next enemy approaches. The one that will claim my life.

Outside the *Dauntless Honour*, the storm abates.

Liesl crawls from a narrow, filthy discharge chute and into the gently blowing sand. She braces herself to fight or to run, but no heretics await outside except those dead upon the desert's white surface, and the wind is already beginning to bury their corpses.

She stumbles forward into the night.

There is no grace in her steps. There is no bravery in her heart. She has cast such things aside.

'Come now–' she calls out of habit, before remembering that nothing moves beside her. She left her father there in that bloody corridor to await whatever evil came, alone.

The Lord Apothecary's words ring in her ears.

See to it that you are brave, not out of fear of punishment, but for the sake of the honour that you bear.

She had tried. She tries, still.

Liesl limps forward, her arm burning as she swings her lasgun gently with each step. Dark blood seeps from the edges of a wound upon her shoulder, stuffed with filthy, ragged strips of cloth from the edges of her faded robe. The flesh will fester – if it has not begun to already – but perhaps she will survive long enough.

In the distance, the smouldering ruins of Saint Ofelias glow dimly. She turns away from the shrine city and out into the desert. There are other archologies on this world, some of them still standing. Perhaps one will have chirurgeons of its own.

She sighs and begins to walk into the sands, lifting her eyes to the sky as she whispers a prayer. From beneath, the void appears a simple thing. Beautiful, perhaps, in its own way, but distant. She yearns for its simplicity once again.

Among the stars, something flashes in the darkness.

Liesl pauses.

Again, bursts of light in the black overhead.

Liesl strains her eyes, perhaps imagining shapes moving there in the void. Great, dark silhouettes among the stars. They circle one another like birds locked in combat. And beneath them, bright streaks rain down towards the sand.

Her breath catches.

The ground shakes. Liesl falls to her knees as plumes of sand erupt around her, the glowing metal of drop pods crashing into Tempest's endless desert. As she watches, black silhouettes burst from their doors.

A Space Marine approaches in the dim, blue starlight. He stands before her, his dark armour gleaming, the white cross of the Black Templars emblazoned upon his chest. She does not recognise the markings upon his pauldrons, but the angel's companion could not be mistaken.

'Lord Apothecary,' Liesl says to the white-clad Astartes.

He continues walking. She reaches out and grasps his leg.

'Lord Apothecary, please.'

The Astartes turns towards her, the red eye-lenses of his helm glowing against the dark sky. There is no compassion in them. No pity. But she desires neither.

Liesl fumbles within the folds of her robe, her fingers closing around cool, smooth ceramite and metal. She may be punished for this, but she no longer cares. She grasps Lord Apothecary Alvus' narthecium and holds it out before her.

'Please, my lord. I have carried it far.'

The Apothecary does not speak for a moment. Then he grasps the sacred implement and the gene-seed inside it and turns it over in his massive hand.

The two Astartes speak in muted half-tones that she cannot understand, then turn towards the dark husk of the *Dauntless Honour*.

'Come now, serf,' the angel orders, readying the bolter in his grasp. 'We have holy work to do.'

It must be a pitiful thing to watch me rise. To see a Castellan of the Black Templars crawl from beneath a corpse, and push himself up onto a single knee, groaning.

My shattered arm hangs at my side, and I lift Penitence weakly in my opposite hand, my storm shield discarded upon the floor. Behind me, the gate of my Reclusiam hangs open, my sorry defence the only protection left to that most sacred space.

This is where I will die, just as the Soulrender said.

Here, at least, beside my brothers. Without glory or honour. Without witness.

I curse silently, as I see my enemy approach. Tall. Dark. Clad in the ceramite armour of the Adeptus Astartes. To die is one thing. To be forced to watch Heretic Astartes defile my Reclusiam is another.

'No further!' I bellow, forcing myself to stand. My broken leg crumbles, and I fall forward again.

The footfalls continue as I struggle up onto my knees, my armour painted in the blood of my brothers and my foes.

'No further!' I cry again, raising my power sword before me. 'You will not enter this place while Dorn's sons still draw breath.'

My enemy pauses before me for a moment, gazing down at the wretched display I present. To die like this, crippled and covered in the blood of my brothers. To die like this...

I turn my mind away. To die thinking of shame is a little heresy in itself.

I see the Space Marine raise his weapon, a sword rather than the usual axes of the Blood God's berserkers. I close my eyes and wait for the blow to fall.

But it does not.

When I open my eyes, a brother kneels before me, his blade at his side, clad not in the crimson raiment of the World Eaters, but in the black armour of my own Chapter. My brother pauses as he stares at me, then slowly unfastens his helm. It is a face I recognise well. A face that once stood at my side.

A face I once trained.

Marshal Laise looks around me with sorrow, then brings his grey eyes down to slowly meet mine.

'You were my master once,' he says, 'so your knowledge of Black Templars custom may be greater than mine. But I do not believe that a Castellan may refuse passage of his Marshal into even the most sacred chamber of his vessel.'

The corners of the Marshal's mouth twist up into a sorrowful smile. 'Praise the Emperor you live, Brother Emeric,' he says, setting his hands upon my shoulders and pressing his head against mine.

Chapter 14

My brother's body hangs heavy in my bare, scar-crossed arms, even as his departure weighs heavy upon my soul. The crematorium echoes with the sound of my footfalls, with the whirring, clicking hymn of the rudimentary augmetics that have replaced my ruined leg and arm, crude placeholders crafted by the fabricators of Marshal Laise's fleet until my flesh has healed enough for more sophisticated replacements to be built.

I grunt as I set Hadrick's corpse upon the table of black stone, thin streams of fluid dripping from his pale wounds to soak my black robe.

'You would weep,' I chuckle bitterly in the quiet. 'You would weep to see yourself borne to the plinth and the kilns by an honour guard so broken. And yet, brother, there is no one else.'

Somewhere on a surgical slab, or in one of Chief Apothecary Teffon's auto-creches, the hearts still beat within Brother Kessalt despite his grievous wounds. Whether he will ever wake again is only known by the God-Emperor. Even if he does, what a tragedy has been wrought here.

Two.

Two brothers left alive among the two-score I brought here.

An entire fighting company shattered. A priceless warship of the crusade crippled in the sands. All to purchase what? A small beachhead for the crusade to land upon. And yet, I would pay the cost again, if asked. I pray my dead brothers forgive me for my callousness.

I open the pouch around my waist and sprinkle sand upon my brother.

'Earth from the world upon which you died. I have none from Holy Terra, brother. Nor do I even know the name of the planet that sired you.'

It is a poor parody of my crusade's sacred ritual that I enact here, though it is the best I can manage on my own.

Marshal Laise had insisted upon leaving a Crusader squad with me upon the *Dauntless Honour* to assist with the proper disposition of the dead. I refused. To hold back even a single one of his knights, my brothers, from the campaign that rages across Tempest's surface would have been a dishonour far greater than the one I now commit.

In private, I told him as much, and he acquiesced. He may be my superior now, but it was I who raised him from Neophyte to Initiate, after all.

Slowly, I limp to my brother's head, and press the skin of my forehead against his dead flesh.

'I wish, brother,' I tell him, 'that I might have been there when you died. That I might have seen your last deeds and carried them with me. That your glory might have been recounted as it deserved.'

Simple words. I am a simple man.

When I look up, a figure stands before the doorway beneath the ruined mess of the Reclusiam's gate. A sudden rage rises within me, as I realise that it is a mortal who waits there.

'Turn away,' I growl, stepping towards the door. 'You are not permitted here. To even gaze into this chamber is to defile it with your vision.'

Penitence is suddenly in my hands. The sword hums softly as the human calls back.

'It is fortunate then, my lord, that I no longer possess mine.'

The Missionary Proserpine bows deeply as I approach, her feet just outside the threshold to this chamber. My anger sputters, then dies, and I find my sorrow lessened by her presence.

'I was there,' she whispers. 'I was there when he died. I will tell you of it, Lord Castellan, if you wish.'

A small servitor-cart waits at the missionary's side; within it lies the thunder hammer of my fallen brother.

'It was found within the carnage by one of the serfs assigned to the charnel crews. I had thought it would be better-honoured here with its bearer than there among the corpses.'

I nod slowly, reaching down and lifting the weapon in my hand.

'It is a kind gesture, priest. One I shall not forget. I will enshrine the weapon beside his armour within the heart of our Reclusiam.'

As I turn, she calls out. 'I would stay, my lord. For the remainder of the rite. I would stay here on this side of the gate, if you would permit it. If it would not dishonour him.'

'No,' I reply eventually. 'No, it would not.'

I set Hadrick's hammer beside the slab, then carry his body into the waiting furnace. Gently, I place him beneath its dome, then limp to the great wheel upon the wall.

I nearly call out to the missionary, to warn her to avert her eyes, before I think better of it. Decks above me, Techmarines from the Marshal's flagship labour beside adepts and menials to restore the *Dauntless Honour* to function. The ship will never rise from these sands, but she shall serve as a bastion upon this sacred world long after my crusade departs.

As I turn the great wheel, flame sputters then roars within the crematorium furnace. Its ravenous heat devours the remains of my brother, its warmth flickering against my back as I walk slowly towards the open gate.

A single reliquary vessel is bound around my neck with gold chain, bearing the ashes of Brother-Sergeant Umter. I shall add a second for Hadrick. The rest of my brothers will fade into the sands of this world.

The Missionary Proserpine looks upon me with sadness.

'The vox communications from the Marshal's staff are encouraging,' she says. 'Saint Ofelias has been cleansed, and task forces march on Ciubrus and Saint Gebald. The orbital battle has been all but won for the Imperium. Soon, fire will assail our enemies from both the skies and the surface. As you know, my lord, there are no sureties in war, but it appears that, in time, Tempest will be reclaimed.'

I hold up my hand. Her voice falls silent. We stand together with only the crackling noise of the furnace between us. There was a time I had worried what would be spoken of me when I went to those flames. I had never imagined that there might be no one to speak of me at all.

'I will burn in this chamber one day,' I say. 'Like my brothers.'

The missionary stares at me, then looks to Hadrick's crackling corpse.

'But not yet,' she says, her frail hands meeting to make the aquila before her.

'But not yet,' I echo back into the flames.

ABOUT THE AUTHOR

Steven B Fischer is a physician living in the Southeastern United States. When he's not too busy cracking open a textbook, he can be found exploring the Appalachian Mountains by bike, boat, or boot. Steven's work for Black Library includes the novels *Witchbringer* and *Broken Crusade*, and several short stories.

An extract from
The Lion: Son of the Forest
by Mike Brooks

The river sings silver notes: a perpetual, chaotic babble in which
a fantastically complex melody seems to hang, tantalising, just
out of reach of the listener. He could spend eternity here trying
to find the heart of it, without ever succeeding, yet still not
consider the time wasted. The sound of water over stone, the
interplay of energy and matter, creates a quiet symphony that
is both unremarkable and unique. He does not know how long
he has been here, just listening.

Nor, he realises, does he know where *here* is.

The listener becomes aware of himself in stages, like a sleeper
passing from the deepest, darkest depths of slumber, through
the shallows of semi-consciousness where thought swirls in con-
fusing eddies, and then into the light. First comes the realisation
that he is not the song of the river; that he is in fact separate
from it, and listening to it. Then sensation dawns, and he realises he is sitting on the river's bank. If there is a sun, or suns,
then he cannot see them through the branches of the trees overhead and the mist that hangs heavily in the air, but there is still
light enough for him to make out his surroundings.

The trees are massive, and mighty, with great trunks that could
not be fully encircled by one, two, perhaps even half a dozen

people's outstretched arms. Their rough, cracked bark pockmarks them with shadows, as though the trees themselves are camouflaged. The ground beneath their branches is fought over by tough shrubs: sturdy, twisted, thorny things strangling each other in the contest for space and light, like children unheeded at the feet of adults. The earth in which they grow is dark and rich, and when the listener digs his fingers into it, it smells of life, and death, and other things besides. It is a familiar smell, although he cannot say from where, or why.

His fingers, he realises as they penetrate the ground, are armoured. His whole body is armoured, in fact, encased in a great suit of black plates with the faintest hint of dark green. This is a familiar sensation, too. The armour feels like a part of him – an extension, as natural as the shell of any crustacean that might lurk in the nooks and crannies of the river in front of him. He leans forward and peers down into the still water next to the bank, sheltered from the main flow by an outcropping just upstream. It becomes an almost perfect mirror surface, as smooth as a dream.

The listener does not recognise the face that looks back at him. It is deeply lined, as though a world of cares and worries has washed over it like river water, scoring the marks of their passage into the skin. His hair is pale, streaked with blond here and there, but otherwise fading into grey and white. The lower part of his face is obscured by a thick, full beard and moustache, leaving only the lips bare; it is a distrustful mouth, one more likely to turn downwards in disapproval than quirk upwards in a smile.

He raises one hand, the fingers still smeared with dirt, before his face. The reflection does the same. This is surely his face, but the sight sparks no memory. He does not know who he is, and he does not know where he is, for all that it feels familiar.

That being the case, there seems little point in remaining here.

The listener gets to his feet, then hesitates. He cannot explain to himself why he should move, given the song of the river is so beautiful. However, the realisation of his lack of knowledge has opened something inside him, a hunger which was not there before. He will not be satisfied until he has answers.

Still, the river's song calls to him. He decides to walk along the bank, following the flow of the water and listening to it as he goes, and since he does not know where he is, one direction is as good as the other. There is a helmet on the bank, next to where he was sitting. It is the same colour as his armour, with vertical slits across the mouth, like firing slits in a wall. He picks it up, and clamps it to his waist with a movement that feels instinctual.

He does not know for how long he walks. Time is surely passing, in that one moment slips into another, and he can remember ones that came before and consider the concept of ones yet to come, but there is nothing to mark it. The light neither increases nor decreases, instead remaining an almost spectral presence which illuminates without revealing its source. Shadows lurk, but there is no indication as to what casts them. The walker is unperturbed. His eyes can pierce those shadows, just as he can smell foliage, and he can hear the river. There is no soughing of wind in the branches, for the air is still, but the moist air carries the faint hooting, hollering calls of animals of some kind, somewhere in the distance.

The river's course begins to flatten and widen. The walker follows it around a bend, then comes to a halt in shock.

On the far bank stands a building.

It is built of cut and dressed stone, a dark blue-grey rock in which brighter specks glitter. It is not immense – the surrounding trees tower over it – but it is solid. It is a castle of some kind, a fortress, intended to keep the unwanted out and whatever people and treasures lie within safe from harm. It is neither new and pristine, nor ancient and weathered. It looks as though it has always stood here, and always shall. And on the wide, calm water in front of it sits a boat.

It is small, wooden, and unpainted. It is large enough for one person, and indeed one person is sitting in it. The walker's eyes can make him out, even at distance. He is old, and not old in the same way as the walker's face is. Time has not lined his features, it has ravaged them. His cheeks are sunken, his limbs are wasted; skin that was once clearly a rich chestnut now has an ashen patina, and his long hair is lifeless, dull grey, and matted. However, that grey head supports a crown: little more than a circlet of gold, but a crown nonetheless.

In his hands, swollen of knuckle and weak of grip, he holds a rod. The line is already cast into the water. Now he sits, hunched over as though in pain, a small, ancient figure in a small, simple boat.

The walker does not stop to wonder why a king would be fishing in such a manner. He is aware of the context of such things, but he does not know from where, and they do not matter to him. Here is someone who might have some answers for him.

'Greetings!' he calls. His voice is strong, rich and deep, although rough around the edges from age or disuse, or both. It carries across the water. The old king in the boat blinks, and when his eyes open again, they are looking at the walker.

'What is this place?' the walker demands.

The old king blinks again. When his eyes open this time, they are focused on the water once more. It is as though the walker is not there at all, a dismissal of minimal effort.

The walker discovers that he is not used to being ignored, and nor does he appreciate it. He steps into the water, intending to wade across the river so the king cannot so easily dismiss him. He is unconcerned about the current: he is strong of limb, and knows without knowing that his armour is waterproof, and that should he don his helmet he will be able to breathe even if he is submerged.

He has only gone a few steps, in up to his knees, when he realises there are shadows in the water: large shadows that circle the small boat, around and around. They do not bite on the line, and nor do they capsize the craft in which the fisher sits, but either could be disastrous.

Moreover, the walker realises, the king is wounded. The walker cannot see the wound, but he can smell the blood. A rich, copperish tang tickles his nose. It is not a smell that delights him, but neither does he find it repulsive. It is simply a scent, one that he is able to parse and understand. The king is bleeding into the water, drip by drip. Perhaps that is what has drawn the shadows to this place. Perhaps they would have been here anyway.

Some of the shadows start to peel away, and head towards the walker.

The walker is not a being to whom fear comes naturally, but nor is he unfamiliar with the concept of danger. The shadows in the water are unknown to him, and move like predators.

+Come back to the bank.+

The walker whirls. A small figure stands on the land, swathed in robes of dark green, so that it nearly blends into the background against which it stands. It is the size of a child, perhaps, but the walker knows it to be something else.

It is a Watcher in the Dark.

+Come back to the bank,+ the Watcher repeats. Although its communication can hardly be called a voice – there is no sound, merely a sensation inside the walker's head that imparts meaning – it feels increasingly urgent nonetheless. The walker realises that he is not normally one to turn away from a challenge, but nor is he willing to ignore a Watcher in the Dark. It feels like a link, a connection to what came before, to what he should be able to remember.

He wades back, and steps up onto the bank. The approaching shadows hesitate for a moment, then circle away towards the king in his boat.

+They would destroy you,+ the Watcher says. The walker understands that it is talking about the shadows. There are layers to the feelings in his head now, feelings that are the mental aftertaste of the Watcher's communication. Disgust lurks there, but also fear.

'Where is this place?' the walker asks.

+Home.+

The walker waits, but nothing else is forthcoming. Moreover, he understands that there will not be. So far as the Watcher is concerned, that is not simply all the information that is required, but all that is available to give.

He looks out over the water, towards the king. The old man still sits hunched over, rod in his hands, blood leaking from his wounds one drip at a time.

'Why does he ignore me?'

+You did not ask the correct question.+

The walker looks around. The shadows in the water are still there, so it seems foolish to try to cross. However, he has seen no bridge over the river, nor another boat. He has no tools with which to build such a craft from the trees around him, and the knowledge of how to do so does not come easily to his mind. He is not like some of his brothers, for whom creation is natural…

His brothers. Who are his brothers?

Shapes flit through his mind, as ephemeral as smoke in a storm. He cannot get a grip, cannot wrestle them into anything that makes sense, or anything onto which his reaching mind can latch. The peace brought about by the song of the river is gone, and in its place is uncertainty and frustration. Nonetheless, the walker would not return to his former state. To knowingly welcome ignorance is not his way.

He catches a glimpse of something pale, a long way off through the trees, but on his side of the river. He begins to walk towards it, leaving the river behind him – he can always find it again, he knows its song – and making his way through the undergrowth. The plants are thick and verdant, but he is strong and sure. He ducks under spines, slaps aside strangling tendrils reaching out for anything that passes, and avoids breaking the twigs, which would leak sap so corrosive it might damage even his armour.

He does not wonder how he knows these things. The Watcher said that this was home.

The Watcher itself has been left behind, but it keeps reappearing, stepping out of the edge of shadows. It says nothing; not until the walker passes through a thicket of thorns and finally gets a clearer view of what he had seen.

It is a building, or at least the roof of one; that is all he can see from here. It is a dome of beautiful pale stone, supported by pillars. Whereas before he had been finding his own route through the forest, now there is a clear path ahead, a route of short grass hemmed in on either side by bushes and tree trunks. It curves away, rather than arrowing straight towards the pale building, but the walker knows that is where it leads.

+Do not take that path,+ the Watcher cautions him. +You are not yet strong enough.+

The walker looks down at this tiny creature, barely knee-high to him, then breathes deeply and rolls his shoulders within his armour. He presumes he had a youth, given he now looks old. Perhaps he was stronger then. Nonetheless, his body does not feel feeble.

+That is not the strength you will need.+

The walker narrows his eyes. 'You caution me against anything that might help me make sense of my situation. What would you have me do instead?'

+Follow your nature.+

The walker breathes in again, ready to snap an answer, for he finds he is just as ill-disposed towards being denied as he is to being ignored. However, he pauses, then sniffs.

He sniffs again.

Something is amiss.

He is surrounded by the deep, rich scent of the forest, which smells of both life and death. However, now his nose detects something else: a rancid undercurrent, something that is not merely rot or decay – for these are natural odours – but far worse, far more jarring.

Corruption.

This is something wrong, something twisted. It is something that should not be here: something that should not, in fact, exist at all.

The walker knows what he must do. He must follow his nature.

The hunter steps forward, and starts to run in pursuit of his quarry.